Playing Safe

by Eileen Dewhurst

Playing Safe

EILEEN DEWHURST

PUBLISHED FOR THE CRIME CLUB BY
DOUBLEDAY & COMPANY, INC.
GARDEN CITY, NEW YORK
1987

All of the characters in this book
are fictitious, and any resemblance
to actual persons, living or dead,
is purely coincidental.

Library of Congress Cataloging-in-Publication Data
Dewhurst, Eileen.
Playing safe.
I. Title.
PR6054.E95P53   1987   823'.914   86-19714
ISBN 0-385-23557-7

Playing Safe

CHAPTER 1

He was five minutes late. She recognized him the moment he was through the door, a shabby little man pausing in the shabby little lobby. Matching it, as she matched him. Yes, she had got it right: his flat monotonous voice on the telephone, alternately apologetic and defensive, had been a true guide. His expression, now, was the same.

But he had seen what he was looking for, and was smiling in relief as he hastened towards her, taking an old-fashioned trilby from his sparse hair.

"Mrs. Mitchell?"

"Mr. Redfern?"

"Yes, yes. Mrs. Mitchell, oh, I'm so glad. Thank you, I can't tell you—"

"You've written down for me what I need to know?"

"Yes, oh yes." Apology crept back. "There isn't much, reelly."

"Even so, let's sit in what comfort we can find in this place while I have a look at it." She ought to get the phraseology right as well as the accent, but that could wait. She was aware of a glow of satisfaction that she had so exactly supplied Mr. Redfern's needs, a sensation intensified by the sight of their two drab, middle-aged figures passing the long speckled mirror at the entrance to the lounge.

She selected a chair which seemed comparatively well sprung.

"Would you fancy a drink?" Mr. Redfern looked uneasy, perching the other side of the small table.

"No, thank you, but do go ahead."

"No, ta, no. There'll be plenty later on. Now, here we are."

There was only one sheet—of short, laboriously handwritten paragraphs.

"It's first cousin," said Mr. Redfern humbly, "if you don't mind. I did have a first cousin in Sheffield. You have to get back to your hubby tonight—"

"Yes, I see. Let me just look at it, Mr. Redfern, quietly for a moment. That's how I'll remember it."

"Of course. Sorry." He drew his hand across his mouth. "Wonderful to have a visual memory, like."

Close to, Mr. Redfern did have one distinguishing feature—a disproportionately large and rosy nose which looked as if it had been assumed in conjunction with his spectacles and small moustache. It was hard to imagine that some woman had awakened that morning to the acceptable knowledge that before the day was done she would be Mr. Redfern's bride. As she handed the paper back to him, Helen realized that her enterprise was not only going to amuse her and make her some money. It was going to put her in the way of learning things about different kinds of people.

"Yes, that's fine, Mr. Redfern. How's our time?"

"We've got a few minutes. I hadn't expected you'd take it in so quick. Shall I perhaps just ask you . . ."

"If we've got the time and you're a bit anxious, of course. Fire away."

Helen removed the obnoxious white cotton gloves and sat waiting with her hands folded on her turquoise Crimplene lap. Satisfaction struggling with anxiety as he looked her over, Mr. Redfern asked her how long it was since they'd last met.

"Must be all of eighteen months now, Albert."

"Yes. *Yes*. Do you get up to London much, Mabel? You must come and stay with us. I'll say that half-hearted, like," added Mr. Redfern, dropping the slow loud tones of his interrogation. "Because, no offence meant, Mrs. Mitchell, but, well, I don't want to be needing you again. Not that you'd be available, I don't suppose—"

"I don't suppose I would. Oh no, Albert, I hardly get up to London now. Herbert never feels equal to the journey these days and why should I bother on my own account? I'm no fashion plate and I can get all I want in Leeds."

It was she who had chosen Leeds. Her home town was the one subject on which Mrs. Mitchell would have to be precise, and Helen had played there once in repertory.

"That's wonderful, Mrs. Mitchell, wonderful. I reelly don't think we need . . . Will you excuse me just a moment? Then we might as well be on our way. My car's in the park. Did you come—"

"I didn't come by car, Mr. Redfern."

Because, Julian had reasoned, if anyone wanted to follow her home at the end of an assignment, travelling by car would have made it too easy. Once he'd realized she was serious, Julian had been very firm about adding the cloak and dagger touches. She thought he was being a bit unnecessary, but he had made her promise. . . . Looking round on the sagging red velvet chairs and sofas as she left the lounge, she was suddenly chilled, struck by the thought of being sunk without trace in this milieu where she was dabbling. Quickly she imagined telling Julian about it, smiling over it with him in their green-gold sitting-room. If he was prepared to stop and listen, he'd been distracted lately. . . .

Mr. Redfern was using his handkerchief on his temples when he rejoined her.

"Are you all right?"

"Quite all right, thank you, yes." He waved her into a section of revolving doorway. "It's just," continued Mr. Redfern on the pavement, "that it isn't every day that one marries Vi, you know."

And it wasn't every day that one got married for the first time at—fifty-five? Fifty-eight? Mr. Redfern's age was one piece of information he had not offered over the telephone, or on the sheet of paper.

Unless he was always talkative, he was one of those people who are made voluble by the prospect of unusual experience. As he drove among depressing contrasts of small rundown old property and large new flat and office blocks, he was telling her again what he had told her on the telephone.

"Mr. Robinson from the office agreed to be my best man. Oh yes, there was no trouble there. But, well—you see, Vi has so many friends and so much family, she was always talking . . . And then one day I heard myself mention my cousin Mabel. Just heard myself mention her. I said she was in Sheffield, which she was when she was alive, but I don't suppose that'll matter, I don't think Vi was listening all that hard. But she took you—pardon me, Mrs. Mitchell—she took the idea of Mabel in, she said once she was sure Mabel would agree with her about something or other. And then she said that as my only relative of course Mabel would be coming to the wedding. I said, yes, of course. . . ."

"Wasn't it rather difficult, Mr. Redfern?" He had a hand off the wheel, dabbing the handkerchief at his neck. "I mean, she might have wanted to write to Mabel herself, ring her up."

"I know. I was ever so annoyed with myself. And bothered, too. I wouldn't have wanted Vi to think I didn't tell the truth. At least before we were . . ."

"Yes, I understand." Before he had secured her. But to Helen it seemed that the charade could only be harder to play after today. What if Vi was to write the Christmas cards, for instance? But that was Mr. Redfern's worry, not hers. And perhaps not even his, once Miss Violet Leslie was Mrs. Redfern. Perhaps he was not entirely sure of her. Helen found herself absurdly eager to meet the bride.

But first it was the best man, collected at the gate of a house where Mr. Redfern suddenly stopped without warning. Mr. Robinson, a tall, silent man with shiny black hair, was accorded some deference and no first name, indications that he must enjoy a higher status than Mr. Redfern in the office where they worked. After the introductions Helen offered him her front seat so that he could stretch his legs, but with a brief thanks he squeezed behind Mr. Redfern and they set off again. A few small sounds from Mr. Redfern, and a puckered brow, made Helen think he was aware of *lèse-majesté* in the fact of his superior being cramped into the back of a small car of which he was in the front.

"So Miss Leslie will have a lot of guests, Mr. Redfern?" she asked, to distract him.

"Actually, no. Knowing how small my side would be, she settled for just her sister and husband. Very understanding, Vi."

Or perhaps also given to fantasy? So far the most interesting thing about her new self-employment was the questions it was posing about human nature.

There was a large, rather elderly car in the parking bay outside what must be the Register Office. The front near-side door opened a fraction after Mr. Redfern had opened his. As he helped her out on to the pavement, Helen, to her amusement, experienced the heady sensation which had always assailed her the moment before her entry on stage.

The woman who had opened the door of the other car was having a little difficulty getting out. Even so, Helen thought Mr. Redfern's proffered hand had been repulsed. Standing eventually on the pavement beside him, Miss Leslie topped her groom by two or three inches.

But she was handsome in a large, colourful sort of way—hair hard gold under perhaps too youthful a wide-brimmed straw hat, bosom and bottom generous under the close-fitting pinky-mauve dress and short cape of some whitish fur.

Looking into big but severe blue eyes, Helen hoped it was not a case of the stoat and the rabbit. At least she was now sure that Mr. Redfern would not be entirely able to believe his good fortune until the wedding had taken place.

"This is Mabel," said Mr. Redfern uncertainly. Then, expanding his chest, "And this is Vi."

"Pleased to meet you, Vi," said Helen. "Very pleased."

"Likewise." The bridling motion caused a ripple the length of the pinky-mauve dress. The blue eyes were now absorbed with Mr. Redfern's cousin. "From Leeds, Albert said? I thought he told me Sheffield at first, but he can be very vague."

"I was in Sheffield before I was married." The other two people from the car in front were now joining them, and Mr. Robinson, who had allowed Mr. Redfern to help him free.

"This is my sister Joan," said Vi. She had a good strong voice, not unmelodious. Helen imagined it calling time at the end of an evening. "And Bob, her husband."

Joan was small and dark and nervous, not a bit like the bride. Had she and her large, over-smiling husband also been hired? The idea was diverting, but she must postpone contemplation of it. Joan was asking her a string of little questions, not waiting for the answers.

"Did you have a good journey? Was the train crowded? Did Albert meet you all right? Aren't we lucky with the weather?"

"Don't hang about!" Joan's husband beamed and took his wife's arm. With a large gesture Vi took Mr. Redfern's. Helen had taken Mr. Robinson's, bringing up the rear of the little procession, almost before realizing it.

"Come *along!*" Vi was pushing at the door. But inside the building she curbed what Helen saw as natural qualities of leadership in the interests, no doubt, of the better appearance entailed by the best man making the inquiries as to where they were expected.

In the Registrar's office she sat between Mr. Robinson and Joan.

There was a vase of roses on the desk, the sort that looked as if they had come from the Registrar's garden. Joan wept quietly from the moment they were seated, Vi drew deep, impatient-sounding breaths before she made her responses. But she made them—to Helen's relief and slight surprise—more loudly and positively than Mr. Redfern made his. It was over very quickly.

"Kiss the bride?" suggested the Registrar genially.

"Vi!" Mr. Redfern advanced puckered lips, to which the lady graciously applied her cheek. "Vi . . ."

"Later, later!" admonished Bob. Mr. Robinson took Helen's arm. Outside again, she plunged into the back of Mr. Redfern's car the moment the photographic session was over. She imagined Vi Redfern in the future, puzzling periodically over the figure of Albert's cousin, taking the album or the framed photograph into a better light, commenting on what a shock it was that Mabel should have popped off so soon, or that she didn't look the sort to bolt. . . . Or, of course, informing an ultimately honest Albert that his stupid deception had made a monkey of the record of their day. . . .

In the restaurant she wondered if the exigencies of the space available really demanded that Mr. Robinson's leg should be so noticeable against hers. Then wondered no longer as, spilling a few drops of soup from the spoon close to his mouth, he asked her if they might meet that evening.

"Really, Mr. Robinson, I don't know. Didn't Albert tell you that I was a married woman?"

"A damn fine one." He had turned to look at her, in time for her to see his tongue withdrawing between his red lips. *Julian.* Vi was leaning over the table towards her, a ridiculous panic was mounting in her as Vi spoke. "Albert and I aren't going away till this evening. You'll come back to the house, of course?"

"We're living in Vi's house," said Mr. Redfern, turning to her eagerly, as relaxed as she'd seen him. "It's ever so much nicer than mine. Oh, but of course, Mabel . . ." The light in his face faded to anxiety. "Mabel has to get home."

"Yes. I'm sorry, very sorry indeed." She tried not to make herself sound too resolute. Mabel *would* be sorry. "It's a long journey, though, and the last train I can get is the five-fifteen."

"Come on, now, Mabel." Mr. Robinson, on first appearance, had looked the last man to make so roguish and masterful an attempt to overrule a woman. "Surely you can be spared the one night. It's a long way, as you say—too long to come for just a few hours—"

"I'm sorry, really I am. But my husband isn't so well—"

"Mabel *has* to get back, I'm afraid. What do you all say if we go over to the house when we've finished here, then I'll nip Mabel off to the station. We can have our little bit of family talk on the way." Mr. Redfern sought her eye, and she wondered if he had a sense of humour. "I'll be back in half an hour, dear." Mr. Redfern turned to his bride, who was dividing her intense gaze between him and Helen. She was probably the sort of person who is by nature suspicious. Or perhaps she was unaccustomed to the firm note suddenly in her husband's voice. It must surely have been Vi who had popped the question. And Helen would never know why. All her assignments— if she managed to obtain any more—would leave question-marks as well as the relief which she thought would always come when her charade was over.

But of course, she had at least to go in and see Vi's house, make the appropriate exclamations of surprise and delight. It was reassuring, as it had been through the prolonged courses of the wedding feast, to know that Mr. Redfern, for his own reasons, was as anxious to get rid of her as she was to go. And at half past three, with a five-fifteen train to catch, there was nothing any of them could do but accept the inevitable.

Even so, alone for a moment with Mr. Robinson in Vi's over-decorated lounge, she had to manoeuvre a coffee table between them.

They all came to the gate to see her off, waved, as she waved, until the car was out of sight.

"Where d'you want me to take you, Mrs. Mitchell?"

There was a just perceptible change, she thought, in Mr. Redfern. It was probably the first time in his life that he felt he had something to be proud of. "Thank you ever so much, you were wonderful. Just wonderful."

"Thank you. It wasn't difficult. I hope you'll be very happy. If you drop me at Clapham Junction, that'll be fine."

Through to Victoria in a few minutes, and then the end of Mrs. Mitchell.

"Are you sure? If you'd like me to take you farther in . . ."

"No, that's fine. It was a lovely day, Mr. Redfern, a lovely day."

"It was, wasn't it? I'll never forget it. I was glad you were there, even though . . ."

"Even though it might make life tricky for you later. I hope not, I really do."

"I expect it'll be all right." They drew up near the station. "Forty, you said?"

"Thank you." The notes were old and bulky. "Well, goodbye." They shook hands. "No, don't get out."

She had passed through Clapham Junction so often, but never stood on the platform. She could have gone straight home, she was on her way, but she had promised Julian always to repossess herself at Victoria. Already she felt her performance was over and had to remind herself, on the short journey, to act according to her appearance. The pads in her cheeks had become irksome, probably owing to the eating and drinking, and she was aware for the first time of the tiny coarsening tip to her nose. In the privacy of a cubicle of the ladies' cloakroom she removed these props, along with the hat and wig. She slipped out of the Crimplene dress and into the silky tunic which had gone to nothing in the side pocket of her small dressing-case. The Crimplene dress and the Mrs. Mitchell shoes, to say nothing of the hat and wig, took up more room than her sandals and own slip of a dress, and the case would only just close. It was Julian who had said she shouldn't carry anything which looked big enough to contain a disguise. It would be more difficult in the winter. . . . Out by the washbasins, she cleaned her face of the few lines she'd given it, and touched her eyelids and cheekbones with colour. She combed out her silver-fair hair. In this other long mirror was an attractive woman in her late thirties, slim, long-legged. She smiled at her reflection, before seeing it suddenly solemn as she wondered what she was really like. Then she turned and swung quickly out on to the concourse, joyously aware of her strong natural gait as she moved along.

Even if she encountered Mr. Robinson now she would have no fear of him, he would pass her by—if with a wistful glance.

Yes, she was a conceited snob.

But she had new things to think about and to tell Julian, and a thicker wallet.

CHAPTER 2

They *had* been lucky with the weather. Leaving her own Surrey station, Helen looked appreciatively round her as she sauntered home, feeling the sun still warm on her arms, hearing a blackbird. Another thing she had already learned about her new hobby-job—it made her quite sharply aware of her contentment with her real situation. Of course, other assignments could be of the kind to make her envious but she didn't think they would, she didn't think she had much capacity for envy.

The house was waiting for her, telling her through the cat it was glad she was back. He and she walked round the garden while she took a few deadheads off the roses and just savoured being there, and then she fed him and made some preparations for dinner before rounding up the things that wanted washing and shoving them into the washing-machine for the next morning.

It had always seemed to be while she was banging shut the port-hole door of the washing-machine that she found herself regretting not having felt able to accept the job Julian said could have been hers in what they referred to as the Civil Service department where he worked. It had been a failure of nerve on her part not to have taken up the challenge, they both knew that. But she had gone from idle, useless years as John's elegant chattel to the mortal danger of her one unofficial assignment for Julian with only a couple of years' repertory in between, and although in the course of the assignment she had come to love Julian and had afterwards married him, the fact that her life for days on end had depended on her ability as an actress had taken a toll in nervous energy which had left her lacking the confidence to undertake anything more.

She was over it now, had been over it for some time, but she wasn't always at the washing-machine, and for most of her short, joyful second marriage she had been content to refine on their new

house and garden, produce and act for the local dramatic society, do
a few unpaid good deeds, and read and dream. It had been Julian,
not she, who one evening when she was a bit wistful had said jokily
that if she was really bored with housework and gardening she
should advertise herself in the columns of the more intellectual periodicals as being able to supply a wife or girlfriend, even a mother or
an aunt, to fit a tricky social situation.

"And with your extraordinary visual memory"—that, too, had
stood the Department in good stead—"you'd be able to remember
what you were supposed to know so long as it was written down for
you."

"Oh, Julian, yes! What a wonderful idea. A unique service. I'll
provide it."

She had been so charmed and diverted she had got her horrified
husband to sit down with her there and then to devise an advertisement. The exercise had been highly enjoyable.

> Wife? Fiancée? Friend? Sister? Mother? Aunt? Grandmother,
> even? Could you avert a domestic crisis, save a tricky social
> situation, if you were able to produce one of these, or any other
> type of respectable female? Young professional actress offers
> unique service, will impersonate any of the above. Write "Versa-
> tile Actress," Box. . . , giving telephone number where you can
> be contacted. Reputable situations only.

She could hardly believe any periodical would be prepared to accept such an entry, but Julian—still bemused by the terrible success
of his facetiousness—averred that the more intellectual the publica-
tion, the wider and weirder the scope of its advertisement columns.

He was right. Each of the three periodicals to which they sent the
advertisement accepted it. Smiling, then frowning, as she stepped out
to the garden again for some mint, she recalled the first letter one of
them had forwarded to her. It had taken several weeks to come, and
when it arrived her first reaction had been mystification, she had
almost forgotten the whole idea, at the beginning of a good summer
she was free to enjoy and with no reminder from Julian. The letter
was from a man wanting to produce a fiancée, in order to deter a
girlfriend he had encouraged to believe he was prepared to marry.
She had known at once that she couldn't do a job for such a reason,

but in the evening, while disliking herself for it, she had shown the letter to Julian without telling him of her distaste. It was as if she was testing him, trying to find out if an adult lifetime in work where so often he must disregard considerations of morality had blunted that sense in him. It had been immensely important to her that his reaction had been the same as hers, but unfortunately he had been aware of her motive and between them there had sprung up a novel and unbearable sense of constraint. Trying to cope with it on her own the next day, when Julian had gone to London, she had telephoned the author of the letter and delivered him a short homily. Then hung up feeling a prig. When Julian came home she told him what she had done and it made him laugh. This opened the way for him to say in so many words that she had hurt him, and for her to say that she was still assailed from time to time by a memory of that first cold, ambiguous Julian who had put her life at risk. Then the regret was shared and the breach healed.

When the request came from Mr. Redfern, pathetic but acceptable, Julian made his one plea for her to refuse it, and to refuse any others.

"I'm sorry." She hated to defy him, the more because until this moment he had always been content for her to do, and to be, what she wanted.

He knew she was unwavering. "All right. Tell me though, I think you might tell me—why?"

"I don't know why."

"Is it because you want to be independent?"

"No. Oh no." She was sure about that, too. "I am independent."

"What, then?"

"Yes, I do know. Although I've only just realized. I want to use my skills. I know I'm good and I want to prove it again. Without the risk. Darling, I promise you I won't let there be any risk. I just want to see myself in action again. It's hateful to have to admit it, but this amateur business is worse in a way than nothing, for me. It's too easy, and it makes me think what I'm capable of doing."

"When you were Mrs. John Markham you didn't do anything."

"I never had done anything, I married John from school. I didn't know."

"A sleeping giant?"

"Oh, Julian. But a sleeping talent, anyway. Do you honestly not understand?"

"I understand." The grave eyes held hers. "I won't pretend to you that I'm happy about it, but I'll have to trust to your good sense as well as your talents. I won't try to stop you again, but I'll blame myself if anything goes wrong."

"Beloved, it won't."

But he made her promise to take certain precautions. Wherever her assignment, she must travel to it as the character she was about to play. She must always disguise herself in some way, even where she could play the part straight. She must never reveal her real name or address, which would be confined to the bag which never left her hand and the files of the selected periodicals. She must meet her clients already in disguise, in a public place, and must remain in public unless it seemed absolutely clear there was no possibility of danger. (Vi's house, she had adjudged, fulfilled this proviso—more obviously so, on reflection, than Mr. Redfern's car.) She had teased Julian over these and his other stipulations, putting them down to the mentality engendered by a working life in Intelligence. Admittedly, she had had scared moments today, but they had been nothing to do with her physical safety. . . .

The mint was of the apple variety, and she held its fragrant woolly leaves to her mouth as she came indoors. If Julian were to ask her again, now, why she wanted to do this job, she would give him two extra reasons: the peculiar enjoyment of instant entrée into other people's lives, and the almost painful sense of relief and appreciation when she came back to her own.

She had known that morning, although he had merely wished her luck, that Julian had been anxious.

More anxious than usual would be a more accurate description, she reflected as she moved about the kitchen, his work just now seemed to be making him slightly anxious all the time. She didn't know why—when she had elected not to join him in the Department he had told her it would be best if he didn't discuss anything with her —but she knew the anxiety was there. She told herself she would understand if he forgot what she had been doing during the day and didn't immediately ask her about it, hug her with extra fierceness because she was safely home.

"He's here, is he?"

The cat always heard Julian before she did, looking interestedly towards the hall or making his slow way there, his tail like a walking stick.

There was no doubt the feet were sounding more rapidly than usual.

"Helen?" The call came short of the kitchen door, and there was a question in it.

She followed and overtook the cat.

"I'm here."

"I'm glad you're here."

It wasn't until they were in the evening sun in the garden, with drinks, that she began on the details, the exorcism of the sagging red velvet upholstery and Mr. Robinson's aspirations. Julian was noticeably unhappy about Mr. Robinson. In future—if there was a future in this direction—she should perhaps edit her reports where she knew there was no real cause for alarm.

But she entertained him, made him feel, she thought, a bit less furious with himself for having fed her the original mad idea.

"You know, it made me count my blessings. Didn't someone write about lives of quiet desperation?"

"Thoreau. He said the mass of men led them."

"I suppose that was the feeling it gave me. That if you really got caught you'd suffocate. And I had a funny sort of ashamed feeling that I'd never realized it before. Never realized how privileged I've been."

"I know what you mean." He had his steady gaze on her, the gaze which had summed up her potential usefulness to him when he had come backstage the first time they had met. Then it had chilled and frightened her. Now it was her chief source of warmth. "Look, I'll try not to hope that you don't get any more letters."

One arrived the next morning.

Julian had left, which she was glad of. This time she suspected the unfamiliar envelope as soon as she saw it, lying between a bill and a receipt. The postmark was London and the writing was small and neat. The writer, from Camden Town, was awaiting a visit from his mother, "A slightly dizzy lady who lives most of the time in Switzerland, but whose heart is in the right place. This is unfortunate for me, because so far as Mother is concerned the right place is the conventional one. You see, Peter, the man I share my house with, and I are a *ménage,* and this my mother could not appreciate. She descends on me only about once in three years, and I have a woman *friend* who agrees to be in evidence. At the moment she's away and there isn't another girl I know well enough. That's why when I saw your advert I thought I'd better turn professional. Would you take it on for me? It's the whitest of white lies, designed merely to send my mother away with an easy mind about her only child. The one snag from your point of view could be that she is a great person for questions. Luckily she doesn't really listen to the answers." *Did you have a good journey? Aren't we lucky with the weather?* Already the *dramatis personae* of her first assignment had exaggerated in her memory into grotesques. It had seemed unlikely, until this point in the letter, that there would be anything in common between the two propositions. "I can tell you what more you need to know if you telephone me. I do hope that you will."

The letter was signed "Yours faithfully, Tony Edwards," the name printed underneath the signature, a consideration in keeping with the agreeable tone. If it was what it seemed, there was nothing in it to give her pause. It even promised to be amusing at the time, not merely, as with Mr. Redfern's wedding, afterwards with Julian. She went to the telephone at once, taking her second cup of tea with her. Not everyone would leave for work as early as Julian.

There were only a couple of rings before a man's voice saying hello.

"Mr. Edwards?"

"Just a moment."

The second hello was more cheerful.

"Mr. Edwards, this is Versatile Actress." She said the two ridiculous words with a sort of comic emphasis, pre-empting her own sense of their absurdity as well as his. "I'm willing to accept your assignment."

"How absolutely marvellous."

"Just one thing. I'm not intended to be a fiancée, am I, just the current girlfriend?"

"That exactly. How marvellous to have someone intelligent. Are you tired of the stage?"

"I don't answer questions. I don't even tell you my name or where I come from. In fact you can choose any name for me that you like."

"What fun. We'll have to meet first, though, there are some things you'll have to know, things even my mother will notice if you don't know, or get wrong."

"I have one other talent." Toby had jumped up and was trying to wrap himself round the telephone. "An unusual sort of a visual memory. If you write down what I have to know, I'll learn it off in a few minutes. I promise you. When would you want me?"

"Next Monday?"

"That's all right."

"I'm meeting Mother at the air terminal, I think it's three o'clock. She'll only be here a couple of nights, and she's staying in an hotel. We've got two bedrooms but—well—I've had to say we have one each, of course. How much time can you give me?"

"The afternoon. How about if you take your mother to tea at Harrods or Fortnum's and I'll meet you both there?" She hadn't had tea at either place for ages. "I can be going away the next morning, but you'll have set the tone by then, anyway."

"That's marvellous! I say, put a sock in it, Peter." The laugh was low and tender as he fended off some mock attack, and she was overtaken by a little flare of anger: such a charming and considerate young man should be wrestling affectionately with a *girl*. "Sorry about that. Look, though, I mean, I'll still have to see you before I meet my mother. Even you couldn't—"

"Of course. I'll meet you in an hotel near the air terminal an hour before you have to meet your mother. Write down what your girl-friend might need to know."

When they had agreed an hotel, he asked her if she would go back to the flat with them afterwards.

"I may do, I don't know yet." By the end of tea she would know whether or not this was indicated. She had three qualifications, really, for the job. The third was an abnormally well-developed sixth sense. "That needn't worry you, need it? If I say I just have too much to do before my holiday, that won't sound suspiciously far-fetched."

"No." But the cheerful voice wasn't convinced. "I hope you will, though. I'll pay extra. I suppose I ought to have asked you at the beginning what your fee is. Is it frightfully high?"

"It's fifty pounds." She was going to be a bit Robin Hoodish over her charges. "It won't be affected by whether or not I go back with you and your mother."

"That's all right." There was an audible sigh of relief. "There's just the chance, I suppose, that my mother won't want to bother coming back to the flat on Monday, seeing she'll have all day Tuesday with me, but we'll just have to see. Do you think that's all we have to talk about now?"

"You might tell me the sort of girl your mother tends to favour."

"Yes, of course. How bright you are! I haven't got all that much to go on, but I think she prefers them dark and rather intense-looking. Sensible and reliable rather than glamorous. But expensive, if you know what I mean. You sound as if you would know."

"I think I know." For the first time she hesitated. "How old are you?"

"Twenty-seven. I know it sounds absurd," the voice continued hastily, "to worry what Mummy thinks, but it's for her sake. She lives the sort of life where if she knew about me really she'd have—or feel she had—to make up the conventional story and she'd hate doing that, she's the worst actress in the world."

"I'm not, so don't worry." Through the window she could see a rose which wanted snipping. At the same moment she felt a pang of regret. What for? She would always come home at the end of the day. "Your mother wouldn't mind a girl a bit older than you? I don't have to be older," she said, hasty in her turn, "but in fact I am, and if you thought—"

"I think Mummy would be quite reassured by a slightly older girl," said the voice, not at all put out by a piece of information which she thought would have sent a Mr. Redfern busy with his handkerchief. "I think I'll call you Penelope. Penelope Dale. Nice rhythm."

"That's fine, but don't worry if you forget it and settle for something else. Just so long as everything you want me to know is written down."

"It will be, Penelope, I promise you. How nice to know your name. Will you give me your phone number in case anything changes my end?"

"I'm afraid not. Nothing personal, it's one of my rules. If you just don't turn up, that's one of my hazards. Not that I expect—"

"Of course I'll turn up." The voice sounded injured. "How will I know you, though?"

"You've already issued a rough description of me and I'll be alone, looking carefully at everyone who comes into the lounge, or is already there. You do the same, and we'll be all right."

"You're very reassuring, Penelope. Thank you."

"I'll see you on Monday at two o'clock."

"Do you prefer Harrods or Fortnum's?"

"Fortnum's have a particular cake. Meringue topped with marron purée."

"Fortnum's it is. Thanks again. I know I should ring off now but as soon as I do I'll think of something absolutely vital and I won't be able to get hold of you."

"Just write it down and present me with it on Monday. Goodbye."

CHAPTER 3

There were five days to go before she was due to meet Tony Edwards. This tempted Helen not to tell Julian right away, but not wanting her new job to be responsible for making her less than honest with him she resisted the temptation.

"I see." He had looked quickly away from her. She knew he was afraid his eyes might have said more.

"Read the letter."

She saw his mouth relax as he read. He agreed with her that it was a nice letter.

Rain was falling gently, a good growing rain which had encouraged blackbirds and thrushes on to the lawn. They had their drinks by the window, looking out. Eventually he apologized for his silence.

"It's all right, darling, I know you didn't expect anything more so soon. Neither did I. You feel it's setting too hot a pace. I probably won't get any more letters at all."

"I hope you don't. Oh, I don't think I mean that. If you enjoy it a few times perhaps I'll get used to it."

She said gently, "It's inconsistent, isn't it? You wanted me back in the Department."

"I know. But somehow . . . this is unmapped territory."

"You know my sixth sense. You know how careful I'll be. And how different. Even you would pass me by."

"I wouldn't."

This was an argument they had had before, and which she would resolve in some way if he persisted in worrying. She enjoyed devising her appearance, prevailing facial expression as well as clothes and shoes, wig and make-up. She came out of Victoria station at a quarter to two on Monday with her expression in place as well as everything else. Helen Johnson had disappeared behind the pallor, the large serious eyes and the set mouth which could relax so unexpectedly and agreeably into a quick half-smile. Penelope Dale—if that was what her creation was still to be called—had a tendency to plod when she walked, exaggerated by her low-heeled pumps. She stood in the doorway of the appointed lounge, rather nervously clutching her handbag and small dressing-case and with her other hand pushing back the heavy fringe of dark hair.

She was sure she would have known the young man at once, even if he hadn't sprung out of his chair. Fair hair flopping over his forehead, thin face with tiptilted nose and wide smiling mouth. She hoped too many girls would not be victims of a misapprehension. They met half way, beside a table where they both sat down.

"Penelope Dale!"

Face to face, he was as unself-conscious as he had been on paper and the telephone.

"If you say so. All right?" It was so much more subtle than Mrs. Mitchell, so much closer to herself, she had to hold all the aspects together from the start.

"Absolutely marvellous. But I knew you would be when you telephoned, I have a sixth sense. Why are you smiling?"

"Private joke." And her own private smile. She was not as well hidden as she had believed. "Now, Mr. Edwards"—it was difficult, doing Helen Johnson's business in the guise of the character she was playing, but she ought to manage it—"you have something for me to read?"

"Here it is." There were two pages this time, typed. "Will you have a coffee while you're looking at it? I won't interrupt you."

"Thank you, I'd love one." She gave him that quick, diffident smile, then bent her head over the pages. Penelope Dale was a self-employed secretary who worked from her home in Bromley. *My mother doesn't know anything about that part of south London, or should I call it north Kent.* Penelope and Tony had met at the Churchill Theatre. He had spilled coffee on Penelope's dress in the interval and insisted on running her home afterwards. *Ulterior motive, of course. I already knew I wanted to see her again.* Penelope was an only child whose mother was a widow and whose father had been in industry. "Don't worry, Mother won't ask you what kind of industry, she's far too well bred." He was speaking now, seeing where her finger was on the second page. "I honestly promise not to interrupt again." Penelope was off on a fortnight's holiday to Corfu the next morning, with her mother. *She hasn't been there before. The woman next door is going to feed the cat.* (Here Helen had to suppress a thought of what it would be best to do with Toby when she and Julian went away.) When her father was alive Penelope had had a flat in Hammersmith and had built up a clientele for her work, so managed to keep busy. *It isn't spectacularly well paid, but there was no travelling expenses.* She liked the theatre. "I don't have to dictate to you about your hobbies," said Tony reasonably, when she looked up. "Is that all right?"

"It's fine, you've been clever the way you've made everything precise and vague at the same time."

"I was rather pleased with it." The expressive face exaggeratedly registered smugness. "Pete helped me, we had great fun. I hope you'll come back with me if only to meet Pete."

"That isn't really important," said Helen, not pleased with herself for administering the rebuke. Tony looked snubbed. He really seemed to be a very tender plant. But she was out of character again.

"No, of course not," said Tony.

"I'm sorry, I'd no need to say that. I may come, I'll see. If I don't, I promise you my method of refusal will be entirely acceptable to your Mama."

"I like you, you're not acting now, are you?"

Oh, but she should be. "You'd better go. I'll see you in Fortnum's at three."

"What fun, Penelope Dale!"

It was exhilarating, and something Julian would be pleased to hear, that she was passed at close quarters on the ground floor of Fortnum's by a woman she knew quite well. She even had Penelope Dale's quick smile acknowledged, with no hint of puzzlement. But she must not become complacent. And, of course, there was very little chance that she would. Her heart as she left the lift was bumping uncomfortably about her body and she was wondering if she had any voice, just as if she was in the wings.

The impact of mother and son, animatedly opposite one another at a table in the window, was considerable. It was likely Penelope Dale would be seized with alarm. Mrs. Edwards was fair and pretty, still young but clearly mature. She and her son were behaving like lovers in public, greatly enjoying either each other, or their triennial performances. At least she was confident Penelope fitted in as well as any girl could. Tony rose as she approached the table and indicated the empty chair between him and his mother. As she sat down he came behind it and pushed it close to the table.

"Nice," purred Mrs. Edwards, not quite able to keep out of her large bright eyes the fact that she was making an assessment. She had a charming precision in her light voice, a sign perhaps that she had been born abroad. "Tony tells me you're going on holiday tomorrow. Haven't I been lucky?" Any girlfriend, real or imagined, could have responded to this flattery only with the self-deprecatory murmur Helen accorded Penelope. "I like Pete of course, and he's such a faithful friend, but there are other relationships, aren't there?"

The eyes sparkled into hers, unnerving her for a disconcerting second into wondering if Tony's mother was playing with them both.

Tony had lost the nervous edge she had been aware of when they first met. But he wasn't needing to do any acting, gratitude and admiration had similar appearances to affection, and he was beaming them at Helen as he listened to his mother tossing remarks to them both. He had been inaccurate when he had said that his mother asked a lot of questions. What she did was to make statements in which she lifted her voice slightly as she finished and left a very short space afterwards for the person she was addressing to confirm or deny. Penelope's responses were no more than accepting murmurs, Tony's were enthusiastic enlargements on every subject his mother introduced. Helen was both touched and amused by the confidence he appeared to be drawing from Penelope's presence. The situation was so absorbingly enjoyable she knew for certain, as she bit into her marron-crowned meringue, what it was she liked best about her new job—the temporary but total escape from the eternal prison of herself. If that self had not been so contented she thought the job could become as essential to her as a drug, even if it brought with it the qualms she had felt at Mr. Redfern's wedding luncheon.

When Tony's mother told them she couldn't wait another moment to see the flat, Helen realized she was unready to relinquish this particular charade. In answer to yet another statement ending in a vocal query, she said she would love to go back with them for an hour before setting off home to prepare herself for her holiday.

"That's great, Pen!" It could have been spontaneously that Tony leaned across the table to squeeze her hand. On the platform waiting for the tube train, in the train, he and his mother maintained their well-bred fortissimo exchanges, turning themselves, for Helen, into a second series of grotesques against the background of silent, empty-faced passengers. She saw one or two smiles concealed by hands or downward glances, one or two mouthed parodies on the faces of the less polite. She was glad when they were out in the street again, and the uninhibited voices could escape into the sky.

The flat was behind a bedroom-type door on the first floor of an early Victorian stuccoed terrace house. The door was opened, while Tony was still fumbling for his key, by another slender, nice-looking young man, darker and sharper-featured than Tony and, thought Helen at once, rather more worldly-wise.

"Hello, Mrs. Edwards. Hello, Penelope. Come in."

Pete must, of course, concentrate on Tony's mother, but Helen's sixth sense told her he was more interested in Miss Dale. And when Mrs. Edwards had proclaimed the charms of the large long-windowed sitting-room and Helen had suppressed its agreeable impact on herself, Pete seized her arm.

"You may have had tea but I haven't. I'm going to make myself some and I'm taking Penny to keep me company while you take your mother round the rest of the flat."

Inside the pretty little kitchen, round the corner from the door and out of sight of the hall, he propelled her against some cupboards and moved away, staring at her.

"I don't know how good an actress you are," he said quietly and quickly, "because of course I don't know what you're like really. But I do know you're quite weirdly like my aunt who's bolted."

She would hear more before she told him she didn't undertake the impersonation of real people. She said, smiling, "Oh yes?"

"Yes!" Excitedly he ran his fingers through his thick dark hair. "She's bolted before, and come back. She'll come back this time. But unfortunately my uncle has a job interview next week, and he's pretty certain she won't be back by *then*."

"Need she be?" It was crazy and delightful, the way this job gave her intimate knowledge of family after family.

"Well, yes. You see, he was made redundant, and now the Professional and Executive Register, or whatever it's called, has come up with this super prospect—well, Uncle says it's super, I don't know what it is exactly, but it's for one of those self-important organizations which assess the wife as well as the husband. They want to see that their candidate has a stable background to come home to, to keep him sane through all the high-powered work he has to do, and that his wife can entertain other top executives successfully. You know the sort of thing, personally I think it's a bit yukky but the break is frightfully important to my uncle and—"

"I'm afraid I don't impersonate real people, it's one of my rules."

"What bad luck." But there was scarcely a check. "In this case, though, it's literally just for the length of a dinner, that's the dual interview, you see. My uncle feels confident he's passed the other tests, but this is the last one and he's just got to have Aunt Marian for it."

"Can't he tell them she's away?" There were exotic jars and packets on the shelf behind Pete's restless head, complex chutneys, rare spices, obscure *tisanes.*

"He *has* told them she's away. They just say they'll wait until she comes back, but meanwhile of course he'll understand that they have to see other candidates, etcetera." The continuous background of bright voices was moving nearer. "Look," said Pete, leaning towards her, "of course you couldn't possibly decide now, I wouldn't expect you to, especially as it's against your rules. But could I just ask you to telephone my uncle? Just telephone him, even if it's only to say you can't. Then he'll know I've at least tried to help him."

"Well, I—"

He was scribbling on a piece of paper he had taken from a drawer. "Here's his number, will you take it? Will you ring him? It would be an act of charity, really it would."

She laughed as she tucked the paper down the side of her bag. "All right, I'll ring him. But that's the only guarantee I'll give you."

"Of course."

"Better get that kettle on."

"It'll be nearly boiling. I just had some tea." Peter pressed the switch, and subdued roaring began at once. She was sure he was the dominant partner. Tony and his mother came into the kitchen as he was pouring boiling water on to a teabag in a mug. He carried the mug, sipping from it, as they all went through to the sitting-room.

There was some agreeable chat about the view from the window, the amenities of the neighbourhood and the contents of the book-shelves. During the course of conversation Helen learned that Tony worked for the Arts Council, and was shocked that both of them could have forgotten so central a fact of his life. Perhaps the revelation unnerved her slightly. At least it decided her that it was time to go. Another ten minutes went by before she could find a gap in the talk. When it came she got to her feet.

"I'm sorry, Tony, Mrs. Edwards, but I think I'd better be on my way. I've hardly begun to decide what I'm going to take, let alone to pack, and I won't have much time in the morning."

"Of course, sweetie. I'll run you to Victoria."

Ridiculously, her heart missed a beat before she remembered that Bromley trains also started from Victoria. She would have been wise to have refused Bromley for that reason, although of course she could always take a taxi away from the station, then come back. . . . What unnecessary nonsense was obsessing her? Hastily she refocused on the three smiling faces.

"You'll do nothing of the kind. It's a lovely day and I'll be on a bus in a moment." At least the two typewritten sheets had contained information about public transport serving the flat. She half expected Pete to volunteer to get her to the station, but he didn't. He probably had the intelligence to realize he had taken her already to the point where she had to make up her own mind. . . . It was Mrs. Edwards who was speaking.

"I'll go to the bus stop with Penelope, we'll enjoy a little private chat."

Tony's mother smiled at her son, across whose expressive face a shadow had passed. Pete's face remained without expression. Penelope, above the lurch of Helen's heart, gave Mrs. Edwards her quick smile.

"How kind. Yes, that would be nice. . . ."

"All right." Tony was at the door. "But excuse us a moment, we want to say goodbye."

Behind the closed door of a bedroom he gave her fifty pounds in crisp notes and begged her to be careful with his mother.

"I will, don't worry. I hope she'll be careful with me."

"She'll ask you—"

"I can cope." She had a delicious sense of power. "Don't *worry!*" They joined the other two in the hall.

"I'll leave the door on the latch, Mum. Goodbye, darling, please don't decide to stay in Corfu." Tony put his arms round her, pressed his mouth chastely against hers. Pete laid a hand briefly on her shoulder. The two young men stood on the public landing, watching them down the curving stairs.

As soon as they were in the street Tony's mother said, "You're very kind and loyal. I hope you're not in love with him." It was the only remark, all afternoon, that she had made softly. Helen stood still in astonishment, turning to look at the woman strolling by her side. The warmth and the sparkle were still there, but the mouth looked different. Mrs. Edwards bit her lip as it continued to tremble.

"What do you mean?" She knew exactly what Tony's mother must mean, although she couldn't quite grasp it, despite that second of foreknowledge vouchsafed her at the Fortnum's tea-table.

"Oh my dear." Out of sight of the windows of the flat, just short of the bus stop, there was a wooden seat. They sat down. "I knew last time I came that Tony only cared for Pete. They'd just started to live together. The same girlfriend was paraded who had been paraded the time before, but I knew. I was wretched for a while, but I got used to the idea. The bad thing now is that Tony won't tell me the truth. That he underestimates me." *She'd have to make up the conventional story.* Helen hoped Tony's mother would never learn the full extent of his underestimation.

"You should tell him." It still appeared to be Penelope speaking.

"Perhaps I will, eventually. Perhaps I'll do it in a letter, in time for my visit. Oh, I'll do it. But myself, in my own way. I ask you not to tell him." Mrs. Edwards turned to look steadily at Helen. "Do you know him well?"

"No."

Part of the sparkle, now, was suppressed tears. Helen's sense of power and enjoyment evaporated into the uncomfortable feeling she tended to have when intimate scenes were enacted on the television screen. She felt like a voyeur, and voyeurism was a perversion. She got up, and after a few seconds Mrs. Edwards got up too.

"Goodbye," said Penelope, holding out her hand. "Try to enjoy the rest of your stay."

"I'm glad to have met you." The strong hand held hers for a moment. "I wish you *were—*"

"I wish you would tell him while you're with him. Have a few hours with him without any deceits."

"I think you might be right."

"I think I am. Only"—she remembered the real situation—"please tell him it wasn't anything *I* said."

"That I promise you."

They were able to part with smiles, and Helen with the thought that she might just have done something really helpful, as opposed to helping maintain an unnecessary fiction. And this time, if she got in touch with Pete's uncle, she might even find out.

CHAPTER 4

The ritual of re-establishing herself at home made her forget about the piece of paper in her bag until she had been back almost an hour. For a few seconds she thought she had lost it, and felt a disconcertingly strong sense of relief. But it was there, screwed up under the pocket mirror she had used at Victoria. Besides a London telephone number, Pete had written the name Mark Weldon.

She had the receiver in her hand when Toby raised his head towards the hall. She let the receiver clatter back. No need for such eagerness. Yet the sooner Uncle Mark knew whether or not he could rely on her, surely the better. . . .

"Welcome home, darling."

But Julian had walked at his normal pace into the kitchen, and hadn't spoken until he had kissed her. She hoped this was a sign that already he was beginning to get used to the fact of her new job.

"I'm glad to be home, as always. But it was fun."

And really quite a good little story. Julian obviously enjoyed listening to it, and there was nothing she had to leave out or skate over. She couldn't help, though, being hesitant about the scrap of paper. She told Julian about Pete's request at the end, when she had finished telling him about Tony and his mother.

"It sounds just about as straightforward as it could be," she commented, to his silence. "That is, if after talking to the man I decide to do it. Of course I haven't made up my mind yet. Julian?"

"Of course you'll telephone him. Although you told me you wouldn't be impersonating real people."

She put her hand against the curve of his cheek. "I won't, usually. But this sounds so inoffensive. I promise you now, though, that if I take it on, I'll be wary about going into any private suites."

"What if the high-powered potential boss has booked one for the evening?"

"Oh, Julian. Beloved, I shall *know.*"

After dinner they worked in the garden together until dusk. As they came in Julian suggested Helen ring Mark Weldon.

"You want to hear me in action?"

"You're most likely to get hold of him now. That is, if you've been given a private number. And I admit to a slight interest."

The telephone was answered almost at once, with its number.

"Mark Weldon?"

"It is."

"Mr. Weldon, I was given your number by—Pete." It was ridiculous, the basic things one could forget to find out. Knock three times and ask for Pete, for heaven's sake. "Your nephew. He knows me as Versatile Actress. He told me you have an interview coming up at which your wife is required to be present." She wasn't looking at Julian, this wasn't like so many of her telephone calls when she was saying one thing and facially commentating another to him over the receiver. She was aware of him though, standing motionless, looking out on the darkening garden. A thrush had begun to repeat itself, indignantly defying the twilight. "*I* told *him* that in the normal way I don't impersonate real people, but that I would be prepared to talk to you about what you wanted. Forgive me, perhaps your nephew hasn't—"

"Peter has told me that he met you. He was very surprised and impressed, by your resemblance to my wife. He told you that my wife will not be back in time for this dinner-party?"

"He said . . . Yes." The precision of the voice made her think of Tony's mother. Otherwise, in its colourlessness, it was totally different.

"I would require only two or three hours, over a meal in a restaurant. A good meal." The pale, expressionless face of her imagination could, at that point, have half-smiled.

"There are things I would have to know. I could make it worse for you rather than better."

"That is so. But from what my nephew said . . . You would require your briefing to be written down, I believe. But I cannot send it to you?"

"No. But if we could meet an hour or so beforehand"—was it her apparent willingness to contemplate this third assignment which had made Julian move so sharply that his ankle bone cracked like a pistol shot?—"and you could leave me with the brief, that would be all I should need. I have an unusual kind of visual memory."

There was a slight pause. Straining, she could hear no background sound. "Yes, that could be arranged."

"Obviously there would be precise requirements regarding my appearance."

Out of the corner of her eye she could see Julian sitting down.

"Obviously, yes. But Peter told me—your colouring, your hair, just right. Except that the face—forgive me, your face—was a little too young. My wife is a good-looking woman but she is forty-two"— she didn't recognize the compliment right away—"and the ageing shows under her eyes. White, a little puffy."

"That could be managed. The hair . . ."

"My wife has long hair which she sweeps up at the back and holds with combs. And some pins, I believe." The man must *know*. But if his wife had left him, even temporarily, it probably hurt to think too precisely about such details. "The ends curl on top quite thickly, and there is a half fringe. Could you—?"

"I'll do what I think you've told me, Mr. Weldon, and when we meet on our own you can suggest any changes if I'm not close enough."

She was no longer using the conditional. Had she decided to take on this third assignment? Julian shifted in his chair.

Mr. Weldon had not missed her inference. "You are prepared then to consider my proposition?"

"Yes." Obviously, she was.

"Good. I am grateful. What you suggest about the hair is sensible. As regards clothes . . ."

"Yes?"

"My wife also has elegant legs." This second compliment was delivered with no change of tone. "She wears delicate shoes with heels to show them off. A dress quite plain but clearly good. A very little good jewellery. You have a picture?"

"Yes. When would you want me?"

"The date suggested is next week. Monday. I don't know whether they would be prepared to postpone it. They are being as reasonable as they can be, they tell me." The face could be almost smiling for the second time.

"Monday next week is all right for me." She and Julian stared at one another.

They arranged to meet at Claridges, which was near the restaurant and where she could sit and learn her part when Mr. Weldon left her.

"I will come back for you at half past seven, and we will arrive together at the restaurant. At the end of the meal we will leave together of course, you will appreciate that we must do that, and then I will find a taxi, or take you to your car."

"That's fine." She could tell the taxi to go to another station, then change her mind after a few corners and go to Victoria. . . . She was as bad as Julian.

"Good. I will see you then at six o'clock in the lounge at Claridges Hotel. You will not, I suppose, permit me to take a telephone number to contact you, should my interviewer decide—"

"I'm afraid not." But it would be unreasonable to expect the arrangement to be inviolable, as if only she and Mr. Weldon were involved. "I could telephone you on Saturday evening. This time."

"That would be satisfactory. I hope there will be no change in the arrangements, but it will anyway be sensible to confirm. I gather your fee is fifty pounds."

"Yes." If he hadn't known what Tony Edwards had paid her, she would have charged more.

"Very well, then, Miss Versatile Actress. Good night." The inverted commas were as noticeable in his voice as they must have been in hers.

"Good night."

She went and sat on Julian's knee. Not as any sort of attempt at compensation, which would have been unworthy of them both, but simply because she had sudden need of the contact, and it was a moment in which cheek against cheek was more expressive than words or even eyes.

In that position, she told him the other half of the conversation.

"It sounds as if it's going to be the easiest of my three assignments."

"Perhaps. I don't want you to travel on your own so late without the car, let alone miss the last train. When you've put yourself to rights at Victoria, take another taxi. All the way home."

"I'm quite happy to do that. I have a well-developed sense of self-preservation."

"I hope so."

Of course, he was not entirely happy. It was the one shadow over her new innocent pleasure. It made her uncertain whether he would prefer to be given progress reports on her preparations, or would rather they behaved as if the assignment hadn't been agreed. It was a relief, the next evening, and again the next, when he asked her—over their drinks rather than immediately on his return, as if the query wasn't at the forefront of his mind—how she was getting on.

She thought she was getting on well. She had a wig of the same silky dark hair she had worn as Penelope Dale, but dressed on top. Even without any work on her face the wig aged her beyond Tony's girlfriend, beyond herself. She knew, though, exactly what she would do to make herself into a forty-two-year-old who wasn't wearing too well. And she had just the shoes for the legs which had been the object of Pete's academic admiration. Tentatively, the night before, she asked Julian if he would like a dress rehearsal.

"I'd prefer a reconstruction." She knew he regretted taking so long to be at ease with what was giving her pleasure. "I know you'll be exactly what's required." This, rarely, was a sop, but she accepted it.

"Thank you, Julian."

There were no further sops. It was she, in bed, who put out her arms.

She left in the late afternoon, before Julian got home, after a couple of hours working in the garden with Toby, trying to disperse what felt absurdly like a sense of regret. When she came through the front door as Mrs. Mark Weldon it was hard, as it had been hard with Mrs. Mitchell and Penelope Dale, not to put her head down and make a dash for the road. She had to tell herself, again, that it was because of the neighbours her performance had to begin at that moment. Heart beating as it had beaten each time she had started to make her way from her dressing-room, she walked to the gate and down the road as she imagined Mrs. Weldon would walk. (She couldn't even remember the woman's first name. How could Julian be happy?) A little more tentatively than Helen Johnson, placing the elegant shoes a little more precisely. . . . She passed a neighbour on the other side of the road, her first local encounter in disguise. Although he noticed her—in fact very slightly slackened pace to survey her from head to toe—she was amused to realize that this was from generalized male interest rather than puzzled recognition. For the first time that day she thought she might enjoy the evening.

She was a little early into the lounge at Claridges, but she had hardly crossed the threshold when a man rose as if casually from a chair near the entrance and came to stand in front of her. She stood still, looking at him in silence, and after a few seconds, with the half smile which was not the only thing she had got right about him, he repeated her terrible sobriquet.

"Yes. Mr. Weldon?"

"Yes. You are intelligently circumspect, my dear." In the circumstances she could hardly object to his mode of address. "Let us sit down, and you can peruse your brief. Will you have a drink?"

"No, thank you. But please go ahead."

She thought irresistibly of Mr. Redfern, but Mr. Weldon was nodding and making a gesture so minimal she was surprised that a waiter should be at once beside them. But of course Julian didn't have the monopoly of quiet authority. Mr. Weldon was even more self-effacing than Julian when he was at work, she doubted if she would be sure of knowing him again. Average height, average weight, neat greying hair, pale eyes behind pale-rimmed spectacles, the sort of weathered grey-white skin that never seems to respond to heat or cold or embarrassment. . . . She knew the eyes had already taken in her every detail and was suddenly anxious, afraid she had got it wrong.

"Will I do?"

"You will do, Mrs. Weldon. You will do very well indeed."

She felt again that surge of power, hoped it wasn't too large an element in her enjoyment. "Surely there's *something* . . ."

"I don't think so. Everything appears to be right. But if you would prefer me to criticize"—Mr. Weldon paused, then again almost smiled—"I would say that my wife looks tired, that perhaps while I have been sleeping she has been lying awake, that maybe she needs more fresh air. But of course we all change from day to day, I am satisfied." The waiter brought whisky and a bottle of soda water. Mr. Weldon poured some of the soda and took a drink before drawing folded papers from an inside pocket. "Here is your brief. Will you look through it before I go, in case there is anything which is not clear?"

She thought again, as she had thought with Tony's mother, that the precision of Mr. Weldon's speech might indicate he had been born abroad. It was hard to imagine this man being made redundant, suppliant for a job where he must present his wife for approval. . . . The two sheets of typed paper told her that Marian Weldon *née* Simmonds had been born, brought up, and educated in London. After leaving school she had taken a secretarial course, also in London, and gone to work for a firm of City solicitors, now taken over, before meeting and marrying Mr. Weldon at the age of twenty-one. From there Mr. Weldon's own *curriculum vitae* ran alongside that of his wife, a fact to which he drew her attention with a conventional apology. "But it is as important for you to know about the husband as about the wife."

"Of course, I see that. I've had a look at all of it, Mr. Weldon, and it all seems clear. I'll have it by heart when you come back for me."

"Your confidence, and the experience of my nephew Peter, convince me of that. A rare and wonderful thing, to have so remarkable a memory."

"I suppose it is." Despite the reappearance of the half-smile, the intensity of his gaze made her uneasy. "But having always had it, I tend to take it for granted."

"That is understandable, but you should value such a gift, you really should. It must have been useful to you in your work?"

"Forgive me, I don't answer questions." She sounded, to herself, ridiculously pedantic.

"I was not asking a question, I was merely remarking that an actress must be greatly assisted by a memory such as yours."

"I'm sorry, forgive me. Of course, yes. . . ."

"And now, if you have no questions for *me*, I will leave you, and return for you at seven-thirty." Mr. Weldon was on his feet, smiling ironically down at her. "I am very pleased." He made her a little bow and walked quickly away.

Helen turned back almost eagerly to the typed sheets. Mrs. Wel-

don had met her husband at the house of a mutual friend, married
him within three months, and in twenty-odd years apparently borne
him no children. (In that respect, at least, they were alike, unless
Mrs. Weldon hadn't been able to help it. . . . She and John, for
reasons which now, in her late thirties, seemed to Helen appallingly
unimportant, had debarred the arrival of children. She and Julian
hadn't, but time moved relentlessly on. . . . *Not now.*)

Really, Mrs. Weldon seemed to have done very little with her life.
Except, in Pete's words, to bolt. There was, of course, no mention in
her record of the length and frequency of her departures. All Helen
learned from this about her recent life was that she enjoyed enter-
taining at home, played tennis, and was active on a number of chari-
table committees. It all sounded depressingly like her own first marriage and in a few minutes she had mastered its details. Mr. Weldon's
life appeared rather more interesting. He had been a pilot with the
old British European Airways when he met his wife, and after retir-
ing from the air had worked for a time with their ground staff. Later
he had "gone into the City" in a business consultative capacity after
taking a two-year course (the fake Mrs. Weldon was recommended
to say that she had been impressed by her husband's initiative and
had encouraged him), the demise of the consultancy for reasons beyond Mr. Weldon's control accounting for his current joblessness.

All quite easy to absorb, and all strangely difficult to apply to the
neat, self-assured figure who had just left her. But hers not to reason
why.

She spent forty minutes on the typewritten sheets and fifteen in the
cloakroom, making sure her appearance was maintaining itself, and
the persona she had adopted to the apparent satisfaction of her employer. Part of the persona was to be less at home with her reflection
in the mirror than Helen Johnson was with hers. But it was only
since she had loved Julian that she and her image had exchanged
secret smiles. . . .

Mr. Weldon was back promptly at half past seven. She asked him
at once the question which was growing more and more obtrusive.
"My voice—surely you must have something to tell me about that? I
mean—does your wife talk readily, animatedly, or—"

"My dear." Mr. Weldon sat down. She felt a tension rising in him,
as in her, although there were no visible signs of it. "When Peter told

me how like Marian you were, I could scarcely believe my good fortune. And, of course, he had also told me you were unlikely to agree to help me. But when an hour ago I saw you, and saw as well as heard you speak, I was astounded. The only suggestion I can make about your voice is to ask you to speak as you would speak yourself—which I must presume is what you have been doing, as I have given you no brief to do otherwise."

"It seems—too easy." But, of course, she had adapted her voice. "And when you get the job, and your employers really do meet your wife—"

"Thank you for your assumption that I will get the job." Another infinitesimal movement had the waiter again beside them. "I think we should both have a drink now. What would you like?"

"Whisky, please."

"Two double whiskies."

"One thing," she said reluctantly, when the waiter had gone, "you have no children. I wouldn't remark on it, except that perhaps it's the sort of thing which may interest them."

"It did not happen." There was no change in his eyes.

"Thank you. I hope all goes well for you tonight."

"Please do not worry on my account. Or your own. Having reassured themselves that my wife does not eat peas with her knife, has the willingness and the ability to entertain my colleagues, and strength enough for me to lean on, they will not turn the spotlight on her again." That made sense. "And now there is one modification to your appearance I should like to make." Mr. Weldon's neat hand went again to an inside pocket. "My wife has a sentimental attachment to this rather curious brooch." There was a slight hesitation. "In the past, her leaving it behind has reassured me of her return. May I ask you to wear it?"

"Of course." The brooch was a piece of *art nouveau* silver, its centre a girl with flowing dress and hair, the hair curving with leaves and tendrils into an irregular surrounding circle. "It's beautiful."

"I think so. I gave it to her many years ago." Mr. Weldon pinned the brooch carefully to the lapel of Helen's jacket.

"Good luck," she said, as they walked briskly along the pavement.

"And to you."

There was one couple standing in the small foyer of the restaurant, and taking her arm Mr. Weldon led her up to them.

"Good evening, Mr. Davenport. May I present my wife?"

"Mr. Weldon, Mrs. Weldon . . . My wife."

From the doorway Mr. Davenport had appeared to have a young girl on his arm but, closer to, Mrs. Davenport was seen to be presenting herself a little more youthfully than was the fact. She was, though, exceedingly attractive in a vague blonde way. Mr. Davenport was scarcely different from Mr. Weldon, making Helen reflect, as they followed the head waiter, on the chance element in success. The two men could so easily have played each other's parts. . . .

Mr. Weldon, she soon saw, was not very good in the role of suppliant—but perhaps that was a quality in him which his prospective employer had seen as auguring well. It was equally obvious that Mr. Davenport was setting out to make the evening appear the straightforward dinner-party it ostensibly was, his questions seeming to rise naturally out of the general conversation. Mrs. Davenport had a persistent laugh and no views, confirming Helen in her first impression that she was not to be taken into account. For herself, it was easy enough to fall into a routine of readiness to answer Mr. Davenport's questions when they came, and for the rest of the time to add the odd comment to the main burden of talk carried by the men.

It was, as Mr. Weldon had told her it would be, a rather good meal. And her acting ability was being called on at its minimum.

Why then, when the end of the assignment was in sight, was she assailed by a sense of unease, a sense of . . .

It couldn't be merely that Mrs. Davenport had surprised her, leaning forward as she was answering one of Mr. Davenport's questions, to suggest unlaughingly that she thought Mrs. Weldon was in process of contradicting herself. It was in fact as credible that Mrs. Davenport's little-girl role should be a pose to lull an unsuspecting interviewee into a false sense of security, as that she should be as she had seemed. . . .

Roles. She was applying the word to all four of them. For a crazy moment, feeling the reality of good wine in her mouth, listening to Mr. Davenport's explanation of a particular aspect of his consultancy, watching Mrs. Davenport's expertly painted eyes and restored smile, she was feeling herself one of a quartet of actors. . . .

The moment passed. Perhaps, relaxed in the knowledge of how little she was being called on to do, she had allowed herself too much of the good wine, perhaps she couldn't escape scot-free from the monstrousness of entering other people's lives in the way her new job was propelling her. . . .

Everything had come back into focus, she could distinguish again between fact and fancy, but when Mr. Davenport said he thought that perhaps they should be on their way, her relief was greater than at the moment she had left Vi's house with Mr. Redfern.

"You have your car, Weldon?"

"Thank you, round the corner. . . ."

"Good night, then. Good night, Mrs. Weldon. Thank you for joining us."

"Thank you for inviting me, Mr. Davenport, and for a very good dinner."

"My pleasure," said Mr. Davenport perfunctorily. Mrs. Davenport laughed and husband and wife disappeared into the car which a man in a peaked cap had just driven to a stop outside the restaurant.

"I don't suppose you will accept a lift," said Mr. Weldon. The street was well lit and full of people, and she couldn't object that he had continued lightly to hold her arm after she had stumbled on a paving stone.

"Thank you, but I'll get a taxi. There are plenty about."

"Of course. And of course before you do"—they were walking slowly towards the end of the block—"I must give you what I owe you and thank you for coming so superbly to my rescue." Mr. Weldon went into a pocket and brought out an open envelope. "Look inside." It was easy to see that there were five new ten pound notes. "Put it away now, while I'm here. One never knows . . ."

"Thank you. And I hope you'll get the job and that your wife will be home soon." They were strolling on again and she was wanting to look towards the road and secure one of the cruising taxis.

"Thank you. I am sure of your second hope, if not your first. What's that?"

A hoarse voice had shouted close behind them, and Helen, too, was alarmed, springing round as one with Mr. Weldon, who again had his hand on her arm, this time firmly and protectively.

They turned into a blinding flash.

Afterwards, Helen realized she had expected a deafening noise to accompany it. But there was only the back view of a man, scattering other strollers as he raced away from them.

She didn't know what had happened, and stood dazed as Mr. Weldon let go of her arm.

"Oh my God," said Mr. Weldon.

"What was it? What happened?"

"A photographer. Taking our photograph by design, I am afraid, rather than by accident." Mr. Weldon's voice shook slightly, but he appeared to have mastered his shock.

"You mean—"

"My wife, I am forced to assume, has entered a new phase, she has had me followed. I can only hope that when she sees the photograph she will realize why I appear to have her on my arm when she is not here. She knew about my hopes for this job. Oh my God," said Mr. Weldon again.

He was staring unseeingly, a man stricken. But the feeling which had assailed her at the dinner table was on her again. She hailed the taxi travelling slowly by the kerb.

"Mr. Weldon, I must go. I'm so very sorry. But it must mean your wife cares. Think of it that way." She had left Tony's mother on a similarly exhortatory note. But not in the midst of such inexplicable panic.

"Paddington!" she exclaimed as she climbed into the cab, on the reflex of her sixth sense. A similar reflex made her draw back as Mr. Weldon's frozen face followed her inside, but he was merely reaching for the *art nouveau* brooch.

"I'm so very sorry," she repeated, helping him to detach it. "Paddington!" she urged again, as slowly Mr. Weldon's head withdrew, and the taxi moved off. When she looked round she saw him standing motionless on the pavement, but the street behind the taxi was full of other moving vehicles and she thought she saw the outline of a chauffeur's cap. . . .

The taxi had turned several corners when she leaned forward.

"Can you get away from everything that's behind us, and when you've done that, take me to Victoria?"

"I'd given up hoping anyone would ever ask me." The taxi-driver was young and his smile filled his mirror. While they twisted and turned she pulled the wig off and combed out her hair, crouching low on the seat, cleaned her face and changed her jacket for the one folded into her dressing-case. If the driver wasn't successful, she might look sufficiently different for the short sprint into the ladies' cloakroom. . . . Her sixth sense was working overtime, she was out-Julianing Julian with her absurdly melodramatic behaviour. But she couldn't help it, all she could see in her mind's eye was her home and garden and Toby among the roses, and a shadow that hadn't reached them. . . .

"Reckon we're in the clear," said the smiling mouth. "Victoria, you said?" The mouth dipped and wide eyes filled the mirror. "Blimey!"

"It's a dare," she said. "I want to win."

"Lady, you deserve to."

"When you stop I don't want to hang about. Can I pay you now?"

"If you insist. For two pins I'd let you have the ride on me."

"On the contrary, there'll be a big tip."

He leaned back for the money without slackening speed.

"Goodbye and thanks," she said as he drew up outside the station, remembering a childhood day when she and a friend had started chasing each other up the stairs and the one being chased had ended up hysterical with terror. It didn't seem as if she had grown up, but at least she knew not to run now, not to make herself stand out among the men and women grouped zombie-like about the station entrance. It was almost impossible, but she managed to walk slowly on to the concourse, into the ladies' room, into a cubicle. And when she locked the door and began to shake, it wasn't so much that she was still afraid of pursuit, it was more with the shock of her own extraordinary behaviour.

CHAPTER 5

Eventually she strolled out of the station and up to another taxi. The driver was surly, needing to be persuaded he was willing to make a journey out to the sticks. She had been lucky with the other one. Unless . . .

No more of that. Leaning back in the taxi and consciously relaxing, she thought over the evening and by the time she reached home her chief preoccupation was with the woman whose life of tennis and committees hid so unconventional a temperament. Well, she would never have a chance to fathom it. As, now, she would never know if Tony's mother had spoken out. How big a gallery of unfinished portraits would she have hung by the time she decided she had had enough?

Toby was downstairs alone in Julian's armchair. Julian was upstairs in bed, reading.

"Well?" One arm across his book, one behind his head, he turned to look at her as she crossed the room.

"Absolutely and completely well, the easiest part I've ever played." How extraordinary that she should have behaved as she had.

"The lady doesn't protest too much?"

"Of course not." But she had turned away from his steady gaze. "Although there was a bit of a funny ending."

"There was?"

The question sounded mechanical and when she got up to the bed she saw that the worry in his face was not for her. Suddenly and sharply she wanted to be close to him, and as she asked questions she tore off her clothes.

"Are you all right, darling? Is there something extra bothersome in the Department?"

"Yes to both questions. And the Department isn't my life."

"It isn't?"

"Come here."

"When I've cleaned my teeth."

He leaned down to put the book on the floor. "While you've been doing all this I've been remembering . . ."

"What?" She turned back in the bathroom doorway, at something in his tone.

"What you did for me. For the Department."

"What I'm doing now is nothing, to that. But you weren't worried then."

"Even a man in my inhuman position is permitted to worry about his wife."

But tonight it wasn't his wife. She asked him as she got into bed if he wanted her to tell him about the evening.

"Tomorrow? As it was so absolutely and completely all right?"

"Tomorrow. . . ."

Tomorrow, so far as telling each other non-urgent things was concerned, meant tomorrow evening. Although she had not yet failed to stagger downstairs at the early hour Julian had weekday breakfast and share his teapot, this small ritual was usually accomplished in a silence broken only by monosyllables. At least she got her chores finished early, as she had not yet, either, given in to the luxurious possibility of going back to bed. Earlier than ever the morning after her evening as Mrs. Weldon, she found the adrenaline caused by her ridiculous over-reaction had not quite ebbed and was aware of extra energy. She expended some of it on house and garden and some on starting to devise the production of a comedy the local dramatic society had entrusted to her for the first offering of the autumn programme, then went for a walk, enjoying the simplicity of being herself and without anxiety. But product as she was of an upbringing which stressed service as the correct expression of gratitude for privilege, she was aware of a tinge of guilt creeping across her contentment. Probably the time had come for her to think about keeping less of her day for herself. . . .

She was working in the front garden when Julian came along the road, walking from the station on another warm sunny evening. She knew he was still worried before he reached the gate.

"Things haven't resolved yet. I'm sorry."

"No. But I didn't think I wore my mind on my sleeve."

"In the set of your shoulders." This was probably a more reliable indication than that extra sense of hers which had been working so much overtime. "Darling, I don't want the Department to make an old man of you."

"You said, from that first time you saw me, you thought I'd never been young."

"I knew I'd made a mistake about that the first time I saw you with your hair untidy. I said that, as well. Come and have a drink."

They sat near the open doorway.

"That funny ending to last night, if you'd like me to—"

"Of course. Yes." As usual he had the *Evening Standard* on his knees, turned back at the point he had reached on the train.

"We'd said good night to the other two—their chauffeur picked them up at the very door of the restaurant, at the very moment we came out, I was a bit impressed—and were walking vaguely along the pavement. I was wanting to get a taxi and suddenly a man's voice shouted behind us and when we turned round there was a terrific flash. I thought it was a gun and I sort of waited to hear a noise and feel a pain. . . . Julian?"

"Sorry, darling."

He looked up hastily from the paper, but she didn't think he had been reading.

"Are you all right?" He couldn't have heard what she was saying or he would have shown some interest, if not concern. She had another chance to decide not to tell him about the photography. For the time being she'd take it.

"Yes, just not switching off. Forgive me. What did you say?"

"I was only burbling on about the dinner-party. It was a very good meal, but the company wasn't all that easy. Well, I don't suppose a business meeting disguised as a social occasion could expect to be. At least I'm confident I didn't do Mr. Weldon's chances any harm, and I might have improved them."

"Mr. Weldon?"

"The man who wanted the job. Whose wife—"

"Yes, of course." Julian laid the paper on the arm of his chair and got up to refill his glass. "Carry on," he said as he sat down again.

She didn't think he was aware he had flipped over a page of the paper.

"I got a taxi very easily and then another at Victoria." She wouldn't tell him, either, about having changed in the first taxi rather than in the ladies' cloakroom.

"That's good," said Julian, turning another page.

"The second driver wasn't too keen— Darling, what is it?"

Shooting his hands up to devastate his smooth hair, Julian had sent his glass flying from the table beside him and Toby was hissing and shaking himself free of the golden arc of whisky and water which had ended where he sat sunning himself on the garden threshold.

The glass was upside down on the carpet, unbroken but empty, and Julian was throwing himself backwards and forwards in his chair and swearing.

"It doesn't matter, I'll pour you another one." As she got to her feet, Toby, with a reproachful glance, walked stiff-legged outside.

"I know it doesn't matter. Do you think that's what's worrying me? Yes, pour me another one."

She did so, in silence when she had seen his face, and when she had put it down beside him she sat on the floor by his chair and went on waiting without speaking. Either he had suddenly understood or remembered something, or he had actually been looking at the paper.

Eventually she tried to draw it out from under his clenched hands. His angry eyes saw her, and softened.

"I'm sorry." The hand she had taken responded. "Poor old Toby." The cat was in the centre of the lawn, ostentatiously washing.

"Can't you tell me, this time? Is it something in the paper?"

"It's something in the paper." When he took his other hand away to have a deep drink, she saw there was one photograph on the uppermost page, of a man and a woman. He covered it again before she could turn it to face her. "And yes, I'll tell you. A very important physicist, female, British, has disappeared from London. She'd reported some KGB harassment, and we thought we had her adequately protected. But she disappeared five days ago. Something happened subsequently—I won't go into that—and we thought we knew where she'd ended up. Somewhere in this country, not far away in fact, and we're in process of working out the best thing to do. At

Playing Safe

least we thought there was something we *could* do. And we thought our information . . ." Helen picked up Julian's glass as his arms flailed again, and put it into his hand as it descended. He drained it and set it back sharply on the table. "And all the time," he said, coughing and hitting the paper on his knees, "the bitch had defected. Complained to us about harassment by her paymasters and then waltzed off with them. And meanwhile we were told . . . I'll start thinking of the public weal eventually, but just now . . . I wouldn't have believed I could have misread someone so totally. But there she is, against the background of the Kremlin, arm in arm with one of our chief UK KGB tormentors. And how *he* got out of the country . . ." The paper was free now, and she pulled it down beside her to look at the photograph. "There are going to be a lot of inquests, and rolling heads, and—"

"Julian."

"I still can't believe I could have been taken in like that. And we were almost . . . Fools. Idiots. Without the sense God gave geese."

"Julian!"

"I'm sorry, darling. Let me rave. Dr. Susan Bakewell and Vladimir—"

"Julian, stop tearing your hair. That's not Dr. Susan Bakewell."

"For heaven's sake, you know nothing about it."

"It's me."

"What's you? Look, I'm not ready yet for the light relief. Can't you just let me rant and rave myself off boiling point?"

"I can take you off boiling point. Julian, *listen.*"

She imprisoned his hands and, less easily, his eyes. "I told you something when you came in and you didn't hear me, and then I thought I wouldn't tell you again, because on second thoughts I decided it might upset you. But now you're going to listen to it. Darling, when I came out of the restaurant last night with—Mr. Weldon"—already she was sheepish, using the name—"we were walking along the pavement when someone shouted behind us and we both turned round. He grabbed my arm tightly as we did, I thought just from an instinct to protect me, and a man took a photograph right in our faces and then ran off. Mr. Weldon said his wife must have had him followed, and went through the motions of being frightfully upset. It was very well done but somehow I didn't go for it and I actually started to tell myself off for being so paranoiacally suspicious."

"All right, Helen." He spoke coldly and tiredly, laying the paper back on his knee. "Mr. Weldon's wife had him photographed. You were with him. Dr. Bakewell is wearing the *art nouveau* brooch she was never without, it's quite clear. And she's standing in front of the Kremlin."

"Mr. Weldon pinned that brooch to my coat. He said it was a brooch he'd given his wife years ago and the fact that she left it behind always reassured him that she'd come back. He was very insistent I should wear it. All through the dinner I felt things were wrong. . . . Oh, darling, you should have agreed to a dress rehearsal, you might have suspected . . . I'm going upstairs now, I'm going to dress up as I was dressed last night. That photograph was taken in Davies Street, your Vladimir hasn't left London." Still he sat motionless, eyes lowered to the paper. "Julian, I know myself! I know how Mr. Weldon and I were standing, I recognize *my* jacket, the wig *I* was wearing. I always said you wouldn't know me if I was disguised, and now . . ."

He said harshly, "Yes, go upstairs and get yourself up as you were got up last night. Quickly. I hope you're crazy."

"I'm not crazy. You were right about your Dr. Bakewell, she hasn't defected, she hasn't—"

"Idiot child, that's the least of it. Hurry up, let me see you. Go on!"

She fled from the room. Luckily she hadn't dispersed yesterday's props, they were still tumbled together in the top of her chest. Dress, scarf, jacket, wig, shoes. Everything but the *art nouveau* brooch. When she was dressed and made up she ran down the stairs and back into the sitting-room, running until she was standing in front of Julian and staring wide-eyed as she thought she had stared into the shock of the flashbulb.

Julian stared back at her, holding the newspaper in his hand.

She said almost angrily, "Haven't you got some sort of physiognomist in the Department? Equivalent to a handwriting expert, someone who could *see* it's the same face, the same—"

"I can see." Julian dropped the newspaper but went on staring at her. Something in his eyes turned her cold.

"So you can see too, darling, your physicist hasn't defected, what you were working out must be right, you don't—"

"Did you go straight to Victoria? Did Vladimir hear you say Victoria?"

"I said Paddington. I was unhappy, I told you. I don't know why, there didn't seem to be any reason, except that I'd had the extraordinary feeling during dinner that I wasn't the only one playing a part. When we'd turned a few corners I asked the taxi-driver to get rid of everything behind us, and then take me to Victoria. Then I—well, I took the wig off and cleaned my face while I was in the cab. I was telling myself off all the time for being an idiot, but I went on doing it. The taxi-driver was young and keen and entered into the spirit of it. He assured me we'd shaken everything off. I pretended I was doing a dare, I—"

"Did Vladimir hail the taxi for you?"

"No. It was just going slowly past. . . . Julian, you don't think . . . For a moment, *I* thought, he was so helpful. Oh, darling."

She knelt in front of him, clutching his hands. She knew, now, what she had seen in his eyes, because he had passed it to her.

Fear.

But he was shaking his head. "Don't worry about the taxi if Vladimir didn't hail it. Anyway, it wouldn't have dropped you off. Get me the addresses and telephone numbers of those three wretched magazines you wrote to. And find out which of the three that youth saw the advert in."

"Julian . . ." She drew back to stare at him, while the sense of fear spread out like a stone thrown into a pool.

He said impatiently, "Your sixth sense did you proud. It's the rest of the cast I'm worried about. Get me those addresses now. Then get yourself back to normal."

The telephone by the bed murmured twice while she was upstairs, one long call. She went downstairs when she heard it the second time. Julian was pacing the sitting-room.

"I've given instructions for everything relating to you and your Versatile Actress to be withdrawn from the files of those magazines. We've got to think, now, what they'll do if you really did shake them off last night. Which I hope to God you did. And apart from the

skills of your taxi-driver, they were probably being a bit casual anyway, they would hardly expect you to use their tactics."

"But—Julian—why should they bother about me any further? I'd
done what they wanted."

"Oh, darling. You'd done one thing they wanted. Admirably. As-
tonishingly, if you think about it. Can you imagine they'd be willing
to lose so valuable a find? Your memory for a start. Think of the
applications of *that*. The dinner-party—it *was* an interview, but you
were the only interviewee. They wanted to see if your nerve matched
your talents. I gather it did."

"All that stuff about the Weldons . . ."

"They probably lifted that from a couple of CVs. It didn't much
matter. Look, darling, if they lost you at Victoria—no, don't, it looks
as if they did lose you"—*if they aren't waiting for the dark, or for one
morning when Julian has gone to town and I'm beginning to relax, to
think I've been worrying about nothing*—"then one of their hopes is
the files of the magazine where that young man saw your advertisement. I want his address, too."

"You think Tony's involved?" The ripples were spreading wider by
the second.

"If not Tony, then the friend of his who put you in touch with his
so-called uncle."

She thought of Pete, his bright, sharp face and her awareness, in
that small kitchen, of the purpose behind his charm. "Another Rus-
sian spy?"

"Probably nothing so dramatic. But he's homosexual, no doubt
he's been drawn into the network as they hope to draw you in. You
see, darling"—he took her hands again—"you have a weakness, too.
You don't merely possess a range of unusual talents they could make
use of. Last night albeit innocently you helped the KGB to perpe-
trate a fraud, which was hardly in your country's interests." He
leaned forward to put his face against hers. "If they can find you they
have a hold over you."

She held him at arm's length, glaring. "I'd explain to—to the
authorities—how it happened."

"The wife of Julian Johnson would explain. The woman they think
they're after could try. No doubt Vladimir and Co. consider she
might find it easier not to try, and to earn more money than she did

the first time for a second piece of assistance. I said those files were one of the possibilities open to them for tracing you. The other is the letter for Miss Versatile Actress which one of the magazines should shortly receive. Suggesting that it will be in your interests to respond. And that if you don't—"

"I see, I see. Oh, Julian, they mustn't find me!" They mustn't find Julian, or Toby, or the sitting-room in the evening sunshine.

"If they try to break into the files of one of those magazines, or if they address a letter via Versatile Actress, it'll be a fair assumption that you managed to shake them off. They'll hardly expect you to have a husband in my position. But they will, I think, recognize the possibility of your seeing that photograph and going to the police, so whatever they do will be done fast. That's why I gave instructions for the three sets of records to be removed at once. Oh, darling." Her knees had given way and he picked her up and laid her on the sofa.

"I'm sorry. I'm so terribly sorry." She felt dreadful. "I wish you'd be angry. Tell me how selfish I was to insist on satisfying my ego while you were in such a sensitive position. And when I knew you didn't want me to."

"That wasn't anything to do with my position. That part of it's just an appalling coincidence. I was worried about *you.*"

"And now—we're both worried about *us.*" She resisted as he tried to stop her getting up. "Let's have dinner. I'm all right now, I want to do something. It's awful when you dislike yourself, you can't escape. But moving about makes it seem less concentrated." She trailed out to the kitchen, where there was a smell she would once have considered appetizing. The casserole was precisely ready. "Let's have some wine." The sun, low and sharply angled, was dazzling off a ceramic plant pot. "I'm going to be like the people of Dracula country when they saw the sun disappearing. I'm going to be afraid of the dark."

The telephone rang when they'd finished eating and were sitting over the last of the wine. Julian went upstairs to take it, with an apologetic smile. He was soon back.

"There's no record of you now with the three magazines. And in each case exasperated officials hauled back to their offices have been able to tell us categorically that no attempt has been made to break into the filing areas. I was afraid, darling, that Vladimir and Co.

might already have tried to get at your files, before there was any possibility of anyone being alerted. But they haven't. If they do, now, they'll find nothing. So it will be the gently threatening letter. I rather think it will be that anyway. If they try the files—and nothing will be done to make that especially difficult for them—and draw blank, there's a chance they might try to nobble a records clerk. Say two words and offer threats or money—"

Versatile Actress. "Too clever by half. That should be my obituary."

"Don't talk like that!" It frightened her even more, that he should react so sharply. "Certainly there's the likelihood that the records clerks will be able to remember your pseudonym," he said more gently. "But I'll be surprised if they remember the name and address to which they forwarded letters, and our people will have confiscated memo pads, too. I'll also be surprised if Vladimir and Co. take it that far. At least until they've tried the letter and drawn no response. By which time . . ."

She had stopped listening, she had had another memory like a knife thrust. "Julian! When I took the bus away from that flat in Camden Town, Pete could have followed me. I'm pretty sure I took him by surprise but I'm equally sure he's the sort to make the most of any piece of luck."

"If you think you could deceive me, you could deceive Pete."

"But if he was waiting at Victoria, looking . . ."

His eyes slid away from hers. "He's cleared out. Just one injured innocent, now, in that flat, saying his friend left without a word."

Toby hurling himself at the back door made her give a little moan of shock. Julian got up to let the cat in, then shut the door and locked it. Usually he didn't lock it until they were ready to go to bed, after their final walk round the garden.

"Julian, what about the garden?"

"I think, tonight, we'll prefer to stay indoors, although it isn't logical." No. If they had found her, it wouldn't matter whether she was indoors or out. "Let's go to bed early."

But it was impossible to sleep. To accept, without tossing and turning, the watching and waiting role. And Julian hadn't told her what she was to do when the letter came.

"Are you asleep?"

"No."

"When that letter comes, I can play along with it, can't I? Go and meet Vladimir or whoever it is. Meet as many of them as possible and then tell you . . . As you said, they don't know anything about my husband." Yet.

"Oh, darling." He turned towards her.

"I can, can't I?"

"Yes. . . ."

"Julian, I want to help! I want to try and make up a bit for being so vain and putting us into this nightmare."

"If it hadn't been for you, we'd be believing now that Dr. Bakewell had defected." He laughed, a disagreeable sound. "It's a test, isn't it, of my departmental loyalty? Shouldn't I feel that the risk to me and mine is offset by the information about Dr. Bakewell?"

"Don't be like that. It doesn't do you any good and it makes me feel even worse. Where is Dr. Bakewell?"

He put his hand at the back of her neck and pulled her head against him. "If our—information—is correct, at a fashionable psychiatric clinic near Lewes. Patients ranging from catatonics to the mildly dotty. The clinic's recently changed hands, but the manner of its running hasn't altered, nor the majority of its personnel." His steady heartbeat seemed to be crescendoing against her ear. "Doctors admit their patients, and continue to attend them. We've been trying to think how we could confirm Dr. Bakewell's presence, and assess the chances of an SAS-type snatch, without losing our trump card—the fact that, if we've got it right, the new owners have no inkling of our interest in their establishment."

I've been remembering what you did for me. For the Department.

"You've been wanting to ask me, haven't you? Julian, I'll go in for you. Please let me go in. That is if it would be more useful for me to do that than to play along with the letter. Would it?"

"Yes." He groaned. "I wasn't going to ask you, although the Department have been pressing me."

"Perhaps you've told me about the clinic now because subconsciously you knew I'd ask *you*. Please."

"Yes. You can go in. It'll be dangerous, darling, of course it will, but if our information is on the level it'll be invaluable. And if it isn't,

I promise you, although I can't explain things to you now, it won't be you in the front line."

"You could be in the front line here."

"I'll get a colleague to come and stay. Share keeping the house occupied all the time and explaining your absence if anyone rings or calls. We'll be alert." Julian moved restlessly. "Darling, I have such mixed reactions. I'd like you out of the way for a time, and in one sense Hartshorn Manor is the coldest trail I can send you along as well as the hottest."

"Won't the important door be locked or guarded?"

"I don't think so. The practice of the clinic favours the principle of the beach and the pebbles."

"Explain."

"Various comatose patients with various own doctors. No one understanding anyone else's case. Nurses either knowing all or knowing nothing. Why should one case be more significant than another?"

"I see. And one fey lady drifts about among others. . . ."

"Just so."

"Except that they know about Versatile Actress." It was a small penance, just to spit out the two words.

"Yes, but as I've told you, we don't think they know that *we* know about the Manor. And the fact of that photograph, now I can think about it more dispassionately, should rather strengthen our confidence—if they've gone out of their way to satisfy us that Dr. Bakewell's in Moscow, they'll hardly be mounting guard on Hartshorn Manor, or expecting any interest in it. And we'll go out of *our* way to let it appear that the photograph has been swallowed whole. But you'll trust none of the Manor staff, of course, even though some of them will be all right."

"I suppose the Department has already had ideas about my role?"

"Well, yes. There's a bit of luck. . . . Let's try and sleep now, darling, and I'll tell you in the morning."

She thought she would never find oblivion, but Mr. Redfern's nose exploding in her face was the alarm clock ringing. As her confused, uneasy dreams receded and memory rushed back in a cold stream, it seemed incredible that the curtains were golden and the birds were singing.

CHAPTER 6

George Parkinson, a senior Civil Servant, had no children of his own, but for some years had given board and lodging to a niece, the only child of his late sister. The niece, a woman in her mid-thirties who some years earlier had lost her tenuous hold on reality, spent her days at a convent run by an order of nuns specializing in the care of the mentally handicapped, who charitably referred to her as being in their employ. (Sometimes, on a good day, she might manage to pick a few peas and beans, or stuff a cuddly toy.) George and his wife suddenly being offered a villa in Spain for a well-earned holiday, temporary accommodation had to be found for Miss Fiona Spencer. The nuns were of course willing to let her sleep at the convent, but were doubtful of the suitability of the building for someone prone to wander at night. A friend, however, had told the Parkinsons about Hartshorn Manor, a clinic for mentally disturbed patients which was prepared to take cases covering widely divergent degrees of severity. On application, it was ascertained that the clinic could accommodate Miss Spencer for the week of the Parkinson holiday, subject to a mutually satisfactory interview.

"I'm grateful to you for responding so quickly." George Parkinson's kind red face wore a permanently anxious expression. "The chance of this trip came up out of the blue. . . ."

"It's fortunate there is a vacancy." Mr. Jenkins, the Resident Director, had a tight professional smile. The small man sitting silent in an alcove of Mr. Jenkins's office had been introduced more vaguely.

Helen thought the vacancy hardly surprising, in view of the fees. She hummed her way up to the Resident Director's desk and stood twiddling the brightly coloured tube in which brightly coloured pens and pencils leaned like flower stalks. Then danced across to the window, the humming expanding into a light rendering of *All Things Bright and Beautiful.*

"Fiona," said Mr. Parkinson apologetically, "puts on a pretty continuous song and dance act. Very mild, that's as obtrusive as it gets, unless she's really distressed. Hymns, childhood and traditional songs, songs of the day—they all make up her repertoire. But although she must obviously latch on to songs, to be able to sing them, she doesn't latch on to conversations—one can talk across her and the most she makes of it is to catch the odd word sometimes which sends her off on some private tack. She's never tuned in to other people, even when she takes a fancy to someone."

"Takes a fancy . . ." The Resident Director's head turned, as if on a reflex, towards the man in the alcove. There was no responding gesture.

"From time to time," pursued George Parkinson, "she seems to see someone and actually notice them, and then she's likely to spend a few hours, or a few days, following them about. Her attentions are only little offerings—she might take a flower out of a vase—and a sort of fluttering about the person concerned. She can be ignored, she isn't looking for a response and in fact it could alarm her."

"Thirty-six, you say. She looks a lot younger." The smile, when it rested on the shorn blonde head of Miss Spencer, became less marked but warmer. "The—er—innocence, I suppose."

"She's been like Peter Pan," said George, "since she went over the edge."

"She wasn't always like this? That is to say—"

"No. That's what makes it all the more tragic—for us—because we remember . . ." Would it have been harder for George, or easier, if he hadn't been speaking the truth? "She was always—unpredictable—there were always times when she was as she is now. But in between you could communicate with her, please her, make her smile when you caught her eye. You can't catch Fiona's eye now, she's living altogether in her own mind. To her own pattern." George coughed. "The other awkward thing—she goes where her whim takes her, she's no respecter of privacy." Again the Resident Director turned his head, slowly and Helen thought reluctantly, towards the alcove. "On the other hand, she's so unaware of other people one could carry on—er—any activity in the sight of Fiona and she would be oblivious of it."

This time, for the first time, there was a slight movement from the small seated man.

"We can cope with that," said the Resident Director.

"I'm very grateful." But the smile on George's honest face had quickly disappeared. "When I say unaware of other people . . . Of course, she's aware that they're sources of food and comfort. And of fear— Fiona's afraid of anyone speaking harshly or loudly, or if anyone directs attention to her so persistently even she can't disregard it. Try to secure her attention to yourself, rather than to food or drink or something pretty, and Fiona's frightened. And talking of pretty things, she has a little gilt box she likes to carry round with her. Nothing in it, just something to hold on to—in two senses, I suppose. Her skirts and dresses always have pockets and she carries the thing with her all the time. Like a small child and a bit of blanket," said George sadly. "Now, I've told you the worst."

"Thank you. You did assure me she is able to look after herself in the day to day things. . . ."

"Oh yes. She's very clean and neat. Folds up her clothes and makes her bed and keeps herself—in order. She'll cause very little work for your staff on her own account. They're more likely to be aware of her when they're attending to other people." George laughed but Helen, turning her back to the window, could see his knuckles white where he was clenching his hands.

The man in the alcove was facing her as he had faced her when she had stood by the desk. His chair was on a swivel. Feeling herself shiver, she floated back across the room and stood with her hands on George's shoulders.

"Well, Mr. Parkinson," said the Resident Director, "we shall be happy to accommodate your niece for a week." She had missed the signal. "Beginning . . ." He looked down at the papers in front of him. " 'As soon as possible.' Tomorrow?"

"In the hope that you might find Fiona acceptable," said George, reaching up for Helen's hand, "I took the liberty of bringing a suitcase with me. Today?" Helen snatched her hand away and went back to the window.

"Today will suit us, Mr. Parkinson." The Resident Director glanced from Fiona to her uncle. "Will there be any—difficulty—when you leave?"

"Oh no." George's smile was rueful. "Fiona isn't wary of my wife and me, or of the nuns, as she is of other people, but she won't miss me. I've come to the conclusion that the life she leads inside her head is always more dominant than the life around her."

"Interesting," said the Resident Director. "Very interesting." But he looked, to Helen, like a man who lacked the peace of mind to pursue that or any other interest. Unless, of course, in view of the presence in the alcove, she had cast him in the role of bewildered innocent.

The Resident Director got to his feet. He was a man as unmemorable as Mr. Weldon, but in the negative English way of undistinguished features and personality without impact. "Perhaps you would like to see our public rooms, Mr. Parkinson. And the bedroom your niece will have."

"Of course. Thank you."

The Resident Director, followed by George, made brief obeisance to the alcove before leaving the room. Helen, staring through the man who sat there, saw him begin to rise as Mr. Jenkins closed the door. They crossed the well-proportioned hall—the house basically was late eighteenth-century—and entered a large, light room with windows on to the drive. Helen remained more or less with the two men, reminding herself of Toby when he joined her for a walk, diverting behind hedges and into gardens. . . . A woman by whose chair she had paused while she disciplined her thoughts was snatching the book she was reading up against her chest and staring defiantly. Fiona, cringing, backed away.

". . . quite cheerful, we think," the Resident Director was saying. "There's a smaller room off it—here—where our more collected clients can write letters. Or . . ." Fiona joined them in the doorway, looking in on a solitary woman in a voluminous smock who was concentrating on drawing circles with a felt pen.

"That's right, Mrs. . . . er . . ." said the Resident Director heartily. "You'll appreciate," he told George in his usual tired tones as they crossed the lounge again, "that I don't have much personal opportunity to get to know our clients. Administration these days . . ." He shrugged his shoulders and sighed. "Here's our dining-room."

Another pleasant room, matching the lounge the other side of the

front door. George murmured appreciatively, and they returned to
the hall. "To give our clients the benefit of our lovely gardens"—
Helen was sure the Resident Director always used that exact phrase
—"we have effectively enclosed a portion of them to the west of the
house, so that even those with a tendency to wander away—this is a
very common tendency, Mr. Parkinson—can be allowed outside
with impunity."

Helen, in her unnaturally heightened state, saw impunity as a de-
mure young nurse in uniform, and wanted to laugh. But she knew,
without it having been discussed, that Fiona Spencer didn't laugh.
Probably couldn't, a sense of humour was a higher attribute. . . . A
funny time to be making philosophical discoveries. She darted past
them on the stairs, then danced in a circle until the Resident Director arrived on the landing and turned left.

"Here we are."

A small white room at the side of the house, overlooking a piece of
kitchen garden, then fields. Bed, bedside locker, washstand, armchair, small built-in cupboard, small white chest of drawers.

"Very nice," said George Parkinson. "It has an atmosphere like
the convent. Peaceful. Fiona!" He crossed the room to where she
stood just inside the doorway. "This is your room, Fiona. Yours.
You're to sleep in this bed, over here. Come along." He took her
hand and she followed him draggingly, like a reluctant dog on a
leash.

"Will she take it in?" asked the Resident Director, looking more
relaxed than he had looked in the office. Perhaps this indicated that
the room wasn't wired for sight or sound.

"Yes, I think so." George was sitting on the bed, with Fiona wrig-
gling beside him. "Your bed, dear," he said softly, hypnotically
(they'd rehearsed it). "You'll be happy here while Auntie and I have
our holiday. Until I come to take you home."

"A holiday. You have this." Helen took the handkerchief out of
her skirt pocket and offered it to George. It was the first time she had
ventured the rare Fiona speaking voice. As she had hoped, it came
out light and breathy.

"Thank you, dear, but you keep it, you'll need it." He tucked the
handkerchief back in the pocket. Already Fiona had ceased to notice.
She jumped off the bed and went to gaze out of the window.

"Perhaps if you stay with her here a few moments." The Resident Director moved slowly, and she thought reluctantly, to the door. "Have you locked your car?"

"I'm afraid I have. Good habit, though."

"Yes, of course. If you'll let me have your key I'll get someone to bring Fiona's case up."

"Thanks, it's in the boot. Here. Just a small suitcase."

"Perhaps you'll look in at my office before you go, Mr. Parkinson. There are one or two formalities. . . . And you might like a word with Matron. . . . I hope you'll enjoy your holiday, and not worry. The doctors visit twice a day, every day. Your niece will be all right."

It was a difficult five or ten minutes, waiting for the suitcase. Helen felt more and more certain the room wasn't bugged, but it had been agreed no chances were to be taken. George had a look into the fitted cupboard, and through the chest of drawers. He ran the hot tap, then the cold. Eventually he said, "Your room, dear, this is your room. Your bed. Your place. Look at all the interesting things through the window. You can look out of the window, can't you?"

"Bye, bye, blackbird," sang Helen.

The case was brought in by a young nurse, pretty, blonde, and breathless.

"Fiona Spencer?"

"Yes," said George, taking the case and putting it on the bed. "But I'm afraid she doesn't always answer to it."

"I know," said the nurse cheerfully. "I've just had a word with Mr. Jenkins."

"She'll wash herself when you tell her it's bedtime. And in the morning when you tell her it's time to get up. She may get up in the night and wander about, but she won't do any harm."

"Well, not many of our patients are in a state to be upset by her." The nurse had natural colour in her cheeks and a wide smile.

"You have a lot of seriously disturbed people, then?" asked George.

At the window, Miss Spencer stopped singing.

"Some. But what I was meaning, when you're batty yourself, you don't notice other people's battiness the same." There was nothing unkind, only cheerful acceptance, in the choice of words. "Most of them here are in their own worlds, bless them."

"All of them are able to come downstairs, though, get dressed and go through the motions of normal life?"

"Mostly. Some of them prefer to stay in their rooms—the agoraphobics—and some prefer to eat there. Or their families prefer it. A few couldn't come down, they're not really conscious."

"The clinic has its own doctor?"

"Oh yes. Dr. Sandelson. He's been here for years, ever since the clinic started, I think. He looks after everyone whose own doctor isn't around, comes in twice a day. They all do. The clinic's always been open to people who come with their own doctors, if you see what I mean. In psychiatric cases the relationship between doctor and patient is pretty vital. Even though the clinic's changed hands it still works that way."

"The friends who recommended me—they knew it under the old regime. Has it changed?"

The nurse stood perplexed, rubbing her chin. "I don't know, really. There haven't been any changes of practice, and not many changes among the staff. But the atmosphere feels a bit different, somehow. Not quite so free and easy. Discipline tightened up a bit, I suppose that's what I mean. Which reminds me, I'd better get on with unpacking Miss Spencer's case. Hello!"

Fiona was executing a dance round the nurse, singing *Ring a Ring o' Roses.*

"I think she's noticed you," said Mr. Parkinson. "I'm sorry, she may follow you around for a bit, try to give you something. There won't be any more to it than that."

"We shan't worry, shall we, pet?" The nurse put her hand out at the same moment Fiona put out hers, and the tips of their fingers met. Miss Spencer shied away.

"Nervous as a thoroughbred filly," said George Parkinson. "I'll leave you then, Nurse . . . ?"

"Evans. I'll look after her."

"I'm sure you will. Goodbye, dear." Helen let herself be approached by George and secured by the shoulders. He kissed her forehead. "I'll come and take you home in just a week's time. Sunburned, I hope."

Fiona went straight back to the window, humming and staring out. The nurse began to put things from the suitcase into the drawers and hang up the few skirts, blouses, and dresses in the cupboard. Eventually Fiona became aware of the operation and started picking things up and walking round the room with them before putting them carefully down on bed or chair. Nurse Evans retrieved each object with good humour.

When everything was put away Helen followed her out of the room and along the corridor. They had done well to give Fiona these temporary attachments. . . .

Into a bright room with three beds, tidy and empty. On into another similar room, a woman lying on one of the beds, foetally curled.

"Come along now, Freda pet, come downstairs for your tea." The woman took her thumb out of her mouth, but stared expressionless. Nurse Evans sat down on the bed beside her, while Fiona danced across to the dressing-table and picked up a hairbrush backed with *petit point* embroidery protected by transparent plastic, crooning over it. Helen knew the nurse had seen her, even while her attention was unstinting for the woman on the bed. Here was a bright, intelligent girl.

"That's right!" There was a wavering ascent.

"Shoes!" came the fretful command.

"Here are your shoes. Can we manage? Good. Now, shall we brush your hair?" The nurse went straight to Helen without looking on the dressing-table. "That for me, pet?" Fiona held the brush out. "Thank you."

Freda was small and very thin and of indeterminate age, probably quite old. The nurse couldn't do much with her sparse grey hair, but while she was gently brushing Freda's hand stole up to take the brush and continue the exercise.

"That's the ticket!" said the nurse. Freda walked docilely at her side on the way downstairs, while Fiona played backwards and forwards, reaching the hall at the same time. There were the sounds of crockery being set out and a group of people, predominantly female, was being encouraged into the dining-room under the close supervision of a sister and another nurse.

"You come here, pet, beside Freda," said Nurse Evans to Fiona. The dining-room was arranged as in an elegant hotel, with tables for four. Most of those using it, Helen thought, would be oblivious, but

no doubt it assuaged the consciences of the affluent relatives who had
not felt themselves able to cope at home. . . .

Nurse Evans was indicating a vacant chair, and after going past
the table to examine a stretch of wall, Fiona floated back and sat
down, flinching when assistance was offered.

"Gentle persuasion," announced Nurse Evans, "with this one."

"We've heard," said the other nurse. She was small and dark and
moved and spoke mechanically, as if tired after a late night. Sister
was a tall, well-made woman, handsome when one had absorbed the
unadorned austerity of her face.

It had been agreed that Helen's attention should be focused on the
staff. Nevertheless, of course, she noted her table companions. In
addition to Freda, there was a prim-looking lady in a good suit who
kept pursing her lips and shaking her head, and a young man with
large sad eyes and a prominent Adam's apple who kept saying he
was sorry.

To her surprise she was hungry, and the food was good and well
cooked. No one at her table needed help with eating, although Freda
tended to forget about it and had to be reminded by a nurse. The
disapproving lady snatched the salt at the beginning of the meal and
put it closely against her plate. Once or twice she said, "No, oh no, I
certainly don't!" and vigorously shook her head. The sound of the
room was a series of quiet running monologues, murmurous background to the bright talk of Sister and the nurses.

It was just as she was finishing her meal, scraping the last of the
apple pie and cream from her plate, that she suddenly felt sick. So
sick she thought she must either race from the room or reveal a
characteristic of Fiona which had not been confessed.

"You all right, pet?"

Nurse Evans was at her side. Noticing her again. Fiona leaned into
the centre of the table and plucked a carnation from the slender vase,
holding it out to Nurse Evans. Fiona was consolidating her role, and
Helen was expressing her gratitude that the sickness had passed as
quickly as it had come, its only aftermath a new source of fear. She
could have sworn that the plates had been set before the patients in
order of seating. . . .

There was enough to worry about without inventing more. There was no possible way anyone at Hartshorn Manor could know Fiona Spencer was not what she seemed. Not yet, at any rate.

"Thank you, pet, it's lovely!" Nurse Evans put the bloom to her nose, sniffed ecstatically, and returned it to the vase. Fiona was humming, turning away to stare at the next table. "Shall we go into the lounge and see what's on television?"

Helen wondered if George Parkinson, before leaving, had told the Resident Director and the Matron that Miss Spencer's attention could sometimes be caught by the television screen. That no one was sure whether this was brought about by the programme being shown, or her own state of mind. . . .

Fiona sat quietly for a while, her head against the back of the second comfortable armchair she had been steered to. (Her occupation of the first, which she had chosen herself, had been disputed by a stout lady who Helen suspected might have tried violence if Nurse Evans hadn't been hard on their heels.) Through her drooping lids she saw Sister moving about the room, stopping to speak to one or two patients or try and make them more comfortable. When the severe face relaxed it took on an expression of concern and concentration which was reassuring. Nevertheless, when the tall figure passed Helen's chair and she felt a hand briefly on her shoulder, she found herself flinching in her own persona. Probably her actress's reflex, bringing Fiona to life. . . .

The programme was a repeat of an episode of a serial she'd seen a few days earlier, in that safe world which had so suddenly blown apart. Her eyes half closed on the images before them, she was seized by an anguished love for her home which was a physical pain. Sunlight, peace, freedom . . . Toby the small dark totem at its heart. Betrayed, endangered by her stupid pride, because she had thought it wasn't enough for her. . . .

Fiona got up and drifted out to the hall. She went up to the window beside the closed front door and stood softly singing, staring towards the drive and the grassy bank which dipped beyond it before rising again, tree-dotted. When Helen had subdued her regret, the new effort was to refuse to recall the moment she had thought she was going to be sick and had looked down at her empty plate. . . .

"I'm sorry." The young man with the Adam's apple had followed her, for goodness' sake, and was standing close. Surely he couldn't be a serious menace, he wouldn't be allowed to go freely about. Fiona started back like a frightened fawn—Helen kept seeing her in animal images—and the little dark nurse was there, standing between them as expressionless as she had been in the dining-room but making Helen aware, now, of her authority.

"You're saying hello to Miss Spencer, are you, Geoffrey? That's all right, but she's rather shy."

"Of course. I'm sorry." The young man blinked rapidly, as if he was going to cry.

"That's all right," said the nurse again. She turned to Helen. "He won't hurt you, lovey, he just likes to be friendly." A car scrunched into view, and the nurse turned to the window. "Ah, it's Dr. Webster. Sister said he would be late tonight."

She unlocked the front door with a key from her pocket. Helen, still leaning at the window and watching the young man return with drooping head to the lounge, heard the murmured exchange of greetings and flitted to the nurse's side as the door was closed and locked behind the man who had just come in.

"Your lady hasn't said anything yet, I'm afraid, Dr. Webster, but the pulse rate is holding up. If you'd like to come upstairs . . . This is a new patient, Miss Fiona Spencer. Staying for a week while her family's away. She's not really aware of us."

"No? That's interesting."

But thank heaven the precise voice was indifferent, belying the words, and the pale eyes were on Helen so briefly. Yet she really had to congratulate herself for managing to look through them and continue singing.

What had Julian said? *Some people will be all right.*

But not Mr. Weldon.

CHAPTER 7

The only thing to do was to stay with Mr. Weldon—Dr. Webster—
and the nurse, flaunt the irrelevant figure of Fiona Spencer, make
them realize it was as uncomprehending as the figure of the blacka-
moor at the head of the stairs, holding up a miniature palm tree.
There wasn't much she could do with the palm, but on a table
against the wall where they turned along the corridor away from
Fiona's room, a large bowl of roses offered her a gesture. Pulling one
out, spiking her thumb painfully on a thorn and sending an entwined
second rose to the floor, she held it out to the nurse.

"Oh Lord!" The nurse took the rose and bent down to pick up the
other one. "She gets crushes on people. I thought it was Daphne.
. . . Thank you, lovey. I'm sorry, Doctor. . . ." Jamming the two
roses roughly back into the vase (Helen had to restrain an absurd
impulse to arrange them properly), the nurse hurried after the disappearing figure of the doctor, who might have been a horse in blinkers
for all he appeared to notice of the incident with the flowers. Even
when Helen, forcing herself to be unhesitating, followed him and the
nurse into the dark room whose door he had opened, he continued to
act as if she was invisible, striding across to the window to make a
gap in the closed curtains. Light fell on to the one bed, spotlighting
the woman lying motionless with closed eyes, her dark hair sprawl-
ing on the pillow.

So easy? There was no doubt who the woman was, on a quick
glance Helen could have been looking at herself as a brunette. Dr.
Bakewell was on her back and breathing heavily, the face which
Helen knew to be habitually pale now grey-white.

"Is there anything I can do, Doctor?"

"Thank you, Nurse, no. Except to tell Sister that I am here. So
that she will have her usual excellent tea ready for me when I come
down."

And talk? How many of the staff did Dr. Webster talk to? She must start a list in her head. At this stage, the small dark nurse would not be on it.

"Yes, Doctor. I'm sorry the patient hasn't shown any responses."

"I had not expected them. Take this woman with you, please."

Helen was by the window and Dr. Webster had not appeared to look at her.

"Come along, dear," said the nurse. Helen began to sing, to cover her dilemma. Did Fiona for once understand something in the real world, or did she wait for force?

She went round the bed and began to fiddle with the few things on the bedside table. A water carafe. An enamel bowl. A bottle half full of liquid.

"Come *along,* dear," said the nurse a bit desperately.

"I'll take the high road," sang Helen, drifting away from the bed-side table. Dr. Webster met her at the foot of the bed. She had to look through him without seeing him because that was what Fiona Spencer did. So when he put his hands on her arms and said "Out!" she didn't know what his face was like. But the word and the gesture were enough to send Fiona shying out into the corridor.

"I'm sorry, Dr. Webster."

"It's all right, Nurse." The voice was preoccupied and not ill-humoured. Murmuring further apologies, the nurse followed Helen out of the room and closed the door. "You're a naughty girl!" she said, smiling.

Helen held out her handkerchief. It seemed that this nurse was the one to be keen on for the time being.

"Lovely!" said the nurse, taking the handkerchief and tucking it back in Fiona's skirt pocket. (Fiona carried no bag, there being nothing apart from the handkerchief and her small gold toy she could possibly need.) Helen ventured a quick pull at the roses as she danced past, then chided herself for less than total dedication. Whenever she came out of Fiona she had to get back into her, and there were to be no moments at Hartshorn Manor which lent themselves to this process, apart from those spent in bed.

The room marked SISTER was beyond the dining-room. The nurse's knock was answered at once, and Helen went in with her.

"Oh dear, has it started already? Matron, this is Fiona Spencer, who lives in a world of her own and whose uncle I think you met."

"Yes. Mr. Parkinson, wasn't it? Well, we've had them more upsetting, Sister." Matron was plump, with a face on optimistic lines and fair curly hair turning grey. She had not disturbed in any way her relaxed pose in what looked like Sister's most comfortable chair.

"We have, yes. Oh, she's all right."

"Doesn't hear what you say, and wouldn't have anyone to pass it on to, anyway."

A veiled reassurance? Or simply something to say? However innocent and unaware, the irruption of Fiona Spencer into private rooms and private gatherings must be unnerving in its effect.

"I presume *you* had a reason for knocking at my door, Rogers," said Sister.

"Oh yes, Sister, I'm sorry, Fiona made me forget." There was one school of thought which would advocate Fiona hanging about the offices and corridors of power as much as possible, to distract people less and less from their real business. "Dr. Webster's here, he's with one of his patients. Mrs. Hughes. He said if you were making tea . . ."

"I'm making tea."

Sister's calm voice was suddenly faint and far away. Fiona darted to yet another window, and Helen stood with her forehead against the cold pane. *One of his patients.* One of two, three, four? One of two was bad news enough. If there had been another Dr. Webster patient only a few days ago, wouldn't Julian have known of it? She'd spent only two days at the convent observing George's niece, and Julian had said the next step would be the letter. But he had also said that at some point a records clerk . . . Approached in his favourite pub, her favourite café—would he, she? And if he or she wouldn't, drinking a certain glass of beer or a certain coffee and not making it back to the office . . .

And if he or she *would* . . . Then Dr. Webster's other patient or patients would be nothing to do with Helen and Julian and the house and Toby, but one records clerk would be richer and all her ingenuity would have been in vain. . . .

There were so many terrible possibilities, how could she ever have imagined she could retrieve her home and her life from the jeopardy into which her vanity had plunged them?

It was a bad moment, standing at the window of Sister's office humming *Robin Adair* and staring over the manor garden while she saw her own house and garden vanish into shadow. . . .

"Put the kettle on for me, will you, Rogers, I'll just go and see to one or two things before Dr. Webster comes down." Just go upstairs and join Dr. Webster and his patients? "Will you excuse me, Matron?"

"That 'one or two things' applies to me too, Sister." Upstairs for Matron, before Dr. Webster came down to have tea with Sister? Both questions could be answered, but it would be absurd to push it too far on the first of seven days. Or perhaps she meant that the revelation that Dr. Webster had more than one patient had temporarily sapped her strength and confidence. Or that she was feeling sick again.

Matron was heaving herself up from the armchair.

"Won't you have a cup of tea before you go?" Sister's face, as she, too, got to her feet in one quick movement, was expressionlessly courteous. Impossible to tell if she was hanging on Matron's response. The little dark nurse, having filled an electric kettle from the tap of the sink in a recess and plugged it in, had slipped out of the room.

"Thank you, Sister, but I must carry on. Even though I can't pretend I'm as busy these days as I was. I rather think I miss the hurly-burly. I don't really like being above the battle."

"I think that's something you only appear to be, Matron."

"I don't know." Matron paused in the doorway. Standing up, she was magnificently hefty, handsome as a contralto in Gilbert and Sullivan. "You're so competent, Sister, I'm beginning not to feel the need . . . I suspect I've one eye on retirement now, anyway."

Fiona Spencer made a sudden dash from the window and slipped through the doorway before Matron had advanced sufficiently to fill it. Helen knew that Sister, too, had come forward to watch her pirouette round the hall.

"She's a strange one," said Matron. "I'll encourage her back to the lounge."

"Thank you, Matron." Sister pulled her door to and moved quickly out of sight to the back of the house. Another set of stairs?

"Come along, dear," said Matron. She approached Fiona in the steady, sensible way one is advised to commend oneself to domestic animals. After an initial shrinking, Fiona even allowed Matron's hand to rest on her shoulder as they walked across the hall.

"I should sit here, dear." Helen let herself be settled in a chair between the woman who disapproved of everything and a man of about forty with a loud American voice. He appeared to be having a conversation with the woman sitting opposite to him, but seemed undeterred by the lack of response during his short and infrequent pauses. He was talking about the deterioration in public manners, substantiating his argument with illustrations of specific cases of discourtesy.

"Shall we perhaps have some television?" asked Matron, after watching the American for a few moments. She clicked among the channels until she found a nature programme. As soon as a voice was heard the American subsided. "There we are!" pronounced Matron. "We're as right as rain!"

It was surprising that someone enormous and middle-aged could move so youthfully. When Matron had gone Helen relaxed against the back of the chair, her eyes half closed. At least mentally disturbed people could be expected to do whatever they did thoroughly, and Fiona now was thoroughly at rest. It would be wise to establish the poor woman as being subject to abrupt changes of mood, so that nothing she did would seem out of character. But when Fiona relaxed Helen's worries tried to force themselves forward, and she was glad when Nurse Evans came in, looked round the room, and noted Miss Spencer's lethargy.

"Hello, pet, are you having . . . Whoops-a-daisy, then!"

It wasn't happening on her left, the American appeared to have gone to sleep. Turning the other way, Helen saw that the disapproving lady had spilled a glass of orange juice over her blouse and skirt and was being mopped up by Nurse Evans.

"It's all right, Mrs. Lockett, it's all right."

But Mrs. Lockett was weeping as she shook her head, holding the front of the skirt away from her. "You like things nice, don't you?

Well, it is a pity. We'll go upstairs and change and we'll have every-thing all nice and clean for you before you can say knife."

Crying more and more noisily, Mrs. Lockett was led away. The American said, "It's my pleasure!" and slumped back to silence. The television was announcing the news and with a slight sense of shock Helen remembered there was such a thing as time and saw that it was nine o'clock.

There were no reports of untoward incidents in the Home Counties. But how could she live through the uncertainty, the unknowing-ness, of a whole week?

"Here we are, then!"

Another determinedly bright voice. Perhaps nurses in psychiatric institutions had to keep their own spirits up.

"Hello, dear, you're the latest lady, aren't you? Nurse Chadwick at your service. D'you like Ovaltine? Try it, anyway. And a biscuit."

Two layers of a trolley carried steaming mugs and two dishes of shortcake and wafer biscuits. Yes, a warm drink, even on a brilliant June evening, would be a distraction.

Except that she felt sick again, and hadn't chosen her own mug. . . .

Her sixth sense really was taking her over the top. If they knew enough about her to try to poison her, they wouldn't have let her get as far as Hartshorn Manor.

Fiona's hands were closed round the mug, she was smiling fitfully through the kind face of Nurse Chadwick, which was surmounted by curly red hair almost obscuring her cap. Someone else for her list? So far the small dark nurse was the only one she was inclined to leave off, and her seemingly innocent conversation with Dr. Webster could have been merely the practice of the doctrine of vigilance at all times, as with herself and George Parkinson in the bedroom. . . . How she was dreading going to bed, even while she longed for the respite of it. . . .

"Asleep already, are we? Can't leave you here, pet."

Nurse Evans was beside her, smiling and patting her arm, and thank goodness Fiona was recoiling. Helen had a feeling that some time had just passed unaccounted for. Well, she had drained the mug of Ovaltine, and there was no doubt that an increase in docility would add to the smoothness of the general ascent to bed. Had Uncle

George been consulted over this easing of the staff burden so far as Fiona was concerned? If so, he would have suggested that in his niece's case it was not recommended. But whatever families said, it was likely that the mugs would be equally spiked. Mildly, she decided. Now she was awake her mind was clear. But she was unnaturally lethargic, as never at home at half past nine at night. At home, the shadows lengthening across the garden. . . . Tomorrow night, she must refuse the mixture or contrive to get rid of it another way.

"We're ready, then?"

There was the royal we, and there was this, the idiot's, we. In that other nursing home where Julian had sent her they had used it for people whose only disability was to be old. Here it was used for everyone. But perhaps it had begun merely through a kindly intention of appearing to identify with the plight of the patients . . . clients. . . .

She *was* affected mentally, she was indulging in incoherent and inessential wanderings about her mind, seeing Nurse Evans vaguely, the mahogany stair rail in minute detail, everything else further away and merely as out of focus background.

"We'll see how you get on," said Nurse Evans, advancing into Fiona's room. Someone had turned the bed down and arranged Fiona's nightgown across the fold of the sheet. No doubt the gesture would put another hundred pounds on the Department's bill. She had to make a sudden desperate effort not to laugh. She flitted past Nurse Evans and sat down on the bed, letting her yawn show.

"So we're tired. Well, it's been a bit of a day for us, hasn't it? I'll leave you now, pet, and come back to see how you've got on."

At least "pet" appeared to be an endearment exclusive to Nurse Evans. Who was rather a pleasant girl. Wasn't she?

Nurse Evans laid one of the fluffy towels beside Fiona and went out leaving the door slightly ajar. Helen sang her way round the room, stopping at drawers and cupboard to move a few things about, then undressed and washed still in the character of Fiona. She was as convinced as she could be that the room wasn't bugged, but she must play her part until she was actually lying under the bedclothes.

Did Fiona bother with a dressing-gown? The modesty of her nightdress made it easy for Helen to decide to wear nothing over it. Nor shoes, on the continuous expensive carpet.

Nurse Evans was undressing Freda. Almost as simple a process as undressing a large doll. She greeted Fiona with less enthusiasm than she had shown in their encounters hitherto.

"To *bed,* pet! You're ready for bed—that *was* a good girl!—and you must go and get in. Right away! I'll come and say good night."

Nurse Evans didn't exactly make a threatening gesture, but she advanced purposefully and Helen turned and fled along the corridor, away from her own room and past the head of the stairs, along the corridor beyond, grateful to Nurse Evans for providing the impetus to a flight which would seem so naturally to peter out by the door through which she had followed Dr. Webster.

It was closed, and was flanked by other identical closed doors.

After dancing a nervous circle (the equivalent of turning her head each way to see if she was observed), Helen opened the farthest door and danced on inside, leaving it wide open.

The room was unoccupied, but otherwise looked and felt like the room where Dr. Bakewell lay. Why was this corridor so different from the one where her own room was, where Nurse Evans and her colleagues were cheerfully and audibly cajoling and controlling? Was it only her knowledge that Dr. Bakewell was so near, that on this side of the stairs there were no open doors, no comings and goings?

Fiona was tidy, and Helen pulled the door to behind her as she came out. One more door would do for tonight, she mustn't risk a stronger sedative, or being locked in if Fiona was considered to be too wayward. After she had danced another round she tried the door on the stairhead side of Dr. Bakewell.

The same sensation again, and a young man lying on the bed, as motionless as the woman next door and as unhealthily pale.

Fiona circled the bed singing, but there was no response.

It was an effort to take the time and care to close the door. There was no one in either corridor or on the stairs. Helen fled to her room and into bed. When Nurse Evans came in full of remorse and congratulation, she took no notice.

Dr. Bakewell or the records clerk from *The Contemporary Review* —who would talk first?

CHAPTER 8

The sedative in the Ovaltine had been a corrective to her dangerous sense of Fiona's immunity to any form of restraint. It was perhaps the sedative, too, which enabled her to fall asleep, into a long allegorical dream where the night was a heavy book whose pages, however steadily she turned them, seemed never to come to an end. When the dream eventually faded, it was because Nurse Evans had a hand on her shoulder.

Fiona cringed down into the bed, and Helen rejoiced that she had been spared the awful clarity of a sleepless night.

"All right, pet, all right. That's better!" Fiona was still lying down, but she was humming. "You must have slept well, your bed's hardly disturbed. I'd like you to sit up for me now, and I'll get you ready for your breakfast. Breakfast in bed's the order of the day at Hartshorn Manor. Well, they've got to do something to justify the expense." Nurse Evans grinned, but glanced behind her towards the slightly open door. The unknown quantity of the new ownership? "Let's just put this jacket on. There. . . . And swing the table over. Now don't go away, and I'll fetch your tray."

On the tray was a small pot of tea, hot water, four triangles of toast in a china rack, butter in curls, marmalade in a slightly-cut-glass jar, and a boiled egg. Shrewdly, in Helen's judgment, the nurse stood back when she had set the tray down, watching to discover what Fiona's habits might be. Helen shook salt on to the egg plate, put milk into the teacup, then appeared to struggle with the teapot.

"Perhaps I'd better. . . . All right, pet." Nurse Evans poured weak tea and added water to the teapot from the similarly flower-sprigged jug. "You'll be able to manage it yourself, I'm sure, if you want another one. Let's see how you tackle your egg."

Fiona cut the top off the egg with the knife, making a hole too small to be of service. Clucking cheerfully, Nurse Evans advanced again and broke off some further pieces of shell. Helen was impressed, even while she was unnerved, by the conscientiousness of the busy young woman, by the way she gave the impression of having plenty of time. But perhaps Nurse Evans had discovered that the mentally sick were worse affected by nurses in a hurry than those patients whose problems were physical.

To her surprise and somehow her shame Helen was hungry, and Fiona crammed toast into her mouth.

"No hurry, pet. I'll leave you to it." But first Nurse Evans inspected the clothes lying quite tidily on the chair. "All right for another day, but let's have a change of blouse."

Fiona took no notice, smacking her lips over the egg, whimpering as some yolk fell on the sheet. The inspiration for this came from Mrs. Lockett and her reaction to the cascade of orange juice. Nurse Evans hastened back to the bed.

"Don't worry, pet, it's nothing. I'll use your flannel to wipe it. See? Now I really must go."

It was half way through the third piece of toast that Helen was suddenly no longer hungry, and no longer thinking about home. She managed to reach the basin before she was sick, then leaned against it, her eyes streaming, her heart racing.

Boiled egg, toast, and tea. . . . They couldn't be poisoning her—they *couldn't*—so perhaps they used a sedative on other occasions as well as bedtime, and she was allergic to it. But how to isolate the preparation on a breakfast tray? The tea was the most likely candidate, but it could be folded into the butter, added to the milk or the marmalade. . . .

She pushed table and tray aside and got back into bed. Just for a few moments until heart and stomach calmed down. . . . She didn't seem to have any control over the sickness, but if she could contrive to be sick in the presence of a member of staff, they might decide to take the chance of withdrawing the sedative in her case. . . . She still felt awful, the nausea not really relieved by the sickness, her head in a whirl. . . .

Julian had said the Department might be wrong—but that, if they were, it wouldn't be she in the front line. She didn't really know what he had meant, but she must hold on to it. . . .

Sun was shafting through her window, across the pretty flower-patterned cover of the duvet. Was it shining on the usual tranquillity of her home, Julian feeding Toby, preparing for his Saturday mowing. . . .

"We're still in bed, then? We've even gone back to sleep?"

She wasn't asleep, it was panic which had made her deaf and blind. She sat up in bed and heard her voice softly singing *Early One Morning.*

"Which it isn't any more," said Nurse Evans a trifle briskly. "Shall we get up?"

She took hold of the bedclothes and pulled them gently back. Fiona got out of bed and went and stood in the middle of the floor.

"That's the ticket! You just see what you can do. I'll come back to see how you've got on."

Nurse Evans bounced out with the tray and Helen began slowly to wash and dress, pausing every few moments at the window to look across the fields sparkling out of sight under an already strong sun. The nausea had almost gone and she didn't feel mentally nobbled as she had felt the night before. So perhaps it had been nerves—she had far more at stake, now, than she had had the first time Julian had sent her into danger. At least she had learned that the effect of the bedtime narcotic didn't persist into the morning. Perhaps, if she had a fruitful day, she would drink the Ovaltine again.

When she was ready she sat down on the bed, forcing her thoughts into coherent and practical shape. She had a week, and what else did she have to do in it?

First of all, she had to discover how many patients were being treated by Dr. Webster. And to be thankful that her experience with Mr. Weldon had set a bound to those in whom she should be interested.

Then she must learn the geography of the Manor vis-à-vis the rooms where the catatonic patients lay—at least those to whom Dr. Webster was ministering. Julian had said it would be useful if she could pinpoint these from outside the house as well as within, to offer an alternative means of access. She thought she had already learned something useful here, too: that the patients under duress were all in the quiet corridor the other side of the stairs.

She should also make an attempt, at least, to discover those members of staff who were working with Dr. Webster and the little man in

the Resident Director's armchair—if only to tell Julian something
about the people who could be missing the day after the rescue of Dr.
Bakewell. And the records clerk. And anybody else who by the end
of her week she would have discovered in the same immobility and
darkness. . . . The best way was to try and find out who seemed
familiar with Dr. Webster's patients. So far, on these grounds, she
had exempted only the small dark nurse called Rogers. And on the
grounds of her sixth sense, the Resident Director and Nurse Evans. . . .

It helped her morale, trying to be constructive. And it would help
her to use her time as well as she could, now she had set up in her
visual mind the orderly bold type of her plan of campaign. Singing
softly, she danced round the room, examining it in the way a team of
Julian's had once taught her, finding no evidence of bugging devices.
Then she took her pretty gilded box from under her pillow, pushed it
down into her deep skirt pocket, and went out into the corridor, her
own bright corridor, zigzagged with sunlight from all the open
doors, full of the sounds of incomprehension and encouragement.
The other corridor, when she glanced beyond the stairhead, could
have been a black door, until the little man she had seen in Mr.
Jenkins's office came out of a room on the front of the house, allowing a brief bar of light across the darkness.

Helen sped to the first wide door, where Nurse Evans was busy
with Freda but greeted the nervous entrance of Fiona with more
pleasure than pain.

"Goodness, we *have* done well! Look at Fiona, Freda, all ready for
the day! Although perhaps we could do better with our hair."

Oh yes, we could. Except that every time she caught sight of the
ragged remains of her hair, her vanity was secondary to her sense of
a punishment deserved.

Nurse Evans came up to Helen and gently smoothed the short
tufts on the top of her head. When Fiona tried to duck the nurse
persisted, and eventually there was humming and a comparative relaxation.

"I always say you can make contact." Nurse Evans was openly
pleased with herself, and it was an effort for Helen to dismiss the
sense of hope that she had nothing to do with Dr. Webster. . . .

In the next room Mrs. Lockett was sitting on her bed dressed but for her stockings, one of which she held aloft in either hand.

"No. Oh no." Mrs. Lockett was continually shaking her head, bringing her hands together, gazing at the stockings in juxtaposition, then once more dangling them at the length of her arms. "They're not matching. They won't do."

"Let *me* have a look." Nurse Evans whipped the stocking out of each waving hand, shook her head over them several times as decisively as Mrs. Lockett herself, then went over to a chest of drawers which she opened and plunged her hands inside. Helen, dancing a half circle behind her, saw that she was moving her hands about without letting the stockings go, before producing them again with a cry of satisfaction. "You were right, Mrs. Lockett, they wouldn't do, wouldn't do at all. These are the ones we want, these are a pair. On with them, now, you can manage."

Still shaking her head, but with noticeably less assertion, Mrs. Lockett began laboriously to ease her foot into the first stocking, and Nurse Evans turned away to the assistance of a diminutive woman with a shock of black hair, sitting listless and almost naked on the chair by her bed and no more resistant to being dressed than Freda had been to being undressed. The progress of Nurse Evans in that room was predictable, with two more half-dressed ladies to go. Helen decided to move on.

"Hello, young lady!" Matron speeding past the door towards the stairhead was too strong a temptation to resist. Fiona backed away from the greeting, but followed Matron in her usual indirect way, reaching the two facing doors at the end of the other corridor just as Matron was opening one of them. Matron, like Dr. Webster a few doors away, strode briskly across to the window and pulled back the curtains. Then, abruptly diffident, slowly approached the bed on which another young man lay, his wide eyes staring at the ceiling.

Fiona went to the other side of the bed and mimicked Matron's cautious movements—head bent towards the pillow, hand stretched out and withdrawn, finally urgent on the yellow-white cheek.

It was more in unison with Matron than in imitation, then, that Helen recoiled, her fingers rejecting contact with that cold waxy surface.

Matron looked up at her. "Oh, for an innocent soul!" she exclaimed, then closed the eyes of the man on the bed and drew the sheet up to cover his face. Tears glistened on her own and she shook her head and made the sign of the Cross. There was death in this room, but not dread, and it was no surprise to hear Matron, after she had stood a few moments at the window before pulling the curtains together again, murmur the name of Dr. Sandelson.

"I knew it, I knew it," said Matron, recovering. "But it's none the less of a shock. Come along, my darling." Fiona, grasping the bed rail, had begun to whimper. "Yes, the dog would feel it, why not you? Come along."

Fiona allowed her arm to be taken as she and Matron left the room. There was a key in the lock and Matron turned it, then put it in her pocket.

"Nurse Evans!" The nurse was just coming out of the room where Helen had left her. "Our Mr. Lowe has gone in the night. Peaceful. It's a blessing. All the same . . ."

"Oh, Matron." Could these two women really have other vital professional preoccupations? But the question was arrogant, in the light of her own skills. "Do you want me to . . . ?"

"I've locked him in. I'll go up with Dr. Sandelson when he comes. In the meantime I'd better telephone the lad's mother. Unless Sister feels strong."

Helen and Nurse Evans stood at the top of the stairs as Matron plunged heavily down. Nurse Evans pulled herself together with a gusty sigh. "Poor Mr. Lowe. Well, I'm going off duty now, pet, and I'm not half sorry, Mrs. Gregory gave me quite a night."

"Gregory!" warbled Fiona. Dr. Bakewell had the temporary name of Hughes, but it would always be as well to clear things up if she could.

"Yes, you go and sing to her, she could do with that. Mrs. McLeod's gone downstairs but I can't get Mrs. Gregory to move, even though she's all nicely dressed and ready. Along here, pet, come on, I'll introduce you to Mrs. Gregory. Perhaps you'll come down together—"

"Garden," said Fiona, her mouth turning down. "Flowers. *Outside.*"

Nurse Evans was trying to lead the way along the bright corridor which had no secrets. And the sun was still shining.

"You want to go outside, pet? Nothing easier. Come on, I'll show you the way. Try not to change your mind, there's a good girl, before we get you there."

Helen took the rose out more carefully this time, to present to Nurse Evans. Nurse Evans, after looking round, broke the stalk in half with her teeth and pushed the bloom down between her plump breasts. "Thanks, pet. I'm out to lunch today and it'll just set me off. Come along."

The way into the secure garden lay through a door towards the back of the hall, on the opposite side of the staircase to Sister's office, past a door marked MATRON.

"There you are, pet. All to yourself. Come back in when you're ready."

Fiona danced blithely into the sunshine, but Helen's spirits were already drooping as she noted that the surrounding conifers formed a square the precise width of the west end of the house.

This, then, was to be the extent of her external view.

The patients' garden had a pretty sunken centre, with seats on crazy-paving among small symmetrical beds of roses and low bushes, and there were seats at intervals round the edge of the lawn. Helen made her devious way across the centre, pausing to examine flowers and shrubs, and turned to face the handsome stone end of the house only when she had reached the far boundary. There she took stock.

Door towards the back with short flight of steps down which she had just danced, window of the annexe to the lounge which the Resident Director had almost called the writing-room, two more windows, one of which had to be Matron's. Above, on the first of the two upper floors, two windows only, one for each of the rooms at the end of the dark corridor which corresponded with the two rooms at the end of the busy light corridor. One of those was Fiona's. Behind one of these a young man had just died. Strange, how she had known he was no more than what he seemed, a voluntary patient in a psychiatric clinic. Her sixth sense again, and working more reasonably than when it had tried to tell her she was being poisoned. . . .

She didn't have to concern herself with the two windows on the third floor: the door at the top of the main staircase which concealed the stairs up to it was marked *Private Staff Only*, and she knew already where Dr. Bakewell and the records clerk lay, and where at

least one other room was waiting. These rooms were all in the long
south garden façade of the house, to the left of the dark corridor as
she had come upon them. What of the doors to her left now, overlooking the drive, none of which she had yet opened?

Skipping, singing, Helen moved erratically along beside the
boundary trees until she was back at the house. Attached to it, and
to the stout fence which was almost obscured by the thick growth of
the ornamental boundary conifers, was a tall, elaborately wrought-
iron gate, twin to the gate at the front angle of the house which gave
on to the drive.

Standing close against it, holding an elegant but strong black curl
in either hand, Helen gazed through at the inaccessible Capability
Brown austerity of the long green sweep which led away to slopes
and parkland trees. Mingled with the birdsong was the crescendoing
of a petrol-driven mower, and in a moment its driver came in sight
two or three swathes beyond the gate, decrescendoing out of earshot
again as she stood trying to subdue an awareness of imprisonment
far stronger than she had yet felt inside the house. It sent her, eventually, running rather than dancing about the allotted space until she
dropped breathless on the farthest seat.

There was no need to feel frustrated so far as her mission was
concerned. Entry through one of those two first-floor west windows
would give access to all the quiet dark rooms. The running had made
her feel sick again, and as if she had run for miles rather than yards.
The lawnmower was working its way back. Julian should have finished mowing by now. Fiona didn't wear a watch, but her inbuilt
clock said somewhere round eleven. Toby would be hanging about
for a mid-morning snack and Julian would be making himself coffee. . . .

It was a relief to see the verbose American crossing the lawn.

"Hi there!"

He was coming to sit beside her on the seat, making her fidget
away towards the very edge of it, so that she was half leaning over
the arm.

"It's all right, ma'am, I know how to treat a lady, there's no need
to be alarmed. I'm not one of those folks that bang doors in your
face, don't give you a seat, tread on your toes and expect *you* to say
you're sorry."

The American appeared to be launched on much the same tack he had followed in the lounge the day before, talking somewhere in her direction but not expecting a response and looking mainly, as she was, at the wall of the house in front of them. Not a bad-looking man, tall and well built, strong wavy hair, a straight nose and brown skin, sad that he should be afflicted. . . .

"I know what we'll do now, ma'am, we'll play I Spy. That's a game I learned here in England, in your great little country. I'm not a man, ma'am, to insult a woman. I spy with my little eye something beginning with C. There you are. You going to be able to guess it? Have a try." The American's attention was still only partly on the mesmerized, cringing figure of Fiona Spencer. It could be that, so far as he was concerned, there was another woman present. "Well, I guess I'll tell you. Anyway, it's not there any more. Cloud. That was it, C for cloud. And the sun's chased it away. You want a go now? No? All right, I don't mind going again. And don't worry, I'll hold the door for you. I spy with my little eye something beginning with I. With I, that's it. Bit of a hard one, this is, but it's fair. I can see it. Go on, have a try. But don't worry, I'm not going to keep you standing when the tube fills up. No, sir, I'll see that you get a seat. I. Want to give up? Okay, okay. It's ivy. I for ivy. Your turn. Don't worry, ma'am, I'm not one of those folks shut doors in people's faces. No, sir. I'll go again then, shall I? Righty-ho. I spy with my little eye something beginning with A. That's it. A. This is a beaut, this is. You comfortable, ma'am? I'm not one of those folks who only consider their own comfort, no, sir! You just tell me, and I'll go fetch your coat. Something beginning with A. You can get it? No? Okay, okay, I'll tell you. I don't mind telling you. It's arm. This here I'm holding out. Or this here that I'm leaning on. See? Not bad, eh? But I know when a lady's tired. I'm not one of those folks keep a lady talking when she's tired. I know when a lady's had enough. But you think about it, ma'am, you think about it."

The American stirred, perhaps preparatory to getting to his feet, and for a brief unnerving instant his eyes, as restless and visionary as those of Fiona, interlocked with Helen's as each glance swooped past the other. Then, although she still felt abnormally tired from her short exertion, Helen was running across the lawn, slipping through the door into the house and closing it behind her. She had wasted too much time on the ridiculous American, she should be attaching herself again to a member of staff, as she had been instructed.

Was the American ridiculous? From instinct and the intensive training of that other time, she had tried to write his nonsense down in her visual mind to look at later. . . .

"There you are, Fiona." Sister was certainly the most superficially severe member of the staff, but there was something to be said for being spared the idiot we and the excessive cheerfulness. "There's a fruit drink for you in the lounge, if you would like it. Nurse Baines will show you."

Nurse Baines was thin and pale with a long face and long lank hair. She asked Sister in a lacklustre voice what kind of tactics were recommended.

"As a start describe what's on offer, she likes food and drink." The front doorbell rang, and Matron came from the direction of her room as Sister slowly crossed the hall, bustling past her to open the front door.

"Dr. Sandelson. . . ." The tall grey-haired man Helen hadn't seen before was subjected to immediate intensive whispering. Sister stood close by but not, Helen thought, closely attending to the monologue.

"Lovely fruit juice," said Nurse Baines wearily. "In the lounge. Come and see."

Singing softly, Helen waited while Nurse Baines performed a perfunctory mime, then showed a willingness to follow her. As they reached the door of the lounge there came sounds behind them of further arrival, another male voice, loud enough to echo up into the small rotunda.

"Yes, he's all right, Sister, but rather pressed this morning and as he wasn't expecting any real developments . . . He'll be here tonight. Anyway, you know you're always pleased to see me. Nurse Evans is, at any rate."

"Aren't you coming? The drinks are in the lounge. That's a good girl." Fiona was following Nurse Baines with the sudden obedience of a well-trained dog, standing by the trolley while Nurse Baines selected a glass of orange juice and transferred it to her. "Careful now, you're going to spill it. I should sit down."

Holding the glass as steady as she could in both hands, Helen wavered to the nearest vacant chair. She was prepared, of course, for shocks. For danger. Even, in her worst moments, for death. But not for another encounter with the enigmatic Pete.

CHAPTER 9

Mrs. Lockett had fallen asleep in her chair and was nodding her head instead of shaking it. One of the women who had been waiting for Nurse Evans to dress them was knitting laboriously with big needles and thick cream-coloured twine. Probably a dishcloth like the dishcloths interminably knitted by Helen's grandmother in the year before she died. . . . The jugs and glasses had been cleared away and the marble clock on the mantelpiece had ticked on forty-five minutes.

The thing which had impressed Pete, which had fixed his steady eyes on Helen's face, had been Penelope Dale's likeness to Dr. Bakewell. Pete had never seen Helen, any more than he had ever seen Fiona.

But however many times she told herself this, however reassuring it was, there was the fact that focused eyes couldn't be disguised. To catch Pete's, even for a few seconds, would be to throw him a memory, however puzzling and oblique. Yet although she had ducked out today, tomorrow or the next day she would have to be ready. . . .

It was nearly an hour after his arrival that she heard Pete's confident voice again in the hall, laughing with Nurse Evans, punctuated by the quiet voice of Sister. Had one or both of them accompanied him on his rounds? However open the drugged imprisonment of Dr. Bakewell was being made to seem, treatment would have to be carried on, the physicist medicated towards betrayal. And the records clerk . . . (This was the point at which she had almost trained herself to stop, the point just before her mind began to run an anguished course round her house and garden.) The so-called doctors could hardly be working alone. *There haven't been many staff changes.* So said Nurse Evans. Therefore there had been some.

But it was no good continually posing questions which she might be able to answer if she got herself moving. All was quiet now in the hall, and Fiona had sat still long enough.

There was nobody on the stairs. Nobody, for once, in the east corridor. The room next to hers, when she danced inside, she discovered to be similarly appointed and as cheerfully, differing only in the predominant colour of the sprigs of flowers on curtains and duvet. There were signs of male occupancy in the absence of cosmetics, the presence of a razor and shaving cream. Before leaving the east corridor, Helen opened the doors of the rooms facing over the north front of the house: the one she had already been in which was shared by Mrs. Lockett and three other women, one with three beds, two singles with private bathrooms. Each as unsinister as the rest.

All was superficially the same when she had passed beyond the stairhead, the west corridor a mirror image of the east. But again she was aware almost physically of the change of atmosphere.

Fiona danced a few rounds the length of the west corridor, then tried one of the doors of the rooms on the front of the house. Helen's first awareness, even before she was inside the room, was a smell of paint, which her imagination intensified as she saw the fresh white walls of the smallest bedroom she had entered at Hartshorn Manor. It was the first time, too, for the queasy sense of imbalance. When she looked up to the white ceiling she understood it: at one side the elaborate stuccoed cornice disappeared abruptly into the wall.

The room had been divided; where she stood had been part of the eighteenth-century space which on the other side of the stairs held Mrs. Lockett and three other women. Here there was no dressing-table or chest of drawers, merely a white cupboard built in. No shelf for personal knicknacks, no mirror. There was a door in the new wall, opposite the bare bed, a narrow unadorned door unlike the heavy panelled door on to the corridor. Helen, her heart unruly, slowly opened it, turning up the volume of Fiona's singing.

Beyond was the remainder of the original room, so small it was cell-like. In the windowless gloom she could just see another bed, a table, another built-in cupboard. There was no access apart from the narrow door, and the smell of paint was stronger.

Also the smell of fear. Even though she was sure the room's latest history had not yet begun.

Singing, Helen passed through the two doors and back into the corridor. There was still no one about, no sound beyond a reassuring clatter of crockery from below, and she opened the two other doors on the same side of the corridor. Each led to suites identically basic and white with drably curtained windows and unadorned beds. Each, she was certain, awaiting the same sort of patient, the same sort of process. The outer room for the doctor (the monitor, the manipulator). The inner for the patient (the victim), doubly disorientated.

Closing the last of the doors behind her, Helen fled the length of the house to her own room and cast herself down on her bed, leaving the door ajar. She had to absorb her realization that Hartshorn Manor, under its new ownership, was in process of being turned into a psychiatric hospital on the Soviet model. Not, in Britain, for the treatment of those who refused to conform, but of those from whom certain information was required. And when the western corridor had been filled in the new way, a start could be made on the east. (It occurred to her that the compass points were wrong, and she had to restrain her mad desire to laugh.) And as the old style of patient left or died, he or she could be replaced by the new. As with the staff. Unless, of course, to run the dual systems side by side was considered the safest, most unobtrusive way to maintain a Soviet-style mental institution in a non-totalitarian state. . . .

"We found our way home then? That *was* a clever girl!"

Matron was filling the doorway and Helen discovered, with a small stab of pride as well as relief, that Fiona, although temporarily out of mind, was sucking her thumb and crooning.

"All right, lovey?" Matron now was by the bed, and attempting to stroke Fiona's forehead. As with Nurse Evans, after an initial recoil Fiona permitted the gesture, although her eyes roved wildly. Helen's sixth sense had been known to work through touch, and it could be she was applying a supplementary test. . . . There was no warning sensation from Matron's soft fat hand. "Good," murmured Matron. "I'm sorry you saw poor Mr. Lowe. I was afraid it might have upset you. There was a horse in a book by Dorothy Sayers, wouldn't go past the spot where it had seen a man done to death." There was scarcely an accent, the Irishness was in the lilt of the voice. "I'm sorry, lovey, no offence."

And none taken. Before she could discipline herself, Helen was hoping Matron might be as nice as she seemed. Fiona had begun to sing *Three Blind Mice* and Matron was smiling, showing a gap between natural front teeth. Wasn't that supposed to indicate sensuality? Yes, she could imagine this woman . . .

"You've got a pretty little voice, darling. How about coming down to lunch now? It's roast chicken."

"Chicken."

There were a few words which could be expected to provoke an oral response from Miss Spencer. Fiona got off the bed.

"Wash our hands?" suggested Matron.

And be sick, Helen found as she reached the basin. It was so quick, she could have swallowed a block of salt. She backed away gasping.

"Now, now!" said Matron, frowning as she moved swiftly round the bed to look into the basin and then run the taps. Although Fiona ducked and wriggled, Matron managed to look at her eyes and her tongue. "You seem healthy enough, my darling. I don't know." Helen knew that Matron's shrewd grey eyes, sunk in flesh, were gazing at her thoughtfully. One thing she had learned, from Fiona as well as from that earlier time, was to make the most of enforcedly fleeting impressions. "I expect it's the shock of Mr. Lowe. And of being away from the places and the people you know. Poor darling. Come along with Matron, and we'll see if we can't manage some chicken. You'll be all right."

Fiona was singing again, if tremulously, and Helen *was* all right, as abruptly as she had been all wrong. Was it the fruit juice? If there had been another drug it had totally misfired, she was still in charge of her mind. But if Matron could compare Fiona with a horse, she would hardly have balked at mentioning the possible effects of a narcotic added to the fruit juice. So it must be nerves, which in a way was no less alarming, she wanted to be in charge of her body, too. . . .

At the lunch table Geoffrey of the Adam's apple seemed to have lost all awareness of his surroundings, although he ate each course with a steady rhythm. Freda on the other hand was comparatively lively for the first part of the meal, bringing out slithery rushes of words only one or two of which were intelligible and ending them with cackles of laughter. But with the pudding came a pall over her high spirits and she, too, lapsed into staring-eyed silence. Only Mrs. Lockett, shaking her head in continuous prim disapproval, offered the occasional comment on the numberless dissatisfactions of human existence. The most surprising event at the table was that Helen was able to eat and enjoy her meal, as if that violent few seconds in the bedroom had never taken place. It was known, of course, that no two people had precisely the same reaction to modern drugs, but it would have been reassuring to hear of, or to see, at least one other inmate of Hartshorn Manor who was similarly afflicted.

She said no—by shaking her head and waving her arms—to the coffee on offer in the lounge afterwards, and dozed unaided through some television sport. Half an hour was enough to refresh her, but she continued slumped in her chair, reading the notes she had written in her mind and assessing her progress against them.

The geography of the house, both outside and within, had proved simple and straightforward, and she had found so much she could hardly believe any undiscovered doors could be hiding more than staff bed and recreation rooms, apart from some sort of local headquarters in which the little man resided. There was nothing further she could accomplish in this direction, but she still had no idea of the extent of Dr. Webster's authority, or of those members of staff who understood what he and Pete were doing. . . .

"All right, then?"

Nurse Rogers was on duty, walking about the lounge to see that all were as contented as their situations allowed them, stopping beside, and touching, only Fiona. Looking wild-eyed round the room, Helen felt her wariness turn to amused understanding of the probable reason Nurse Rogers had chosen to sum up her general concern in a specific question to Miss Spencer, why she had put out a hand in that one direction: it was simply that the other people in the lounge were less appealing. The disguise of Fiona, she had seen for herself in the glass, was a taking away instead of a putting on, a taking away of the veneer Helen had built up over the years on her natural good looks, presenting her in a basic state, her hair cropped, her face unadorned, regressed to girlhood, deprived even of the changes of expression with which normal people protect themselves, distract or mislead. It was clear from Nurse Rogers's compassionate face that the effect was evocative of the instinct to protect, and aesthetically pleasing.

Well, she could do with a bit of help, something to predispose the members of staff, innocent and guilty, in her favour.

And if Julian and the Department had got it right, there was something else with which she should be solacing herself: the fact that the new owners of Hartshorn Manor believed themselves to be inviolate, needing to deceive only busy doctors and nursing staff not looking for anything beyond the changes of emphasis inevitable in the aftermath of a change of regime. So there was no reason why Dr. Webster, having established the easily believable situation that he was treating patients with serious mental illnesses, should dissemble to the point of refraining from taking into the sick-rooms with him the nurse or nurses who understood what he was about. There was no reason for him not to insist, in his absence, on his patients being attended where possible by those same nurses. The appearance of things would be the heart of them.

Whoever those nurses were, they were bound to have joined the staff round about the time of the change of ownership. Matron had talked about being on the verge of retirement; if only she could see the files on the others! But this would involve behaviour beyond the capacities of Fiona Spencer and threaten the priceless advantage of being accepted as a kinetic part of the background.

If the Department had got it right. And if they hadn't, Julian had promised it wouldn't be *she. . . .*

"We *are* quiet this afternoon, aren't we?"

It was time she did something. Once she had drunk the mug of tea being handed to her off the trolley by the red-haired Nurse Chadwick, who wore a green rather than a blue uniform and seemed not yet to have graduated to full nursing status. She would do well, though, if she was what she seemed, she had a word and a smile for everyone, provoking responses in those Helen hadn't yet seen animated.

One of these was a small, depressed-looking man with an enormous moustache which blew upwards with a regular muffled whistling during his frequent dozes. Nurse Chadwick had greeted him by name—"Mr. Fortescue, no less!" Nurse Chadwick had said —and he was craning his thin neck up towards her, trying to tell her something in a hoarse, weak voice. The American's loud tones discouraged him before Nurse Chadwick was able to understand what he was saying, but she waited for him to sink back in his chair before turning away.

"Yes, Mr. Colburn?" The only touch, here, of impatience. But Mr. Colburn seemed unaware.

"I was just thinking a game of I Spy would be a good idea. I'll go first because I've got one ready. I spy with my little eye something beginning with C." It could only be her imagination that the American's continuously roving eye had fractionally paused as it passed over Fiona. Nurse Chadwick started to say all right, yes, she'd hang on and have a game, but as in the garden the American didn't seem to be looking for a response, he had stopped speaking only to gather breath and began again while the nurse was still agreeing to humour him. "An easy one to start with," said Mr. Colburn, "just to give you a bit of encouragement."

"Who? Me?" grinned Nurse Chadwick, but Mr. Colburn had still not slackened pace.

"Too difficult? Yes, I thought it might be. Clock, the C was for clock. Let's make it a bit harder now, shall we? Let's say I spy with my little eye something beginning with I." She was imagining his glance had paused again, she must be. "This is a corker, this one is, I reckon you'll have to give it up."

"Inkwell!" said Nurse Chadwick loudly and with a triumphant smile, pointing to the handsome leather table and its brass accoutrements.

"Yes, you'll have to give it up. . . . What's that? Inkwell, I said inkwell, nobody else guessed inkwell. We're not going to play any more, we've played enough. I was going to say I spied with my little eye something beginning with A, but I won't, now. Nobody could guess it anyway. Nobody. Nobody."

"Yes, well, I think we might have the television on." Nurse Chadwick looked contritely at Mr. Colburn's angrily staring eyes and flushed face. "Thank you very much, Mr. Colburn. You're quite right, you're far too clever for the likes of us."

Helen, watching the American's face as the television screen brightened to life, saw the colour subside and the eyes grow abstracted as he relaxed back into his chair. Nurse Chadwick, anxiously alert, saw it too, and turned away with a rueful shrug. Helen got up and left the lounge with her, crossing the hall at her side and following her past Sister's office and the comparatively mean flight of stairs which must continue its rise behind the forbidden door on the first landing on its way up to the staff rooms. Then for the first time she was in the kitchen.

"You come to sing to us, then?"

The angular lady making pastry at the scrubbed central table was smiling indulgently. Within twenty-four hours it appeared that Fiona Spencer had established herself as a character. Helen hummed her way to the table, picked a few currants from a bowl beside the cook, and after cramming them into her mouth darted back to the hall. It would have been a sort of rest, to stay for a while in the kitchen, but she would not hear, there, the evening arrival of the doctors. She rather hoped Dr. Sandelson would arrive first, it would be less nerve-racking to eliminate patients than add them to Dr. Webster's tally. But she would attach herself to whoever came.

Sister, innocent or guilty, would be ready for the doorbell. Helen opened the door of Sister's room and forced herself to go unhesitatingly inside.

"It's you, is it?"

Sister had turned round quickly from her position at her desk with her back to the door, but it was reassuring to see her relax as she registered Miss Spencer. Helen took an overblown rose from a vase and presented it, the petals billowing to the floor between them in a scented pink fall.

"That's very nice. Thank you." Sister hesitated before throwing the stalk into her waste-paper basket. The doorbell rang as she was picking up the petals. Helen followed her out to the hall, where Sister slackened pace as she saw the man who had just been let into the house by Nurse Rogers.

"Dr. Chalmers," said Sister. "Good evening."

"Good evening, Sister." Dr. Chalmers was a thin, small man with quick movements and a lot of dark hair. "How is my patient?"

"There doesn't seem to have been any response yet, I'm afraid. Nurse Rogers will have looked in on him in the last hour. Nurse?"

"No response, no," said Nurse Rogers.

"Disappointing. Shall we go up. Sister? Nurse?"

"Nurse Rogers will go up with you," said Sister, "if you will excuse me."

"Very well, very well. Come along, Nurse."

Dr. Chalmers's mobile face would move easily into bad temper. Helen kept behind him and Nurse Rogers up the stairs, along the west corridor.

The nurse led the way to the room at the end, next door to the room where that morning the young man had died. Dr. Chalmers found it difficult to restrain himself from overtaking her.

"Thank you, Nurse, thank you."

A woman on the bed this time, tossing and muttering. Medicinal paraphernalia on the bedside table. Closed curtains which Dr. Chalmers pushed roughly back. Flowered curtains and no menace. But somehow she hadn't thought this doctor was another of Dr. Webster's deputies.

Helen wavered across the room as Dr. Chalmers turned from the window.

"She's no trouble," said Nurse Rogers quickly, smiling on Helen. "She's in a world of her own and doesn't—"

"Nevertheless," said Dr. Chalmers, "out!"

The pressure of his fingers hurt her upper arms. Fiona, shaking herself free when she had been propelled a few steps towards the door, fled whimpering.

Almost to collide with the tall calm figure of Dr. Sandelson at the top of the stairs.

"Who's this, then?"

Dr. Sandelson was unaccompanied and was not really asking a question. Helen handed him a rose from the useful vase. Smiling, he put it in his buttonhole, ignoring her in a friendly way as she trotted along the east corridor at his side.

"How's Bessie, then?"

A stout-faced young blonde was sitting up in bed in a room for four, listening to pop music on a transistor. Dr. Sandelson tried turning it down but the reaction was so extreme he shook his head and restored the volume.

"We'll have a look at the legs, then," yelled Dr. Sandelson. Bessie's legs, when the bedclothes were pulled down, were revealed to be grossly swollen. Tutting, shaking his head at Fiona as she danced round the room, Dr. Sandelson gave Bessie an injection in the arm which Bessie, intent on her programme, seemed scarcely to notice. Leaving the doctor to tuck her up again, Fiona danced out to the corridor, in time to see Dr. Chalmers and Nurse Rogers come out of the room from which Dr. Chalmers had evicted her.

"I'll look in again in the morning, Nurse. Don't bother to see me out."

"Thank you, doctor."

Nurse Rogers, standing at the top of the stairs, put her tongue out after the rapidly descending figure of Dr. Chalmers, then went bright red as she turned to face Dr. Sandelson.

"Good evening, Nurse Rogers," said Dr. Sandelson genially. "I've attended to Bessie and I'm just going in to see Mrs. Jones. Is there anyone among the walking wounded you think I should have a look at this evening?"

"It's been a good day for most of them today, Doctor. Geoffrey's been a bit miz and Freda a bit lively, but neither beyond their bounds. You haven't met Fiona, have you? She came yesterday but she's only staying for a week."

"Matron was telling me about her." Dr. Sandelson advanced towards the shrinking Miss Spencer, succeeding in placing a hand on her shoulder. "She's been superintending my round." Dr. Sandelson looked at her so searchingly Helen was forced to stare through him. "There is a certain poignancy . . ." continued Dr. Sandelson, "but I suspect it is in our minds rather than in the condition of Fiona. She seems happy enough. She's physically fit?"

"Oh, I think so." She hadn't been sick, yet, in front of Nurse Rogers. "She'll probably come in with us to see Mrs. Jones. It doesn't matter, though."

"Of course it doesn't." Dr. Sandelson patted Fiona's shoulder. Nurse Rogers opened another door in the east corridor, just as the bell pealed again.

Helen, her heart suddenly noisy, skipped back to the head of the stairs, aware of the kindly amusement she had left behind her.

"As curious as a cat," said Dr. Sandelson.

It was as she saw Pete smiling at Nurse Baines that she realized she was glad it was he rather than Dr. Webster. Was it the necessity of pursuing her researches that sent her down the stairs to meet him, or her pride, her vulnerability to a challenge?

Nurse Baines said, weary again, "This is Fiona, Dr. Irving, she's much in evidence but she's not really here at all, if you get my meaning."

"I've had experience of it, Nurse. Hello, Fiona."

For the second time, those shrewd eyes were upon her. Looking through them, she was unable to see if Pete had changed, was playing a different personality as well as a different role, but the light confidence of the voice was the same.

"Let's go up, then, shall we, Nurse?"

He was turning away. Helen used the window ledge by the front door as support for the weakness of her relief.

Nurse Baines fell into step behind Pete, and Fiona eventually behind Nurse Baines. Helen was going to push her luck, because she wanted to test Pete's reaction to her actually inside the room where he might be intending to advance treatment, and because she must find out if Dr. Bakewell and the records clerk were maintaining their silence.

At the top of the stairs Pete held back, allowing the nurse to lead the way. Helen, not knowing if she was a heroine or a fool, took another rose from the vase and held it out to him. She was able to see, in the oblique glance she was cultivating more and more usefully, his impatient reaction turn to amusement.

"Thank you, darling." Pete looked appreciatively at the fine short-stemmed bud Helen had inadvertently chosen, and eased it into his buttonhole. Fiona twirled in a circle, singing the National Anthem on a thin high note. With a snort of laughter Pete turned to follow Nurse Baines, waiting blank-faced at the door of the records clerk's room.

It was an effort not to enter fearfully, to continue singing and dancing as if she was still in the corridor.

Neither Pete nor the nurse appeared to be paying her attention. Pete, like the other doctors real or bogus, had crossed the room to draw back the curtains, and there was a sudden dazzle from the south-west sun. He adjusted the heavy brown fabric to bar the sharper rays, then moved over to the bed. To Helen, still leaning at the window where she had followed him, the motionless face on the pillow looked as it had looked the other time she had seen it. And it was still silent.

"No response?"

"None."

And none of the courtesy titles whose use must be second nature between doctors and nursing staff. Helen had no doubt, abruptly, of Nurse Baines's involvement in the unadvertised purpose of Hartshorn Manor.

"I think it's time for another injection. Prepare it, will you?"

"Give me the case."

Hardly looking away from his patient, Pete handed over his slim black case and the nurse laid it on the foot of the bed before opening it and taking out an unmarked bottle and a syringe.

"You don't think we're trying to move too fast?"

"I do not. We're hardly going to let him die, or lose his mind, after taking so much trouble. This state is normal."

"The whole thing's experimental. . . ."

"It is no longer experimental. Are you ready?"

"Here."

The man on the bed reared under the pressure of the hypodermic and gave a short cry which Helen heard herself echoing, bringing about the real test she felt had still not been reached.

Pete moved towards the window as he spun round, and the wet tip of the withdrawn syringe was inches from her bare arm. His face was close to her, too, a blur because she was staring desperately through it and couldn't read its expression. She would never know how long it was before the snort of laughter came again, and she learned that from the most dangerous direction she had nothing to fear.

Fiona was cringing back against the window as Dr. Irving advanced his empty hand.

"All right, girl, all right." He was no more alert, now, than if she had been a cat. Toby . . .

"There's nothing happening," said Nurse Baines, intent on the face on the bed.

"I hardly expected there would be. Have they taught you nothing? It's because it's slow that it's so effective in the end. But I'm not here to reassure *you*, Nurse." The use of the title at last was surely ironic. "What of the other one?"

"Nothing. Nothing."

"Let's see, then."

"Check this one over," said the nurse, immovable at the side of the bed. After glancing at her face, Pete went to the case and with an irritable gesture twitched out a stethoscope. Then, when he had used it on the shallowly breathing chest, the equipment for testing blood pressure. A doctor? Or a man who had taken a basic course enabling him to ensure that the victim stayed alive? She had forgotten to find out what Tony, her client, did for a living, so she would hardly have known if Pete was in fact a doctor. . . . *The other one.* She knew now that so far Dr. Webster had only two patients at Hartshorn Manor.

"All right, I told you. Are you satisfied?"

"Yes."

"Good. Now the other."

Pete strode impatiently to the door, Nurse Baines following more slowly. Outside, he stood back for the nurse to resume the lead, but when she opened Dr. Bakewell's door it was Fiona who went in first and danced up to the bed.

No change here either. The appearance of death, except for the tiny regular sigh of the breath.

As the light streamed in Fiona skipped over to the window.

"She gets crushes on people," said Nurse Baines.

"What? Oh, her. . . . Prepare another injection, will you?"

This time, although her mouth tightened, Nurse Baines said nothing. And this time Dr. Irving, after the injection, made his cursory examination unprompted.

"I'll check this one," said Nurse Baines, and Helen absorbed the moment of antagonism. *When thieves fall out* . . .

"Better close the door."

But the nurse was already doing so, after glancing at Pete with cold disdain. Yes, it would look strange, to anyone passing in the corridor, for the doctor to be standing by while the nurse wielded the stethoscope.

As Nurse Baines, with a curt nod, put the equipment away, Fiona swept to the door and began wrestling with the handle, whimpering the while.

"Born free," said Pete, laughing again, and Helen winced as Nurse Baines moved her out of the way while she opened the door.

Fiona ran headlong past the little man who had sat in on the business of her acceptance at the Manor and who was emerging from one of the freshly painted suites, down the stairs and across the hall. She was standing staring out of the window by the front door when the doctor and the nurse reached it.

"Any extra attention necessary in the night, then, Doctor?" Nurse Baines asked deferentially. Matron was appearing from the back of the hall.

"I don't think so, Nurse. They will both be allowed to wake tomorrow for food. Meanwhile ring Dr. Webster, of course, if there's— any change."

"Of course, Doctor."

"Dr. Webster will be here in the morning. Good evening, Matron."

"Dr. Irving."

Nurse Baines shut the front door, and Matron turned to the window which matched Helen's the other side of it.

"Cheer up, Mr. Colburn, now! Things aren't as bad as that, you know. Dear me, we're usually so cheery! But they did tell us. . . ."

Helen hadn't noticed the American when she ran downstairs, but now she saw he was standing gazing out on the drive, as silent and withdrawn as he had been expansive and verbose. No doubt he had entered into the second of those two states which seemed to constitute a dual existence for most of the voluntary clientele of Hartshorn Manor.

CHAPTER 10

All things bright and beautiful,
All creatures great and small . . .

And still something in the world to make Helen suppress a smile
—Freda and Geoffrey standing side by side in front of the lounge
window, the ginger tufts of Freda's hair on a level with Geoffrey's
elbow where it was crooked to hold the hymn book.

The tall trees in the greenwood,
The river running by . . .

Matron was playing the upright piano which was normally kept
locked.

"Just a couple of hymns," Helen had heard her say to someone's
relative arriving a few moments before the service began. "And a
prayer or two. No sermon, of course, and in the circumstances the
vicar doesn't offer Communion. I'm a Catholic myself, but if I'm
here, I play."

. . . and forgive us our trespasses, as we forgive those who trespass
against us . . .

The thud had been Freda's hymnbook falling as she turned away
to look out of the window. Geoffrey was joining in the Lord's Prayer,
his Adam's apple travelling frantically up and down. One of the
dishcloth-knitting women had turned her book over and was examining the cover.

Now thank we all our God . . .

Tune and words were just recognizable through the efforts of Sister and Nurse Evans. Also, suddenly realized Helen, Mrs. Lockett,
who sang assiduously and true.

Now unto him who is able to keep us from falling . . .

She would have liked to stand still and pray that particular prayer,
but Fiona had been unobtrusive enough for the ten minutes of the

service, joining in the singing if not of the announced hymn, moving about only on the spot near the window where Nurse Evans had encouraged her. It was time she went her own way. Also, Helen was feeling sick, and although she was half hoping one of the nursing staff would be there again to witness the outcome, she hardly wanted the entire population of Hartshorn Manor and it came so suddenly. . . .

She had several obstacles to get by and Fiona never used force, so that she only just made her room and basin. She didn't feel ill, but it shouldn't be happening, she was receiving something in her food or drink to bring about these protestations of her digestive system. Five days to go and if the authorities went on administering whatever drug it was, by Friday she could be more than briefly sick.

And if the Department had got it wrong and it was a drug designed exclusively for Helen Johnson . . .

It wasn't. It couldn't be. All the same . . .

She had had Ovaltine the night before and once again gone quickly into heavy, dreamladen sleep, waking only to a nurse's hand and no opportunity to think and quake. If the Ovaltine was giving her the sleep as well as the sickness, it might just be worth the risk of taking it. . . .

Would the records clerk withstand for another five days the drugs *he* was receiving? Would Dr. Bakewell? She couldn't help asking the questions in that order, fear began at home . . .

It was almost a relief to have to dash again to the basin, and when she had recovered a second time she went back downstairs, to find the service over and her fellow patients drifting out of their additional confinement. Mrs. Lockett, being congratulated on her singing voice by staff and vicar, had not left her prominent seat and was smiling in self-satisfaction, her head still.

As Fiona flitted in, the tall, thin vicar leaned down to hear Nurse Evans's commentary.

"Very sad. Very sad."

Nurse Evans looked even more healthy and cheerful than usual, her eyes very bright. "Hello, pet," she said.

"Happy days are here again," sang Helen, not lingering to see any further reaction because of a sudden dizziness which sent her into the nearest vacant chair. The fruit juice, perhaps, which had been

distributed before the service? But why was nobody else afflicted? If anyone was she would know, none of them had her ability, or her motive, to conceal what was happening to them. . . . She reminded herself yet again that no two people had the same reaction to a drug. Yet nearly all the people at Hartshorn Manor stared somnolently in front of them, exhibiting the desired effect. . . .

Even with a clear mind she was finding it difficult to keep her thoughts in order. She would go into the garden. It was fine and she could run off, and be seen to run off, some surplus energy, so that a relatively easy afternoon of it in an armchair would be the less remarkable. And before that, just before lunch, when whatever Dr. Webster had done that morning might have had its effect, she would wander upstairs and in and out of the rooms in the west corridor. There were just two prayers, really: for the safety of Julian and their home, and for the continuing silence of the records clerk and Dr. Bakewell. . . .

"Who's for a game of I Spy? I'll go first, shall I? Let me see now." Mr. Colburn was leaning forward, looking vaguely from Helen to a Mrs. Lockett once more shaking her head in disapproval. He appeared to have recovered his predominant, mildly manic, mood.

Something beginning with C.

"Something beginning with C."

Helen had said it first, in her head, reading the mental notes she had made of the first and second times Mr. Colburn had played I Spy. Strange that it had been C, in the garden, with which he had begun the game. C for cloud. And in the lounge, C for clock. Not so strange, perhaps, C was the first letter of his name.

"Clock!" said Mrs. Lockett severely, shaking her head.

"Not clock, no. I'm sorry, ma'am." Mr. Colburn's manner was a mixture of triumph and regret. "It's a shame, ma'am, that you didn't get it right, I'm not the man to want to score over a woman, no sir, but I'm afraid that's how it is this time, it isn't clock, no, ma'am, you'll have to try it again and I don't think you're going to get it."

"I can try. Carpet," said Mrs. Lockett. She had to talk through Mr. Colburn, who allowed no space.

"It's curtain," said Mr. Colburn. "C for curtain. I knew it would be too difficult, I'm sorry you didn't get it but there it is. I'll have to

take another turn, in the circumstances. I'm sorry, ma'am, truly I
am."

Mr. Colburn, now, was partially addressing an empty chair. Mrs.
Lockett, trembling with indignation, muttering the words "imperti-
nence," "impudence," and "insolence," had got up and left the
room.

I spy with my little eye something beginning with— No, she
couldn't remember what letter Mr. Colburn had used for his second
word, or if it had been the same both times.

"Something beginning with I, now," said Mr. Colburn. So steadily
blank was his gaze she had risked looking at his eyes, and there was
another unwelcome second, before her own eyes veered away, where
his almost seemed aware of this. But Mr. Colburn had already struck
her as one of the few people at Hartshorn Manor who might have a
chance of being cured.

I for inkwell, yes. Nurse Chadwick had guessed and had upset
him. Well, it would have to be inkwell again, she couldn't think there
was anything else in the room beginning with I, except for all the
imperfectly submerged Ids, abstractions hardly within Mr. Colburn's
competence.

He was indulging in a long, rich chuckle. "This is the best one
yet," he said eventually, wiping his eyes on his handkerchief. "I
reckon this is one nobody could guess. I reckon this is the cleverest
one that's ever been thought up. I'm sorry, ma'am"—it was hard to
know whether Mr. Colburn was addressing her or the dishcloth-
knitting lady on the other side of her—"I wouldn't want you to think
I was showing off, no sir, I'm not a man to show off in front of
women, I admire the little lady and respect her, always have done
and always will do." His discourse had the soothing cadences of
United States presidents on television. "But I reckon not one of you's
going to get this something beginning with I. No sir, not one of you."

"You playing your little game again, Mr. Colburn?" Nurse Evans
crossed the lounge and leaned on the back of the knitter's chair,
smiling delightedly. There was something about Nurse Evans this
morning which made Helen feel she could be delighted by anything.

"I it is," said Mr. Colburn, not noticeably enlarging his audience.
"And I reckon I'll just have to tell you. Get ready for it. I for
information. In those books over there." Mr. Colburn gestured

across the room, chuckling again, to the three shelves where some
elderly novels, too few to the row, dispiritedly slanted. Fiona had
picked one up once and Helen, longing to distract herself by reading,
had noticed the old Boots library label. "Information," repeated Mr.
Colburn, and again Helen had been lulled into a second of visual
contact. "Books full of it."

"That's very clever of you, Mr. Colburn. And very encouraging."
Nurse Evans came round the knitter's chair to pat an unresponding
Mr. Colburn on the arm. "We'll soon have you right. Your son told
me you'll be having more treatment when you go home, and that
could just do the trick." Helen thought Nurse Evans glanced instinc-
tively around her, as if looking for someone to make it worth while
continuing her interpretation of Mr. Colburn, before shrugging her
shoulders. "Want anything, pet?"

"I spy with my little eye," said Mr. Colburn, "something beginning with A."

"Garden!" sang Fiona, twirling to the door.

"There's a good idea!" Nurse Evans overtook her and led the way
down the hall. "Here we are, pet, we've got almost an hour before
lunch, and it's nice and sunny."

Helen ran down the steps and went on running about the lawn,
testing herself for any signs of weakness and finding none. Merely,
after a few minutes, a dizziness which sent her posthaste to the nearest seat. At least she could still think and hear and see and move
according to her will.

Couldn't she?

Dear Lord, she had been at Hartshorn Manor less than forty-eight
hours and for a dreadful moment she had already doubted her san-
ity. An absurd moment—if her mind was affected by a drug or drugs,
the anguish in her thoughts of Julian and home would be dulled and
it was not, it was keener each time it broke her guard.

Nothing must break her guard. Nothing must prevent her getting
successfully away from Hartshorn Manor with the information
which would enable Julian to take action and keep them safe. And
Dr. Bakewell's secrets. . . .

She was on her feet again, dancing and singing her way round and
round the lawn, aware that one of three woman wedged together on
a seat was waving to her. She stopped eventually in the sunken gar-

den to examine the plants and discover a black kitten lying in the
shade of a white-flowering viburnum. As she stroked the writhingly
appreciative body she found she was in tears. Consolation rather
than catastrophe—Fiona might not laugh but she would certainly be
able to cry. . . .

Not so long now before lunch, she must get upstairs. She met
Geoffrey in the doorway and braced herself for an approach, but he
passed her unnoticing, with drooping head. Another matter for the
future, if it came, was compassion for the bona fide inmates of the
Manor.

She began in the east corridor, seeing Freda curled up on her
bedspread, Bessie with ear to her transistor, another woman throwing everything out of a drawer. None of them aware of her, and no
nursing staff to observe. Any minute, though, a nurse would be up
with a tray for Bessie, to coax Freda downstairs. Singing and dancing, Helen crossed the stairhead into the corridor where silence and
stillness no longer felt innocent, and, thwarting her instinct, went
into the room where Dr. Bakewell lay, leaving the door ajar behind
her as she tiptoed up to the bed.

It was a shock to see the wide-open eyes.

"Water," whispered Dr. Bakewell.

"Spring," warbled Fiona, *"will be a little late this year."* There was
water by the bed and someone must be coming to administer it—
Pete had put into words his anxiety that his patients should not die.
Dr. Bakewell wasn't moving more than her head, perhaps that was
all she could move. "Water," she said again. Twirling about the room
Helen opened the drawer of the bedside table. Paper handkerchiefs
and a couple of unused bandages. Nothing in the cupboard below it.
Nothing in the long cupboard but a white coat on a hanger and some
contraption on the floor which looked as if it might be a straitjacket.

"Water," pleaded Dr. Bakewell, turning her head into the pillow,
and Fiona ran out of the room.

All quiet still in the corridor, and she opened the other significant
door.

This patient, too, was in a species of waking state. Brown eyes
instead of blue, and not so widely staring. Only the head agitating
above the neat straight line of the sheet. The eyes following her about

the room, but merely as a baby's eyes might trace a shadow on the wall. Nothing in the bedside cupboard, the hanging cupboard—

She heard her choked cry as she sprang back, and that was Fiona's correct reaction as well, but there had been a second in which she and Mr. Colburn had stared at one another in comprehending horror, before Fiona had her knuckles to her mouth as she whimpered, and Mr. Colburn was walking out of the cupboard as if it was the doorway from another room, closing it behind him and asking her genially if she would like to play I Spy.

Helen heard a groan from the bed as she sped away. She didn't stop until she was almost at her own door and bumping against Nurse Evans who was opening the door of the room where Freda still lay curled on her bed.

"Hoop-la! We are in a hurry! Have you seen a ghost, pet?" Helen ran past Nurse Evans, headlong into the room, surprised at her relief that the nurse immediately followed her, at her instinct to cover the American's retreat. "They do say there's a ghost at the Manor, a little girl, but I don't know that anyone's seen her. Unless some of you have, and you wouldn't tell us, would you?"

Nurse Evans chucked Freda under the chin, and Helen was glad to feel, in the midst of her shock, the warm sense of pity which welled in her as Freda's hand crept up to slide itself into the hand of Nurse Evans.

"Come on, then, on our way. Lamb chops today, the sort without any bones."

The woman emptying out the drawers of her dressing-table was scooped up en route along the corridor, and the four of them took their varying paces down the stairs. In the dining-room Mr. Colburn was already at table, assuring the woman beside him of his chivalrous instincts. Helen, in her keen oblique glances, saw no evidence that he was aware of her entry or of anything beyond the making of his oratorical point. So many things were churning in her head it was more instinctive than it had yet been to present the vague humming Fiona façade while she skirted her hopes and fears. Mr. Colburn had been hiding in a cupboard in one of the two dangerous rooms. He could have done this for two reasons: either because he had heard her footsteps and had taken refuge from what he would have thought to be the authorities; or because he had been waiting inside the cupboard in the hope of overhearing what was said during the next visit of a doctor or a nurse—perhaps there had even been a crack to which he had been able to apply his eye. She was horribly tempted, of course, to ponder a third possibility: that Mr. Colburn's extraordinary behaviour was part of an elaborate plot to make the Fiona mask slip. But even her hovering sense of personal disaster had to give way before the unlikelihood of Mr. Colburn knowing the approaching footsteps to be hers. Unless, of course, he had been stalking her ever since she had arrived and already knew she had paid one other solitary visit to the records clerk. . . . If so, she had been out of character for the barest second, her disguise still stood. But if they were on to her it would only be a matter of time, they would try other ways. For heaven's sake, they would try direct, painful ways, and it would not be the short-lived, private-enterprise violence she had withstood that first time she had worked for Julian. . . . She was being absurd again: whatever Mr. Colburn was up to, he could not be an agent of the new owners of Hartshorn Manor.

But why was he interested in the records clerk?

Her pessimism, the taste for intrigue she had absorbed from Julian, they were carrying her on too far. *Was* he interested should be her first question. She had not, after all, been present when Mr. Colburn had been introduced to the Resident Director and the Matron, she hadn't heard the account of his eccentricities as she had heard the valiant George secure for her all her current freedoms. It was a possibility that hiding in cupboards was one of his problems, it was no more extraordinary than a perpetual desire to play I Spy.

I spy with my little eye something beginning with C.

"Come along, Fiona pet, you're not getting on very fast today. Shall I cut it up for you?"

"Nice," said Fiona. *"Sing a song of sixpence!"* She seized each small piece of meat as Nurse Evans cut it free, choking on the last to punish herself for her relaxation of vigilance.

"One extreme to the other," sighed Nurse Evans, "but that's the story of our lives." She was still radiantly cheerful. "Come along, Geoffrey, you can do better than that."

Mr. Colburn might have a tendency to hide in cupboards, a compulsion to play I Spy, and still be a bona fide client of Hartshorn Manor. But in each game there had been that second he had caught her eye, and when she had opened the cupboard door he, as well as she, had known what was happening. After lunch she would go and sit somewhere, give herself a re-run of the three games of I Spy Mr. Colburn had played against himself in her presence. If she had translated them conscientiously on to a mental page she would be able to recall them in their entirety, but of course she hadn't, she had been aware of them—of the first one, at least—merely as welcome diversion from Fiona Spencer. Her mental discipline, though, was probably good enough to have given her something, if she tried hard enough to get it back.

But first she would visit the Resident Director, forgotten since he had left her and George in the bedroom and recalled to mind now merely because she had thought about Mr. Colburn's arrival at the Manor. (When? If only she could look through some files! The temptation, each time she passed Sister's room knowing Sister was elsewhere, was painful, but had to be resisted.)

She chose a moment when there was no one in the hall to suggest she should do something different, but she left the heavy door open behind her. The room was empty and the desk very tidy, the few papers in a neat pile. The Resident Director could be having a weekend off. No one in the alcove, and before she knew she was going to do it she had thrown herself down in the chair there and swivelled through a hundred and eighty degrees. She got up rebuking herself. The gesture was unlikely to have done harm, but even harmless things must be done from decision rather than from impulse while she was Fiona Spencer. . . . Did the small silent man spend all his time at the Manor, and if so, where did he sleep? Behind the door marked STAFF ONLY? As representative of the new owners he might reside there unquestioned by the staff inherited from the earlier regime, and if he kept himself to himself as much as she was persuaded he did, the new owners could afford a slight resentment in the paramount interests of their security. Helen thought she might have seen evidence of such resentment, in what Nurse Evans had said the first time they had met.

There were filing cabinets in the Resident Director's office, too, but they must be as inviolate as Sister's. Sister . . . She'd look in there as well, and then across the hall at Matron. Postpone going out to the garden to think, and to put herself at the disposal of the event for which she was tense with apprehension. *Something beginning with C.*

She was approaching Sister's door when she heard the laugh behind it. The warm choky laugh with the knowing edge which filled her mind at once and exclusively with a picture of the last dinner-party she had attended, a man to each side of her and opposite a woman with elaborate blonde hair and plumply elegant bare shoulders. Mrs. Davenport, non-existent wife of Dr. Webster's non-existent potential employer, was now in Sister's office.

Helen was singing as she went through the door, *Jingle Bells.* Sister was the first person she saw, her face unaccustomedly cheerful. So Mrs. Davenport had perhaps made Sister laugh, too. Helen looked eagerly past Sister to the figure just turning round from the alcove, kettle in hand.

Nurse Baines. Half smiling but not laughing, and anyway Nurse Baines could never have played the role of Mrs. Davenport, she was too short and slight and her face was entirely the wrong shape.

So Sister . . .

"Here's Fiona come to see us. All right, dear?" The concern in Sister's face, now, was ghastly, because Helen had once thought there was compassion in it. She couldn't work things out while she was standing there, she would have to use a mental picture later, but it was all possible, the height, the bones, the timbre of the voice. And the laugh which clinched it.

At least Fiona Spencer didn't laugh. *But was there anything else of Helen Johnson which couldn't be disguised?* She brought her hands together, in a prayer of thanksgiving that Sister had turned away.

"Garden," said Fiona.

"That's a good idea," said Sister briskly, half glancing round. "Nurse Baines, will you?"

"Only too delighted, Sister." Again, Helen was aware of antagonism. Nurse Baines might be pushing it.

Still singing, she allowed herself to be encouraged out of Sister's room and across the hall to the garden door. No nerve left, just at the moment, for Matron. Down the steps and across the lawn at a run, skirting the sunken centre. The door closing and Nurse Baines disappearing.

Helen sank down on the seat farthest from the house, sole occupant of the garden. She had been looking for trouble with Sister, and with everyone else, but had found it only when Sister laughed. Sister wasn't looking for trouble with Fiona Spencer, any more than with the rest of the Manor's clientele. She was as safe as she had been five minutes ago, and with some important extra knowledge. With all the knowledge she was going to get, she would have said before she had opened the cupboard door on Mr. Colburn.

As she sat there, her heartbeat abating, she saw him come slowly down the steps on to the grass.

CHAPTER 11

Already she had her imperfect memory of Mr. Colburn's I Spy monologues spread out on her mental screen. *Cloud, clock* and *curtain,* three Cs for sure. *Inkwell. Information.* What had the second word been in the garden? She saw the tree-trunk and its luxuriant parasite just as Mr. Colburn, with his steady loping stride, reached the seat where she was sitting.

Ivy.

"Good afternoon, ma'am." Mr. Colburn sat down beside her. Fiona edged to the far arm of the seat, half leaned over it. Mr. Colburn, staring ahead of him, appeared not to notice. "I was thinking it would be a good idea if you and I had another little game of I Spy. A very good idea. I'll go first, shall I? I spy with my little eye something beginning with C. You can't guess it? Or you won't? Well, it doesn't matter. It really doesn't matter what it is. Let's say it's cherry tree, I guess there's one somewhere in this hell of a garden. Your turn? You'd like to go?"

Staring resolutely at the house, muttering and biting her knuckles, Helen knew the American had looked towards her.

"No? Not yet, at any rate. Perhaps you're not ready. Well, I don't mind, I'll go again. I spy with my little eye something beginning with I. D'you want to have a guess at that? Not that it matters, it's playing the game that matters, isn't it, that's what you British always used to say. Play up, play up, and play the game. So let's play the game. I. Something beginning with I. Now I reckon this really is the best one I've come up with yet."

Mingling with the sweet smell of some herb hidden nearby was the smell of sweat. Starting a random swivelling of her head, Helen noticed the gleam on Mr. Colburn's temple.

"I," said Mr. Colburn, "for intelligence. Yes, ma'am, I reckon there's some of that in this garden right now. Two lots of it in two heads. Yes, sir. With a small i and a large I, too. We'll have another one, shall we, just one more? I'd better go again, seeing that you still don't seem to be quite ready."

I spy with my little eye something beginning with A.

Arm. Another A either unremembered or unguessed. And again.

"A for Agency," said Helen, and Mr. Colburn's flow dried.

"Good," he said. "Good. Would you like a turn now?"

"M for mania," said Helen softly. "I for ideology. Counted on the fingers of one hand."

"Good," said Mr. Colburn again. "But I hardly expected anything less."

Each of them, now, was looking straight ahead, a pair of careful drivers keeping their eyes on the road from which, whatever of moment inside the car, the real dangers would come.

"Why should you expect anything from *me?*"

"First because you arrived day before yesterday. You're the only arrival since I got here Thursday. Second, because I caught your eye. And third because we don't really consider ourselves all that cleverer than the British."

"It could be said that *I* caught *your* eye."

"Sure, sure. You're great. Just great. Clever, too. Gee, I've envied that harmless crazy kid dancing her way wherever she thinks she'd like to go. No need to hide in cupboards for Fiona. Although this guy's known to suffer from sudden attacks of agoraphobia."

They were several yards from the thick tree boundary behind them, but the rich voice was barely audible.

"Why were you hiding in that room? Why are you here? *Who killed Cock Robin?*" asked Fiona plaintively.

"That's right, yes. I haven't really got an act, but if I'm just seen to be talking I'm OK, I guess. You know already I'm here for the same reason you're here. To look after my own."

"Your own?"

"Positively. Let's not waste time."

"I promise you I've no intention. *I, said the Sparrow, with my little Arrow.* I just thought you might give me some clue as to what interest your organization could have in the records clerk from an obscure English magazine."

"Records clerk? If this is some code, I reckon they forgot to brief me. Forgive me, ma'am, I thought we'd made contact."

"So we have, I believe. But I also believe Dr. Webster's male patient to be British, and my concern."

"Jesus, you British! Pardon me, ma'am, but Dr. Webster's male patient is an eminent citizen of the United States of America. As his female patient is an eminent citizen of the United Kingdom. We won't mention names, although I know both. One step ahead, I reckon. I'm sorry."

"I'm not, Mr. Colburn, I'm not. Thank you for the correction." Julian and Toby and the house and garden. They were still safe. Another patient might arrive for Dr. Webster, but at this moment Julian and their home were safe. Joy was running through her to her fingertips. "I had been making an assumption," she said humbly, "unsupported by any facts in my possession. I'm sorry."

"Sing, will you? Or dance!"

"I'll sing. If Fiona took off she'd scarcely come back voluntarily to a tête-à-tête. *Oh, what a beautiful morning!*" She would have liked to dance as well. And shout to the cloud-flecked sky that Julian was safe. "But how did you know your—case—was at the Manor?"

Mr. Colburn laughed, a different sound from the tolerant chuckle she had heard from him hitherto. "How did your people know yours was? You British, you still think you're the only ones. We knew from the same source that you knew. And we knew first. I told you I'd been watching for you."

She wouldn't tell him she didn't know the source. "How long are you staying?"

"Thursday. We reckoned a week would give me all I needed. At least all I'd have a chance to find out."

"You've been round all the patients' rooms?" The luxury of talking sense, of having the prospect of talking out her discoveries and her fears, was dizzying. "Excuse me."

She was sick into the border, out of sight and sound of him. Discreetly for her own sake as well as his, she didn't want a nurse coming out to be concerned at that moment. Not that she could see one at door or windows—which was just as well, Fiona was going uncharacteristically back to sit near someone who had been paying attention to her. Mr. Colburn didn't look at her as she sat down gasping, but appeared to know what had happened.

"Don't tell me they've put you on something to help the illusion? Well, I lost a good molar once when I was impersonating someone else's dental record."

"My people haven't put me on anything. It must be the drug generally prescribed at the Manor."

"Which drug's that, then? Sing, for Christ's sake."

"I'm for ever blowing bubbles, pretty bubbles in the sky. The one in the Ovaltine, I suppose. Or it might be in the fruit juice. Or the tea. Or all of them. Doesn't it affect you in any way?"

"Nothing's affecting me. Except I sleep better at night than I do outside."

"I see." She was disappointed. "Well, drugs take different people different ways." It felt like a very familiar phrase.

"You've thrown up before?"

"Several times."

"Jesus, if your people have loused it up—"

"They haven't. I tell you, it's just something that doesn't agree with me. If it was anything really bad I wouldn't feel all right in between. I wouldn't!"

"Okay, okay. And don't get so het up. A job like this, I can't believe it's your first."

"It isn't. And it's easier than my first. And I'm amateur. I'm being used because I'm rather a good actress."

"For Christ's—"

"I'm Julian Johnson's wife."

Each word was an electric charge on her heart, offered up to the enemy's garden. But there had been no alternative. The American whistled, long and low.

"Okay. Okay." She had done the right thing. No need to say anything more. Anything about the debit side of her case sheet. "How long are you here?"

"Till Friday. How long will they hold out?" He would understand, now, her patches of ignorance.

"If we've got it right, it's a slow process as well as a good one. Takes quite a few weeks to gain the control that can open the brain. Metaphorically, ma'am, I'm speaking metaphorically." Before she'd told him what she had about herself, he wouldn't have bothered with the reassurance. "Within thirty-six hours or so they can be let wake up and eat, etcetera, they're unaware of their surroundings. If the treatment's not maintained they gradually come back. The thing we don't know—whether there's any permanent damage."

"The treatment's new?"

"Very. And we haven't got it. But we'll get it."

She supposed they would. She would rather neither side had it.

"Will you organize something for Thursday night?"

"I hope so."

"Both of them?"

"Of course both of them. And via one of your outfits. You'll have to lie low."

"I realize that." It was hard to introduce disdain into a whisper. *"Who'll toll the bell?"* sang Fiona. *"I, said the bull, because I can pull. I'll toll the bell."* She hated the way her subconscious threw her Fiona's librettos. "Fiona will know nothing of what goes on." Disdain was a foolishly indulgent sentiment to want to introduce. The discovery of this prickly ally was too wonderful and too important to be jeopardized to the defence of her pride. Her pride, again. "I expect we're at the same place, and I know it's been easier for Fiona. You'll be able to tell them the geography? How they can get to those two rooms both ways, from inside and out—"

"Sure. I know."

"You know the two people who'll try not to be there the morning after?"

"Two people? Nurse Baines—"

"Nurse Baines, yes. And Sister." She managed to keep any sense of triumph out of her voice.

"Sister? Fact or assumption?"

"I call it fact. I've come up against her in another disguise. Both of us. There's no doubt, although I only got her from her laugh."

"Which she doesn't make with all that much. Jesus, Sister! I've got to confess I never really thought . . . I thought of Matron."

"I didn't." But she wouldn't say anything about her sixth sense, which she had learned didn't work for her all the time. "I didn't really think of Sister, either. D'you think there's anyone else?"

She sensed the shrug. Her quick glance showed her his forehead was dry. "There could be. But two would be enough."

"Particularly when supported by our small silent friend. He was in the office when you arrived?"

"Yup. And now and again in the corridors. I tell you, that part of it's hairy for me."

"I appreciate. But you're marvellous. I was especially impressed the way you managed to go red with rage when Nurse Chadwick guessed inkwell. *Gone are the days when my heart was young and gay.*"

"Actually, ma'am," supplied Mr. Colburn, clearing his throat, "I started my career on the stage, too. But this is my profession today."

"Clearly. *Every bear that ever there was is gathered there for certain because today's the day the teddy-bears have their picnic.* Any idea where that little chap sleeps? I presume he's always with us."

"I suspect so. I've seen him coming out of the Staff door."

"Anywhere else?"

"I saw him go into one of those new places on the front of the house this morning."

"Perhaps he's moved down, or keeps two establishments. You'll tell whoever's sent in to look out for him?"

"Will do. This is becoming self-indulgent. We'll meet again."

"We'll meet again. Don't know where. Don't know when. But I know we'll meet again some sunny day."

"If it's sunny tomorrow, out here sometime. One will see the other."

"I'll probably give you a rose." It was as wonderful to be able to laugh softly as to be able to talk.

"If it's not sunny and you see me go upstairs, apart from bedtime, go too. My room's the right-hand door, end of east corridor. Fiona's got entrée."

"She's lucky that way. And in the fact that she's next door to you."

"I haven't seen you."

"I've been in your room, once. I don't go into single rooms on our side of the stairs, unless I'm pretty sure they'll be empty. There isn't any bugging, is there? I haven't been able to find anything, but I'm not professional on that, either."

"I'm certain now there's nothing. Not that I really expected it, it wouldn't fit with the method of concealment. So open you couldn't imagine there was anything to hide."

"That's what Ju— Yes, I know what you mean."

"You'd better go. They're fathoms deep here in self-satisfaction, but we mustn't push it."

"Of course not." She hesitated an amateurish second. "Thanks."

"Get going," he said, and Fiona went circling the sunken round before dropping on her knees on the central granite, grazing them. The kitten wasn't there.

"What have we been up to, then?" scolded Nurse Rogers, as Fiona went whimpering up to her. "Hurt our knees, have we? We'll wash them, shall we, and put on something comfy?" Nurse Rogers opened the door between Sister's room and the kitchen, where Helen hadn't yet seen. It was a small sick-bay, in no way alerting her sense of danger. When Nurse Roger had washed the grey-brown stains away there was in each case only a small area of damage, concealed by a sticking plaster.

"No tights to ruin," said Nurse Rogers, tidying the turned-down tops of Fiona's white ankle socks. Helen had to pull away from her and head for the washbasin to be sick, before realizing how good her timing was.

"Oh dear," said Nurse Rogers, looking from Helen to the basin and back again. "Oh dear," she repeated as she ran the taps. "Matron told me . . . She said it was almost as if . . . And we laughed. Well—it *couldn't* be."

The expression on Nurse Rogers's face was very strange, half smiling, half serious, too full of interest. Helen put her hand down to a knee and recommenced whimpering. Nurse Rogers's face cleared.

"You'll live, chick. Not to worry. Off you go, now."

She pushed the door open and, as Helen flitted out, turned decidedly away as if dismissing her most recent thoughts as well as Fiona Spencer.

Helen ran across the hall into the lounge, feeling the pull of the plaster on her knees. *Almost as if* . . . Almost as if what? Almost as if she was being poisoned? *And we laughed.* But they wouldn't laugh at *that.* Perhaps they had had some pretentious theories spouted at them in a lecture, something about people—even mentally deficient people—who made themselves sick in order to gain attention. They'd laughed, and then there was one of their own patients actually appearing to do it. And they'd laughed again. Nervously, this time. Half amused, half serious. . . .

Her exhilaration at having been able to communicate again had disappeared, and she was realizing how tired she was. Fiona's little accident would tie in well with that. And with the idea of nervous energy being used up to bring on the attention-seeking sickness. . . .

She felt so very tired she was leaning back in her chair and closing her eyes. Not just tired but actually at rest. It was wonderful, how she had got back into her own garden, where all was well and she was walking with Julian, telling him she had had a bad dream and had decided not to take on any more assignments for Versatile Actress. Toby was darting about in the borders, she was saying she'd been worried about anything happening to Toby. She could feel Julian's hand in hers, and then Toby had jumped out in front of them and was growing bigger and bigger, blotting out the bright sky and taking her breath away. . . .

"That's not very nice, Mrs. Merrivale, not very nice at all."

Toby leapt away as suddenly as he had sprung, and Nurse Chadwick was standing there with a cardigan in her hand, looking in exaggerated dismay from Helen to the small woman with the mutinous jaw who was swinging her diminutive arms and looking for something else to throw. Perhaps the woman who had been emptying out her drawers, her manic phase not yet worked off? Fiona picked a piece of wool or hair from her lip and whimpered, expressing Helen's continuing forlorn awareness of Julian's hand and the fantasy that nothing had gone wrong.

"There you are, you see," went on Nurse Chadwick severely, "you've upset our lovely Fiona, and I'm sure I'm not surprised. Oh no you don't!"

One of the arms had fastened on a nearby cushion, and Nurse Chadwick caught it as it flailed in mid-air. She was wrestling with an unapparent strength as Nurse Baines came into the lounge, her lagging walk breaking into a run.

Between them they got Mrs. Merrivale back into her chair.

"We may have to take her upstairs," panted Nurse Chadwick. "Dr. Sandelson had better be told, she's on experimental tablets."

"It's all right," said Nurse Baines, backing off.

Mrs. Merrivale was sitting meekly in her seat, her feet together and her hands motionless in her lap, smiling a propitiatory smile.

"For the time being, at any rate," said Nurse Chadwick. "Thanks for your help."

"I'll help you with the tea."

Suspicion again, always spoiling the thought, now, of anything to eat or drink, especially when Nurse Baines or Sister was involved. But she took the mug as usual into both hands and as usual enjoyed a good China tea, properly made and with no strange taste about it. But of course, drugs for innocents would have to be tasteless, they wouldn't take anything for their own good if it displeased them.

For their own good?

It probably was, in most cases, but also for the good of the nurses. And they worked so hard and devotedly, they could do with some help, so long as it was ultimately harmless.

Friday was ultimately, so far as she was concerned. If the American did what he said he would do, she would know before she went home that Dr. Bakewell and the important American were safe. If she was fit to go home. . . .

Mr. Colburn appeared to be in the depressive phase of his cycle, staring down at his knees and impervious to the blandishments of Nurse Chadwick, who was perhaps remembering the I for Inkwell with regret as she tried to get him to start another game.

"My pleasure!" he said a couple of times, abruptly, but she could provoke him to nothing more and, sighing, she wheeled her trolley to the side of the room and, after switching on the television, trundled it out.

Snooker. One of the better ways of getting through the stretch until dinner and the prospect of bed. Rather like watching a tankful of tropical fish, the flowing colourful movements within the confined bounds. She would risk letting Fiona relax until the announcement of the last meal of the day, passing up on the doctors' visits, now there was nothing more to learn. Although tomorrow, if not tonight, she would have to dance again, prevent any anxiety for the dog which didn't bark. . . .

Her mind's eye pictured those sterile white cells waiting upstairs.

Always, at every moment, there was the prospect of a new patient for
Dr. Webster. . . .

". . . You can see it in his face now. Even in the way he's holding
his cue. He knows it's all slipping away from him. . . ."

Perhaps the most luxurious thing about everyday life was being
able to pin all your hopes and fears on the outcome of a game.

At supper, everyone seemed a bit subdued.

"Have you noticed," commented Nurse Rogers to Sister, "how
mania or depression tends to go through them all? I always think it's
strange."

Sister smiled, but bustled by without comment. Fiona got up from
the table early and went to dance about the hall. When it was bedtime she spent some time with Nurse Rogers as she helped the occu-
pants of the east corridor to get undressed. Helen decided against
crossing the stairhead—and there was the warming new knowledge
that Mr. Colburn might manage it.

When Nurse Rogers eventually edged her into her room she
stayed there. Ready for bed, she stood humming by the window,
lifting the curtain. Light was streaming out on to part of the vegeta-
ble garden and the bit of the path to the back door which she could
see. Perhaps from Mr. Colburn's window or the staff rooms above.
Suddenly across the weird growths which the electric light made of
the vegetables, there slanted two long black shadows. Side by side
they hovered, fused at one end, separated, fused again. Then blended
along their whole length, withdrawing at last as one. The next moment Helen heard quick feet on the path and Nurse Evans came
briefly into view, patting her uncapped hair, a shawl over her shoulders, before disappearing into the building.

Helen slipped into bed and lay hugging herself against an unruly
loneliness. So Nurse Evans was in love, it had shown all day in the
cheerful brilliance of her face. Confirmation, surely, of her sixth
sense that Nurse Evans was precisely what she seemed. A potential
ally, should one be needed in the four days that lay ahead.

Four days. At least, the morning and the evening were the second
day.

CHAPTER 12

Nurse Evans stayed with Helen next morning while she had breakfast, after encouraging her to use her commode rather than go along the corridor as Fiona usually did. Helen didn't like this much, even though Nurse Evans stood looking out of the window, any more than she liked her remaining in the room without any pretence of doing anything but sit gravely regarding Helen while she had the tray in front of her and saying from time to time "I hope not, pet, I hope not."

Helen at least felt confident it was to do with Fiona rather than herself, but Fiona's body was her body, and she was rendered too apprehensive by that kindly brooding presence to be able to give more than token attention to her breakfast. Then immediately she had pushed the tray aside she had to leap out of bed and be sick.

"Oh, pet," said Nurse Evans, and when Fiona attempted a song and dance act, arrested her with a hand on her shoulder. Not only that, Nurse Evans pushed her hand down Helen's arm so that the wide-necked nightdress went with it, and then on the other side, catching it at the waist so that Helen was half naked.

She then looked closely and severely at Helen's bosom, there was an indefinably dreadful moment in which Helen wished she had been granted a glimpse of Nurse Evans's partner of the night before in the garden, and then Nurse Evans had replaced the nightdress and was turning away, murmuring to Fiona to get dressed.

Helen dropped back on the bed in the weakness of her relief, pleased to see Nurse Evans reaching for the breakfast tray. But she changed her mind and came and sat on the bed too, putting her arm round Helen's shoulders and looking sadly into her face.

"Poor pet," crooned Nurse Evans. "Poor pet. It isn't right." She got up again, this time seized the tray. "Well," she said in her usual vigorous tone, "I'd better be getting on, don't want Mr. Mute smil-

ing on my tail. You get dressed, darling, go downstairs. I hope I
haven't upset you."

Oh, but she had. Looking at the door Nurse Evans had closed
sharply behind her, Helen found herself trembling. There seemed to
be only one possible explanation of the nurse's strange behaviour: she
had seen further symptoms of the poisoning which was making
Helen sick.

Standing up and letting the nightdress fall round her feet, Helen
surveyed her upper body in the mirror above the dressing-table, but
saw nothing amiss, her skin was as clear as it had ever been, her
outline as firm. And when, in an access of panic, she pressed her
hands over her breasts, there were no lumps or pains.

But Nurse Evans had seen something. Would she confide her anxi-
eties to Matron or Sister, and if she didn't, how significant would be
the deterioration of four more days?

She went downstairs without monitoring progress in the other east
corridor bedrooms (if there was something wrong with her, it would
account for Fiona's lack of enterprise). The weather was holding and
she ran straight out into the garden. She hoped Mr. Colburn
wouldn't be ready for another conversation—it would be as difficult
to avoid her latest preoccupation as to define it. While she was sitting
on the farthest seat she saw him looking at her through the window
of the annexe to the lounge, but to her relief his turning away didn't
signal his arrival on the steps. In a few moments, though, Nurse
Evans was there, calling out to her as she crossed the lawn. Helen
realized she had been awaiting clarification of their scene in the bedroom, and that it was about to come.

"No fruit juice this morning?" Nurse Evans greeted her. "Well,
perhaps you didn't feel like it, pet. Will you come inside with me
now? We'll go and call on Matron."

Matron at least, not Sister. Humming, Helen allowed herself to be
coaxed indoors. She pulled back on the threshold of Matron's room,
but Nurse Evans urged her forward. Standing beside Matron was Dr.
Sandelson. That grave, severe look Nurse Evans had turned on her in
the bedroom was on both their faces. But how could anyone pass
moral judgment on Fiona Spencer? Terror crept like ice down her
spine.

"Ah," said Dr. Sandelson. "I was afraid this was the poor woman you were meaning. Can you persuade her to let me look at her?"

"I think I can." Nurse Evans closed the door.

"The urine test," said Matron solemnly to Nurse Evans, "is positive. You acted wisely, Nurse."

"I knew when I saw her bos. The nipples . . ."

"It is highly unfortunate, to say the least," commented Dr. Sandelson. "Now, if I might just try to examine her."

Helen, after a weak show of resistance, was persuaded to lie on Matron's couch. Dr. Sandelson sounded her chest, felt her stomach, gently investigated . . . *Julian, will I ever be sure the worst is over?*

"Yes," said Dr. Sandelson. "Yes." He turned to speak to the solemn, waiting women. "It's at an early stage, but I'm afraid there is no doubt that this unfortunate woman is pregnant."

Once in her life before, Helen had heard words so momentous they had at first had no meaning for her. Her father had been waiting when she had been called out of a lesson at school, he had said, "Mummy died this morning," and it had been in that exact moment that the portrait of a former headmistress at the top of the stairs swung sideways and she had known she would never see her mother again. It had been a few seconds—or hours—later.

"It's dreadful!" burst out Nurse Evans.

"Mr. Parkinson did not give us the full facts," said Matron, her lips unaccustomedly pursed.

"He probably didn't know them. It's *awful!*"

"There is no evidence," said Dr. Sandelson, "of an earlier pregnancy."

"I suppose that's something. But whoever it is will get away with it," said Matron in vigorous disgust.

Helen swung her mysterious, exciting body to a sitting position. At the age of almost forty she was going to have a baby. It hadn't happened with John and she had thought it wouldn't happen with Julian, despite those absurd hopes she had for some time successfully buried. She could not remain mute. Sitting on the edge of the couch, Fiona began to whimper.

"Poor pet!" Nurse Evans was sitting beside her again, holding her in the half-circle of a protective arm. "It isn't her fault!"

"Of course not," said Matron and Dr. Sandelson on an indignant instant, and Helen had to clamp her teeth together not to burst into hysterical laughter. Dr. Sandelson asked Matron how long Fiona would be with them.

"She's being taken home on Friday. Her uncle's on holiday abroad. In Spain, I believe. Not likely to be able to be contacted. No parents."

"Obviously a termination," said Dr. Sandelson. There was a look of guilt on each face as it turned towards Helen, staring through them in the most horrible as well as the most wonderful moment of her life.

"I can't go along with that personally, as you know," said Matron. "But I realize . . ."

"There might just be complications anyway," said Dr. Sandelson soothingly. "The poor woman is nothing like so young as she looks."

"Thirty-six," said Nurse Evans sombrely, stroking Helen's hair. "*We* won't have to—do anything, will we?"

"I think *not.*" Mercifully, he hadn't hesitated. *Deo gratias,* he had been decisive. "In four days' time the situation will not be significantly advanced, and it will be up to the unfortunate woman's uncle to set the necessary—ah—wheels in motion. Had there been more time before she is to be collected, so much as a week I might say, then I think we should have to have taken on ourselves the ethical problem. But as things are—as they thankfully are, Matron"—Dr. Sandelson allowed his relief to show in a brief smile—"I think we need do no more than acquaint the uncle with the situation when he arrives on Friday."

"It is a blessing, Doctor, yes. You suggest nothing—conservative —meanwhile? The poor thing's been sick a good deal and looks slightly woebegone, I fancy. You don't think something . . . a sedative, perhaps?"

"I don't think she needs a sedative!" interjected Nurse Evans warmly. "Forgive me, Matron, but I think she's perfectly all right. Just a bit overawed by being brought in here and looked at. The atmosphere's been a bit serious and Fiona picks up atmospheres, she's really very sensitive."

"Well, no need for anything unless she shows signs of distress or unusual behaviour, Matron."

At least her immediate future was still in her own gift.

"One thing," said Matron, smiling at last and scratching into the thick fair-grey curls under her cap. "It didn't happen *here*. We don't have to look suspiciously at Geoffrey or Mr. Colburn or Mr.—Goodness, though! It *could* happen here, couldn't it? I mean . . . if it's happened once . . ."

"It might perhaps," said Dr. Sandelson as Nurse Evans helped him into his coat, "be politic to turn the key in the lock tonight. In the interests of your—er—male patients, if not of Miss Spencer herself. After all, so far as she is concerned the—er—damage is done. But any—forward behaviour—on her part might upset the gentlemen—"

"I'm sure Fiona's never shown any forward behaviour," protested Nurse Evans, cuddling Helen's drooping shoulders. "Some unspeakable beast has taken advantage of her and she could hardly be expected to fend him off."

Julian. I have your baby inside me and these people—these apparently nice, civilized people—have the power to take it away from me. And if I was true to the code you live by, I'd have to let them. Or betray you. Did any agent—and I'm not an agent—have such an issue to face? That I'm not facing it, that's just the bit of luck that George is coming this week instead of next. Unless you change your minds.

And there was still the terrible chance that someone else, someone forceful enough to influence doctor and nurses, hearing this outrageous piece of news might have different views on what to do about it.

Fiona was on her feet, circling the room and singing *Praise the Lord, Ye Heavens, Adore Him*, taking a coloured pencil out of the coloured container on Matron's desk and offering it to Nurse Evans.

"Thank you pet. You see?" said Nurse Evans triumphantly as she replaced the pencil. "She's all right. I promise I'll keep a special eye on her and report to Matron if there's anything to worry about."

"That should see to things nicely." Dr. Sandelson's smile was staying in place, the tension in the room had eased. Then suddenly tightened inside Helen. Her hitherto disregarded tête-à-têtes with Mr. Colburn would be invested, now, with a dreadful significance.

But there had to be one more, to tell him why it might have to be the last.

"Thirsty!" said Fiona.

"Of course, pet. There'll still be the fruit juice trolley in the lounge. Let's go. All right, Matron?"

"All right, Evans. And thank you again for your vigilance. Will you show Dr. Sandelson out?"

"You've got the right idea," said Dr. Sandelson in the hall, patting Nurse Evans's arm. "No need for any action, just keep that eye of yours on her."

"I will, Doctor, I will."

Fiona was already pouring herself some fruit juice when Nurse Evans caught up with her and took the jug out of her hands before more than a few drops were spilt. Helen circled the lounge, an inner circle including Mr. Colburn's chair, singing *Up, Up and Away.*

"Tired," she said when she got back to Nurse Evans, and danced out of the room and towards the staircase.

"All right, pet." Nurse Evans came no further than the lounge door, calling after her. "You go and have a nice little rest. I'm off duty in a minute but I'll see you tonight."

Helen went quickly to her room and cast herself down on the bed, leaving the door ajar. She found herself looking in a sort of surprise even at her fingers and her toes. The slight sense of sickness and dizziness, now, was a comforting reassurance that what had begun was continuing. Lying back, she stroked her flat stomach with a reverence which could have made her smile.

Something thudded against her door and there was the sound of a door opening nearby. Tucking her contemplation away, she slid off the bed and moved softly across the room, looking out along the empty vista of the two corridors to the far-away identical door made matchbox size by perspective. Then, with no more than three or four steps, she was through the open door next to her own.

Mr. Colburn was standing by the window, and turned sharply as he heard her. His face was annoyed and she remembered no suggestion had been made that she might ever be the one who summoned.

"It must be important," he said coldly.

"It is. I've found out why I've been sick. Or rather, the nursing staff have found out. I'm pregnant."

"Jesus!"

"Couldn't you find any irreligious expletives? For the first time in my life, at almost forty, I'm going to have a baby. It's been agreed of course that the pregnancy must be terminated, but at least they've decided not to do it while I'm here."

Mr. Colburn whistled, the annoyance leaving his face. "Gee, that's bad. That's awful." He moved a few steps towards her. "You don't look that good. Sit down."

"I'm all right, I'd better be poised for flight." But she leaned against the chest of drawers. "The thing is," she said, "it's going to mean special vigilance. They're even talking about locking me in at night. I'll get out of that somehow, but meanwhile they're not going to be very happy if they see me in a one to one situation with a male. They think, you see, that I probably got what I deserved."

He was studying her face. "You're tough," he said. "I'll give you that."

"I wonder, if I was an agent, where my loyalties would lie?" That was enough self-indulgence. "I must go back, I'm supposed to be resting. What I wanted to say—if there's any reason either of us needs to see the other, the least risk will be in the night, you to me or I to you."

"But if you're locked in—"

"I've told you, I won't be. I'll make a fuss and Nurse Evans will be on duty. You've got to have a bit of luck somewhere. Anyway, we daren't be seen on our own together, that'll really call for the heavy hand."

"Yes, I suppose so. Gee, I can hardly—"

"Have you been along the other corridor since we talked?"

"Last night, small hours. Only just avoided the gnome, who seems to have taken up residence in one of the new front suites. Second door from head of staircase. Heavy sleep in both cases, no one in attendance. But the gnome had just come out of the woman's room."

"I'll go in some time today, probably just after lunch, no one seems to be about then. No new arrivals?"

"None that I've noticed. Not even innocent ones. You'd better go. Take care. How d'you feel?"

"A bit sick, but now I'm glad of it. I've still got to run the gauntlet of Sister and Nurse Baines."

"They'll hardly be interested. But be careful."

"Oh, I will."

The corridor was still a long featureless diminution. She got on to

the bed again, lying there consciously relaxing as she heard Mr.
Colburn's feet plod substantially towards the stairs and begin their
descent. Her instinct was to stay where she was, brooding on the
process she had begun, but the importance, now, of getting away
from Hartshorn Manor in two pieces was so enormous she must
avoid the least uncharacteristic action which could jeopardize it.
And if she stayed in her burrow too long she might nudge the staff
into thinking about undesirable forms of medication. . . .

Best, for her nerves, to get Sister over. When she had run down
the stairs Helen turned to the right and opened Sister's door.

Annoyance here, again, but only, Helen thought, at an interrup-
tion. Sister was alone and at her desk, and as the annoyance faded it
was succeeded, reluctantly perhaps, by a look of interest.

"You little bitch," murmured Sister, smiling. "Have you been
messing about here, too?"

She couldn't hit the woman, but she could make one gesture towards her. Helen took a rose out of the familiar vase and held it out.
It was a small satisfaction to see Sister wince from contact with a
thorn. But she put the rose back gently enough.

"They won't let you have it," she said. "They wouldn't let me
have mine, either." Having people like Fiona around must be like
owning cats and dogs, offering an excuse to speak one's preoccupations aloud. The expression on Sister's face, for a flash, had been its
own. Helen crossed to the window singing, confused by her involun-
tary sense of pity. She was glad to hear the door open, and to see
Nurse Baines.

"Ah!" said Nurse Baines, advancing. "The innocent!"

"She *is* innocent," said Sister mildly.

"Sure. I wonder if she enjoyed it?"

"Let's talk a bit of business, shall we?"

"That's why I'm here. But we'll get rid of her first, she gives me
the creeps."

It was a pity she would never have a personal chance to even up
on Nurse Baines, who was now beside her at the window, firmly
taking her arm.

"Out you go!" said Nurse Baines.

"Careful," suggested Sister.

"Why? A bit of rough handling might procure the required miscarriage and save a lot of time and money."

Helen, whimpering her way to the door, saw Sister flush, open her mouth, then bite words back. Well, she had learned a little more. Nurse Baines was the senior of the two women in the real hierarchy.

She knew Nurse Baines was watching her as she danced across the hall, but Sister's door shut before she reached the lounge. Mr. Colburn glanced up as she went in, then dropped his head back on his breast. Three women placidly knitted, the man with the moustache was blowing it rhythmically forward, just out of time with the ticking of the mantel clock. George had said he would come at lunchtime. In exactly four days' time . . . Nurse Chadwick was in the doorway announcing lunch, then coming in to encourage them across the hall and give Helen a commiserative look—well, it was the sort of news which would spread quickly to all corners of the establishment. Even, dutifully, to the gnome, although he would hardly share the common interest. Helen imagined the Resident Director, pacing his office, his mood veering between annoyance with George Parkinson and apprehension for himself. . . .

She wasn't hungry but she forced herself to eat normally. *No need for anything unless she shows signs of distress or unusual behaviour.* After lunch she hung about the hall until everyone appeared to be dispersed or settled in the lounge, then ran upstairs. She was aware of a new source of fear, which she defined as she reached the landing: Nurse Baines was on duty, and if encountered in private might give rein to the bullying instinct Helen thought she had recognized in Sister's office. But both corridors were empty, and glancing down the stairs at the empty hall as she spun and sang, Helen took the west, opening and closing several doors before flitting behind Dr. Bakewell's.

Dr. Bakewell was sitting up in bed and there was a lunch tray across her knees, from which she was eating tidily with knife and fork. She seemed unaware of Helen's presence and it took only a turn or two about the room to see that there was no danger of catching Dr. Bakewell's eye—it was as unfocused as Fiona's. To offset the shock of Dr. Bakewell's puppet movements, her white shrunken face, was the fact of her taking food in the normal way—Helen had had to push aside disquieting visions of unnatural feeding. But Dr.

Bakewell, steadily busy, had almost finished her meal, someone would be coming for her tray and that person was likely to be Nurse Baines. Helen danced rapidly and unhesitatingly out of the room, pulling the door to noisily behind her, and continued dancing across the house to the east corridor. On her last turn she saw the small silent man emerge from the doorway opposite Dr. Bakewell's room and cross the corridor. Dizzy with thankfulness that she had been spared a difficult encounter, she closed her door and flung herself down on the bed.

She had been lucky, and she wouldn't push her luck any further. Self-preservation, now, was the imperative, and she would quietly see out the four days she must wait, singing and dancing in insignificant places and doing nothing to earn herself particular attention. Except, of course, if they locked her in at bedtime. Not that she wanted to leave her room in the night, or had any further intention of doing so (except in the unlikely event of learning something to tell Mr. Colburn), but she wanted to be able to.

The rest of the day went as uneventfully as she had wished, to the routine which already felt age-old. Tea in the lounge, where a fire had been lit to counteract the gloom of rain on the windows. Nurse Chadwick chatting them up and not succeeding in getting Mr. Colburn to play his game. Mrs. Merrivale suddenly throwing a cushion which hit Freda and made her curl up so tight Nurse Rogers picked her up as if she was a baby. Mrs. Merrivale immediately running out of steam. Nurse Rogers being grave and chastened when stopping by Fiona's chair, as if at a collective responsibility. Pete's clear voice in the hall, and Dr. Sandelson not looking in on her. Salmon for supper and the embarrassment of sudden attention from Geoffrey. The repeat on TV of an episode of a serial she had watched the first time from inside Julian's arm. Nurse Evans not having reappeared by bedtime and Nurse Rogers, when she left after seeing that Fiona was undressed and getting into bed, turning the key in the lock.

She made herself wait a couple of hours, with difficulty controlling a mounting sense of claustrophobia, before going to the door to knock and whimper. She began the process quite softly, crescendoing to a thin high scream and a barrage of fists against the door. There was no response, and she knew her renewed attempt sounded more authentic than her first. When she was wailing her despair at its height the door suddenly opened and she dropped to the floor, curling up as neatly as Freda.

"Oh, pet," said Nurse Evans, "what are we doing to you? I've never seen you in such a state. We won't lock you up again. Look, if you'll get into bed for me like a good girl, I'll even leave the door open a bit."

Sobbing and hiccuping, Fiona was led back to bed, her continued whimpering bringing Nurse Evans back time and again across the room before she eventually went out. But she was back almost at once, with a capsule and a glass of water.

"Take this, pet, just to calm you down. It won't hurt."

But it just might hurt someone who wanted a pregnancy to run its course, and when she had taken the capsule into her mouth from Nurse Evans's hand, Helen took advantage of the weak light filtering in from the corridor to spit it into the bed as she choked over the water.

"That's right, pet. Off you go to sleep now."

An hour later, as she tossed wide-eyed, Helen was almost regretting her caution. But the door was still ajar, and after tiptoeing across to it to push it more inconspicuously to, she at last abandoned herself to the miracle of the morning's revelation.

CHAPTER 13

The man surveyed himself ruefully in the mirror, passing his hand
over his short rough beard and his scarcely longer bristle of dark
hair. He moved in his underclothes about the bedroom, opening
drawers and cupboards and selecting shirt, pullover and trousers to a
criterion which involved examination in the places where labels are
hung. Eventually, trousers were found without one; the one inside
the casual shirt was cut off; and the one inside the navy-blue pullover, proclaiming "St. Michael", was conceded on a smile.

When he had dressed the man started rummaging, on the same
principle, for socks and shoes. Having found these and put them on,
he turned his attention to the dressing-table and the little pile of
belongings he had taken from his pockets the night before. Scattering
and examining them, he took the coins and the plain handkerchief,
stuffing them into the pockets of his trousers. The wallet he opened
and divested of all but treasury notes, putting it, too, into a pocket.

Then he looked at himself again in the glass, shook his head, and
ran down the stairs and out of the house, slowing at the gate to a
brisk walk.

As he had hoped and expected, mid-morning on a weekday
yielded only a handful of women on the station platform, but by the
time his train reached its London terminus it had gathered enough
passengers for him to be inconspicuous in their midst as he walked
up the platform. A bus next, from outside the station, north-west
from the centre, a twenty-minute ride over a short distance, in the
continuous choke of traffic. A busy road to cross to the building he
had never yet entered—if he was knocked down now, he would not
be identified, his body would have to await the eventual coming of
the one person who knew where he had gone. As it would if he died
in any other way. . . .

The communal front door yielded, as he had known it would at this time of day, the graceful staircase curved up to the first landing, the white door was opposite as he reached the top step.

There was a bell, and a polished brass knocker shaped to a lion head. He pressed the bell.

The silence was painful in the disappointment it brought him, he thought he had chosen the most likely time. But when he rang again he heard footsteps coming quickly, and the door was pulled wide.

"Yes?" asked the young man in the doorway genially. "What can I do for you?"

"Sorry," said the man on the step, moving uneasily from foot to foot, "to disturb you, squire. I was looking for Dr. Peter Irving and I thought—"

"Oh dear, oh dear." The young man shook his head, sadly smiling. "You'd better come in, Mr. . . ."

"Bates. Colin Bates. I don't mind coming in, as a matter of fact, there's a little something—"

"Inside, Mr. Bates, rather than on the landing." The young man spoke in mild reproof.

"Right you are, squire. Sorry." The visitor's voice was in rough contrast to the pleasant, educated tones of the man who had let him in. "You seem to have an idea what I'm here for," the visitor observed, when he had followed the young man on to the pale Chinese carpet of an elegant living-room. "I didn't catch your name."

"I didn't give it," said the young man cheerfully, "but only because the matter hadn't come up. It's Edwards. Tony Edwards."

"Well, Mr. Edwards"—the visitor's eyes were running round the room, in furtive appreciation—"I was under the impression my business with Dr. Irving was private."

"Oh, I'm sure it is. Please sit down, by the way." As if to make the move easier for his embarrassed visitor, Mr. Edwards himself took an elegant small chair, watching in silence as Mr. Bates suspiciously followed suit on to the end of the enormous sofa. "There, that's better! I wasn't meaning to imply that I knew you had business with Peter, I was simply meaning—well, I'm afraid Peter's disappeared, you see, and he's left an awful lot of unfinished business behind him."

"He's—what?" The visitor's brows were drawn together, he was leaning forward with his hands clenching between his knees.

"He's done a bunk and left a lot of unfinished business behind him," repeated Mr. Edwards apologetically. "You're by no means the first person I've had to say *that* to."

The oath was crude and loud.

"I know," said Mr. Edwards, blinking a few times. "You can imagine how it's been for me. I count myself lucky so far to have escaped physical injury. Which is so frightfully unfair, the life Pete led outside this flat was no concern of mine, he made certain of that!"

"Are you telling me—" The visitor got up from the sofa and began to pace the carpet. Mr. Edwards, aware of the heavy feet, looked away from them with a shudder.

"I'm telling you Pete's gone, vamoosed, scarpered. Call it what you will, Mr.—er—Bates, it amounts to the same thing."

"I'll be obliged," said the visitor heavily, stopping in front of Mr. Edwards's small chair and watching its occupant pull slightly back, "if you'll give me his forwarding address."

"But I don't have it!" Mr. Edwards now leaned towards his visitor, in his anxiety to be understood. "Pete's walked out on me, too. That's why I sympathize with your situation. Not that I've any need to sympathize, it's fairly obvious—forgive me, but it's best to be realistic—that your relationship with Pete lacked the stability of mine, but Pete's walked out on *me.*"

Mr. Bates moved away and dropped back on to the sofa. "So you know nothing about where he's gone. There's nothing at all you can tell me?"

"Nothing, Mr. Bates, the proverbial egg is all over my face, I wonder you don't see it. Look, I think we'd better have a scotch, don't you? I don't mean a scotch egg, of course. If you'll do me the favour of just looking at things from my point of view for a moment, you'll perhaps appreciate that your arrival here just now was one teeny weeny extra nail in my coffin? Sharp enough to earn me a whisky before noon?"

"I'll join you in a whisky," conceded Mr. Bates, turning so that he could watch each stage of the preparation of the drinks. "I'm— sorry," he said awkwardly, as the glass was put into his hand, "that things have been done the way they have so far as you're concerned."

"Thank you. It is—rather devastating." It could have been Noel Coward speaking. "He was—very charming, wasn't he?"

"Charming?" Mr. Bates took a second swig. "Sure, yes."

"I thought I was special," went on Mr. Edwards, with a laugh which brought a tremble to the hand with which Mr. Bates was holding his glass, so that he set it down on the exquisite little table by the end of the sofa. "I thought that whatever he did to anyone else, I would be immune, I would be inside his charmed circle. But I was wrong. So far as he was concerned, I was no different from anyone else. No different, it seems, from you, Mr. Bates. I was talking just now about stability. That was rather absurd of me, wasn't it?"

"The flat," asked Mr. Bates. "Which of you owns it?"

"It's in our joint names. Doesn't that sound trusting, and cosy, and happy-ever-afterish? Whether he will surface at some point in the future and claim his share, I don't know. He may of course do it at long distance, through a lawyer."

"You'd quarrelled?"

"*You'd* quarrelled, Mr. Bates?"

"I . . . Look, I think I'd better—"

"No, Mr. Bates, we hadn't quarrelled, and I hadn't known there was anything wrong."

"What about his belongings? You'd have noticed if he'd starting packing them up?"

"I don't know why I like you, Mr. Bates, you're making me say so many disagreeable things." Mr. Edwards transferred himself, in a sinuous catlike movement, from his small chair to the other end of the sofa adjoining it. "Pete told me the last morning I saw him that he was taking a whole lot of heavy stuff to the launderette. I went out, and when I got back the sheets and towels were still there but Pete's books and pictures weren't, and none of his personal things. He must have worked very fast. He even took my photo of him."

"His car."

"He must have packed everything into his car. It had gone, too." Mr. Edwards moved slightly away from the arm of the sofa, into the long stretch of lilac velvet cushion.

"Hm." Mr. Bates drained his glass and set it down. "So there's sweet bloody nothing you can tell me about Master Pete and where he's gone, and why."

"That sums it up very well. But two people left high and dry needn't double the misery, Mr. Bates. One thing Pete and I really did have in common—do still, I must remember that he is in the past only so far as certain people are concerned—is taste in friends. That was the reason, I think, why he never brought any of his home." The lilac velvet gap was rapidly closing. "Do you think . . . You must be emotionally worn out by the dreadful news I've had to give you. Wouldn't you like to lie down? Comfortably on a bed? There's no need for you to hurry away, I'm sure. Did Pete ever mention me?"

"He said . . . I knew he didn't live alone."

"Ah. I do now though, alas. Mr. Bates, shall we go into the bedroom?"

The gap, now, was all on the far side of Mr. Edwards. As he placed a beautifully proportioned hand backed with fine gold hairs on Mr. Bates's knee Mr. Bates uttered another oath which opened a sudden new gap of several feet between him and Mr. Edwards.

"I'm sorry, squire, I didn't mean to give you a fright, and I should have seen sooner but you'll appreciate I wasn't expecting . . . It was money between me and Dr. Irving. A question of money."

"Money!" Mr. Edwards was on his feet facing Mr. Bates, smiling a rather terrible smile. "Please forgive me. Yes, it would perhaps have been preferable if you'd seen a little sooner. Pete did rather tend to go for the coarser type. He used to make me think of those Victorian aesthetes who brought navvies and bargees home and whose mothers used to tell their equally naive friends how kind and generous their sons were, sharing their beds with large rough men rather than let them go couchless. Please don't clench your fists, Mr. Bates, there really is no need for it. What is this question of money between you and Peter? I don't think you will resent my asking."

"No, no. It's just that—I put a bet on for him and the horse didn't come in."

"Put a bet on for him? He wasn't a betting man."

"So he said. We got talking in a bar—he must be inclined to make the same mistakes as you—and in my nervousness I started to go on about this horse that was running that afternoon. Very persuasive I must have been, 'cos eventually your Dr. Irving said he'd like to take advantage of my inside information. Gave me an IOU for a hundred quid to put on for him. To win. I thought the horse was a cert, that's why I said I'd do it. Lost my own money along with that, didn't I? The bleeding horse stopped halfway to look at the view. Said he'd meet me again in the same spot to collect his winnings or pay his debt. He didn't show. I got less relaxed and I phoned a few times, he'd given me the number as well as the address. No reply, or someone telling me he wasn't at home. You, I suppose. So I came round."

There was a short silence, in which the bright, smiling face of the younger man gazed into the dark suspicious face of the older.

"Of course you did," said Mr. Edwards at last, soothingly, "what else could you do? Which was that spot where you were going to see Pete again?"

"It's a new place in Covent Garden, down a level. Can't remember its name."

"Yes. I do have to say, Mr. Bates, that I think you were extraordinarily trusting."

"Seems so. But I trusted the horse."

"Yes. Well, I'm not a gambling man myself. In the normal way."

"I'd better be off," said Mr. Bates, getting to his feet with a little difficulty, out of the low soft sofa.

"Here, let me help you. Mind the edge of the table."

"Ow!" protested Mr. Bates.

"Yes, it's sharp. I warned you."

"I can manage, thanks." But Mr. Bates stumbled a second time, on the fine fringe of the rug. "This place of yours, all expensive boobytraps."

"Boobytraps? Oh, I see. Well, we like a pretty room. All right now, Mr. Bates? You seem a wee bit unsteady."

"I'm all right, just a bit dizzy all of a sudden. Must be that whisky so early."

"It wasn't a very big one, Mr. Bates, and I must say you look strong enough to take it. Would you like to sit down again for a minute?"

"Sit down . . . Perhaps . . . Yes. . . ."

"There we are, then."

The last thing Mr. Bates saw, as he fell back into the sofa, was the handsome face of Mr. Edwards gazing down on him with cheerful attention.

A little later, a taxi drew up at the house next door, and when the driver rang one of the outside bells an elderly lady appeared. She looked up and down the road.

"I'm afraid," she said, "that I've got a tea chest. It's very heavy because it's full of old things I'm taking to my daughter. Goodness, there seem to be all sorts of strong men about the street this morning. Do you think I might ask one of them to assist us in getting the trunk out to your taxi?"

The driver of the taxi, having no wish to dislocate his back, approached a strong man on the lady's behalf, and between them they transferred the tea chest to the interior of the cab, where the old lady was politely insistent it should be placed.

"All your worldly goods in there, ma'am!" said the man from the street, as he straightened up and wiped his face. The chest had been extremely heavy.

CHAPTER 14

At Hartshorn Manor, the surveillance of Fiona Spencer had become far more comprehensive. When Nurse Evans or Nurse Rogers was on duty there was scarcely a half-hour between their concerned seekings out of her, to pat and smile and murmur and shake their heads. Only when Nurse Baines was on duty was Helen left alone—but this might have been because she made sure then that she was in the lounge or close to Matron's room. She could only be grateful that her work had been done before she became an object of such interest and solicitude.

Tuesday yielded no extra revelation, and she managed not to over-rule what she knew had been her wise decision to go no more into the west corridor except to dance and sing its length without pause. She welcomed the few visitors who came in from three o'clock and sat uneasily about the lounge, as losing her some attention for a while. She lost some more in the late afternoon, after tea, when Mrs. Merrivale threw cardigans and cushions and went into a hysterical frenzy until the combined efforts of Sister and Nurse Chadwick removed her from their midst.

In the evening Dr. Sandelson made contact with her again, but only by coming into the lounge and sitting on the arm of her chair while he circled her wrist with his firm hand and looked pityingly into her face.

It was fine all day and she went several times into the garden, sitting on a seat or lying in the sunken garden stroking the cat, dancing and singing her way about the lawn at fairly regular intervals. Indoors, too, she flitted vocally about, visiting the kitchen (where she allowed herself a rest under the fascinated eye of the cook), Matron, and—probably from a misplaced sense of humour—the Resident Director. The Resident Director watched from behind his desk in terrified immobility as she twirled about his office and

twiddled his carton of coloured pencils, eventually getting behind her
and without touching her shepherding her out of the door with a
skill born of unprecedented anxiety.

Nevertheless, Miss Spencer's tendency to wander and to sing was
reduced, and this was remarked on by several members of staff, being
put down in each case to her condition—an illogicality (seeing that
the passage of a few hours had meant an advancement in staff knowledge rather than in Fiona's pregnancy) for which she was further
grateful. Nurse Chadwick even asked Matron if she thought the new
situation might "bring Fiona back," but Matron said sadly that she
thought this unlikely, and that in any case the situation would not
continue long enough for the theory to be put to the test. This last
remark had Fiona on the move again, round and round the hall and
back into the garden.

Mr. Colburn's performance, too, was somewhat lacklustre. He appeared to sleep a good deal, and when he woke he was still drowsy
and disinclined to talk. As he was going home so soon, the nursing
staff were evidently forbearing to be too concerned. Helen, though,
was relieved when after tea he treated a portion of the room somewhere round Nurse Chadwick and two knitting ladies to a little
monologue which could have been entitled How to Behave in the
Presence of the Fairer Sex. It came to an end only when Nurse
Chadwick switched on the television—according to Mr. Colburn's
Hartshorn Manor persona, this meant there was no more for him to
do that day, as the set, once on, remained on until bedtime. Helen
admired and envied his ingenuity or that of his mentors, for securing
him such long regular sessions off stage.

During the day there was only one fresh area of anxiety, which she
dealt with by visiting Sister and dancing past the duty roster on the
wall by her desk. Then out into the hall singing the *Gloria*. Nurse
Rogers was on duty that night, Nurse Evans the night after. Nurse
Baines would take night duty on Thursday, but that was Fiona's last
night at the Manor, and if she was tormented, or locked in at bedtime, Helen thought she would be able to sustain it.

Nurse Rogers didn't lock her in, although she treated Fiona to a
short homily to the effect that it was only thanks to Daphne Evans
and her own appalling hullaballoo that she still had the freedom of
the house.

"But you can't help it, lovey, you can't help it." Nurse Rogers's small pale face in its heavy surround of dark hair looked down at the bed with continuing slight shock. "I just hope they find out how it happened, so they can protect you another time."

But if this time is all right, I shan't ask for another.

Matron looked in as Nurse Rogers was leaving, to take Helen's pulse and endorse the decision to leave her free. Nurse Chadwick saw her through breakfast on Wednesday, and in a normal world Helen would have laughed at the approval in Nurse Chadwick's face as she made a dash for the basin.

In the morning it was fine again and Fiona spent some time in the garden, watched intermittently through the annexe window by Mr. Colburn. She danced round the doctors as they arrived (Dr. Sandelson with a young protégé, Dr. Chalmers, and Dr. Webster), but it was only Dr. Sandelson she followed upstairs and into the rooms where he was in charge. Geoffrey was taken up for a private consultation, no doubt in view of his deepening depression (she would not let herself add another burden to those she already carried by wondering if this might be in some way due to Fiona).

After lunch it grew cloudy, a fire was lit, and a general somnolence settled over the lounge. The strong peal of the front doorbell, about an hour before the usual first arrival of visitors, had several of them starting upright in their chairs. Helen heard the front door being opened, and listened as she always did for the indistinguishable exchange of greetings. Today the voices were too subdued for the usual bright banalities, and instead of emphatic feet on the marble getting louder towards the lounge, there was a thud and then the sound of shuffling movement. She got up and slid across the lounge, reaching the half-open door in time to see a small procession, flanked by Sister and Nurse Baines, starting to climb the stairs. In the midst of it was a stretcher whose occupant was covered by a blanket, turned back to show no more than a motionless dark head. Behind the stretcher, just setting foot on the first stair, was Pete Irving.

Well, she had known it could happen at any moment, she had seen those freshly prepared rooms, it was absurd that the blow should feel so devastating. Without the heart to play a charade round the hall, and knowing anyway that she was of no possible interest just then to any of the people on the stairs, she drifted back into the lounge and

over to her chair. As she sat down Mr. Colburn lifted his head from
his chest and looked across at her without expression. Pressing her
hands on the arms of her chair, Helen turned her thumbs down and,
nodding heavily, he slumped off to sleep again. He was of course—or
should be—symbolically throwing the ball into her court. A new
arrival for Dr. Webster's list would mean an abnormal amount of
awareness and activity in the west corridor, and any espionage could
only be undertaken openly, only by Fiona.

She would, after all, have to take her chance again.

But not now, not until routine had closed over the new patient—
although part of her longed to fly that minute up the stairs and try
the possible doors. Yet what significance could another blank white
face have for *her?* All she could do would be to note any distinguishing features (she pushed aside a memory of Mr. Redfern's nose), for
transmission to Julian after the release now so near at hand. And
perhaps, before then, to Mr. Colburn. She thought he might take the
chance of visiting her in the night. If she found out more than she
had already deduced—that another drugged man or woman now lay
at Dr. Webster's mercy—she might visit him. The only way to make
the waiting bearable, meanwhile, was to reckon that this latest entry
was comparatively lucky—he or she should have only a couple of
days to endure.

She went up to her room before dinner, to lie in relaxation as total
as she could make it, in attempt to prepare herself mentally for
another sortie. Not only had she said finis in her mind, moved imper-
ceptibly away from her state of absolute readiness, she had switched
her priority from her job to herself.

The best thing to do, in the interests both of her safety and the
possibility of learning something, was to go round with either Dr.
Webster or Pete on the evening visit. If there were some more com-
ments to vulgarize what was happening to her—well, that would be
the least of things. And those particular doctors and members of the
nursing staff had more important matters to occupy them. Yes, she
would stay on her bed until she heard Dr. Webster or Pete on the
landing, her inner clock told her it was almost time, then she would
trip along the corridor singing and join them. . . .

She wasn't imagining it, there were unfamiliar noises beyond her door, bangs and thumps and heavy breaths, mutterings and then a hoarse cry.

"Nurse!" A woman's voice, too loud and anxious to be recognizable.

"Trip him up, can't you?" Another female voice, tense and urgent. Feet on the stairs and a further cry, frightened and angry at the same time, starting her trembling before she reached her door.

"Nurse Rogers, thank goodness! Catch that other arm, will you?"

At the head of the stairs Sister and Nurse Baines, now assisted by Nurse Rogers, were trying to subdue a flailing figure in a sort of white surgical gown, a man it must be, the rudimentary beard and short spiky outline of hair showed against the white wall behind him. Sister and Nurse Baines had him by one arm, and Nurse Rogers now by the other, but he was struggling so desperately he pulled away from them and began to plunge down the stairs, still bellowing outrage. Half way down he fell, tripping perhaps, although it seemed to Helen as she watched him try vainly to lift himself by the banisters to which he was clinging that he was suffering a sudden loss of strength. Nurse Chadwick now, too, was running towards the stairs, but turned away as the front doorbell rang.

"Dr. Irving! Thank heaven!" Sister called down from the top of the stairs, where she and her assistant had managed to drag their victim. "He suddenly jumped out of bed and out of his room. We'd done exactly—"

"This can happen." Dr. Irving had taken the shallow stairs in threes and was already on his knees beside the now feebly struggling man, opening his case. "But only with subjects of outstanding strength and resistance."

"What on earth's *his* trouble?" asked Nurse Rogers.

"Believe it or not"—Dr. Irving slipped the needle into a vein in the arm—"a form of melancholia which in rare instances reacts with extreme violence to the first phase of Dr. Webster's new treatment. I assure you it doesn't happen twice."

"Does the treatment always work?" Helen, singing softly half way along her corridor, saw the sudden relaxation of the tense limbs, the head fall back on to Sister's arm.

"Oh yes." Dr. Irving smiled sexily at Nurse Rogers as he got to his feet. "It always works."

Fiona came forward, singing a little more loudly, and took a rose from the vase behind her, presenting it to Dr. Irving.

"For God's sake," said Nurse Baines, but Dr. Irving, his eyes very bright with the adrenalin of challenge, said, "Why not? Thank you, madam," and left the weight of the now unconscious man to his two original pursuers. Between them, Dr. Irving on one side fastening the rose into his buttonhole, and Fiona on the other, they began a slow progress towards the one door in the west corridor which stood open. A door to the back of the house. At least she would not have to negotiate the additional hazards of a suite.

"Polly put the kettle on!" sang Helen, a little ahead of the nurses so that as she gyrated she could observe the man they supported. Although he sagged she thought he was tall, his hair was roughly cut *en brosse,* he had perhaps a week's beard, a pale face, large pale hands, a nose . . . a mouth . . . a forehead . . .

She must not faint. Even in that moment of unsurpassable horror, she must not faint. If she fainted she would be unable to refuse drugs which, however helpfully intended, might harm her baby. Julian's baby.

She must not faint.

The four others were bunching now through the doorway, the three conscious ones had entirely forgotten her and Nurse Rogers had disappeared. Silent, speedy, Helen fled back to her room and shut her door, casting herself down on the bed and lying in instant paralysis.

"Not coming down to supper, sweetie?"

Nurse Rogers had a hand on her shoulder and was smiling anxiously down. So in the end she had fainted, if it was now supper-time. She thought she wasn't going to be able to move, it was only the supreme importance of appearing as usual which enabled her to break through the paralysis. And having broken through, she sat up and got off the bed easily enough.

"That's more like it, lovey. I must say you look a bit pale. And I'd never noticed your eyes were so big. But we can't expect you to look quite as usual, can we? Come along, now, and see if you can manage a bit of supper. It's rice pudding to follow, and you know how you enjoy rice pudding."

If she wasn't careful, she would start screaming her outrage on a scale to make nothing of the afternoon scene in the lounge with Mrs. Merrivale. She had to use every scrap of energy and attention to manage not to do this, to keep her outer self intact, and at least it didn't leave anything over with which to think about what she had seen, what had happened, was happening. . . .

"There! See, Geoffrey's feeling better now, all ready for his supper!"

She had eaten half hers before she got round to thinking she couldn't eat any of it. The meal might have lasted minutes or hours, everything around her was very quiet and very far away, as if at the wrong end of a telescope. When she found herself leaving the dining-room she knew she should be dancing and singing but she didn't dare start in case she couldn't stop, in case it turned into running and shouting. But then she found that after all she was twisting and turning about the hall, as light as an autumn leaf and as vulnerable to the wind, hearing a thin high voice which seemed to come from a long way off but which she eventually realized was her own. . . .

She would certainly be going to see Mr. Colburn in the night. She could go and see Mr. Colburn, where she couldn't go and see Julian. Julian only a staircase away from her, being drugged and damaged and maybe destroyed.

Careful.

At least she was carrying her excuse for any signs of the strain there might be in her face. Each time a member of staff passed her chair (when at last the wind let the leaf fall to rest), she received an understanding nod.

She went upstairs once during the long, long evening, to hover at the beginning of the silent west corridor. It made her tremble so violently she had to run to her room and lie on her bed until the trembling stopped. After that, she sat quietly in what had become her usual chair in the lounge, forcing her thoughts to stop short at the television screen.

"You going to have some of my Ovaltine tonight, lovey? All right, all right, I've got your message!"

She had over-reacted. But how could Nurse Chadwick imagine she would want to sleep? That she could fail to keep vigil for Julian?

"Onward, Christian soldiers!" urged Fiona. If it grew impossible to think about her own security, she must think about the baby's.

It wasn't really a relief to reach bedtime. Nothing could be a relief while Julian was lying a drugged prisoner.

Careful. Mr. Colburn will see that something is done tomorrow night. Tomorrow will come, it always does.

But sometimes too late.

What had Mr. Colburn said, in the other world which had ended before supper?

Takes quite a few weeks to gain control.

But when did the damage set in?

"You ready for bed, lovey?"

She was climbing the stairs, oh so lightly, she was at the top of the stairs and the west corridor was dark and silent. On her own side, shafts of evening sun were slanting across from open doors and illumining the skirting-boards—the telescope had been turned round and she had a strange new tendency to see small things in detail. For the first time she deciphered the *art nouveau* initials on Mrs. Lockett's dressing-table set and noticed a small stain creeping in to one side of the dressing-table mirror. She saw a loose claw on one of the knitting women's garnet ring, the multiple ladder in Freda's stocking.

When the last of them had been put to bed, Nurse Rogers walked along to Fiona's room and stood gazing at Helen from the open doorway. Helen followed her inside and she waited while Fiona got undressed, washed, cleaned her teeth, and climbed into bed. The process was speedier than usual, because Fiona offered fewer diversions.

"You're tired, lovey, I can see."

But Nurse Rogers, in her lifetime, could never see, could never dimly imagine.

"I'll leave the door ajar, lovey. There! Good night."

Paralysis again. As if it was a condition of the bed which had been awaiting her return. She would have to break out of it later, to go and see Mr. Colburn, but for the moment she wouldn't fight, she wouldn't do anything except exist, the only thing she couldn't stop doing. And think about the baby she must keep sane for. . . .

She had moved. She had jerked, unlocking something. Creating a great clear space of peace and possibility. All she had to do was to get up off the bed and go out of the door and a few steps along a corridor and she would be with Julian. That was all she had to do, so why wasn't she doing it? There was someone very close to her, right inside her head in fact, who was telling her that although it was something she could do, it was something she shouldn't do, it wouldn't be good for her or for the baby, or for Julian. But now she was telling that other person, calmly and reasonably she was telling her that it was something she had to do, there was nothing in the world which could or should keep her apart from Julian.

She couldn't understand why it had taken her so long to go, it must be because she had been listening to that other person. All right, she would take her gold toy, she would take it from under her pillow and put it into the deep pocket of her nightdress, under her handkerchief. But she would go. Now.

She let the other person persuade her to dance, the autumn leaf turning and twisting along the corridor, but she couldn't sing, the other person couldn't persuade her to sing. . . .

The room was dark, as the other rooms had been, but in a few moments she was able to see dim outlines and a grey square of window. Before that, though, she had found the bed and the forehead and the spikes of hair and stood silently caressing them. Then as the room took vague shape she went round the bed to the far side and knelt down beside it and resumed contact with the moist cold skin and unfamiliar hair, resting her cheek against them, then against the heart, hearing the beat and the breath, evoking no response. She reached under the neat bedclothes to find the cold inert hand, feel its faint pulse and reverently replace it. . . .

Then, with a jerking movement as violently revelatory as the first one, the two people in her head became one again and she knew what she had done.

And that there was someone opening the door.

The other voice, feeble though it had been, had at least moved her to the far side of the bed. Crouching down she crawled underneath, curling up against the wall at the head of it as the light attacked.

It wasn't a very bright light, only a bedside lamp in fact, she realized that as she watched the legs moving in the small direct cone of it. A man's legs in trousers, and a man's voice asking with a dreadful jocularity how we were getting on. A familiar voice, as it continued speaking, commenting on the rebellion of the early evening and regretting the necessity, as a result, of intensifying the treatment.

"It's your own fault, old man, you should have gone along with it. Just as well you're so fit." Latches thwacked open, there were delicate sounds, unidentifiable. "Here we are, then. Let's have your arm."

"No. Put that down!"

This was worse, far worse, than the thing she had already done, because she was no longer insane, she knew she had made a choice between what was according to all the tenets Julian had taught her, and what would prevent that large full syringe entering his flesh, she knew now that she could never be a professional spy.

The hand stopped short of its target—arrested, of course, by surprise rather than fear.

"That's all I need," said the familiar voice cheerfully, and the man looked hard at her where she knelt with her gold toy in her hand, and failed to recognize her. But that was the only area in which she was clever, and it wasn't enough. "What are you doing in here, woman, in the middle of the night? At any time, for that matter? We'll find where you live in a minute, take you back."

The hand was advancing again, and again she said "No. Don't do it."

But this time the charming face just grinned, so she did the only thing she could possibly do, she pressed the catch on her golden toy and almost simultaneously with the soft sound it made the air and then the sheet were red, the syringe was flying across the room like an arrow and landing like a dart in the wall, the hand was being crooned over and caressed, and the face was ugly with pain and fury.

"I told you," she said, "not to do it."

"You bitch, you insane bitch."

"I'm not insane, actually. At least, not in the way you mean it."

He was managing to bind up his hand quite successfully with his large handkerchief, so he wouldn't bleed to death. Although if he did, it would save her. . . . Julian muttered, restlessly moved his head, gave her new strength.

"You don't know me, do you, Tony?"

He had never heard Helen's voice, but he had heard Penelope

Dale's, and the other new expression in his face, alongside the fear, was uncertainty.

"Know you?"

"Versatile Actress?" Whatever else she gave away wouldn't make any difference, so she might as well learn what she could.

He was staring at her, at a loss at last.

"But it was *us* . . ."

"Yes, I know now that it *was* you. You as well as Pete. And I was quite innocent then. What happened was that you chose someone with the wrong connections." Even now, even when there was no way back, she wouldn't put certain facts into words. "So I've come in on the other side." He had taken a step towards the foot of the bed, and with her gold toy she motioned him back so that they were again directly facing one another across Julian's body.

"But nobody knew . . ."

"Somebody did. And put me in. I was glad to come, even though it's been—a bit difficult." *There will be a termination.* "And now I know it all."

"And are going to have a murder on your hands."

"Yes." It was she, not he, who was trembling. She didn't want to admire his courage, the brave beauty of his smiling face and bright eyes. His hand hung like a broken bird foot, she couldn't look at it. "I've no alternative."

"You won't be able to do it. Not in cold blood. And live with yourself afterwards. You'd escape the law, perhaps, but you wouldn't escape yourself."

"I don't suppose I would, but I haven't got a choice."

"You have, actually. You can just go away from here and back to your cot and nobody but me will know you aren't crazy."

"And—this man?"

"His fate's beyond *me.*"

"But mine would be in your hands and you'd be merciful?"

"I would."

"You say you would." She was playing for time as hard as he was. "You'd have to take my word."

"A traitor's word. Does your mother know—about this?"

"Ah!" For an instant the large eyes closed tight. "No, my mother does not know."

"I'm glad." So there was one small piece of bedrock. "Don't move." She hoped the trembling of her arm wasn't as apparent to him as it was to her, moving up and down against the bloodstains on his yellow pullover. "Is this man important?" She flicked her glance briefly on to Julian's ashen face.

"Could be. We don't know. Yet. He'll tell us eventually. We were just being on the safe side, and he gives us a chance to practice our techniques."

She would have to have brought the conversation to an end sometime, and the light words determined the moment, the great big swollen mutated moment, in which there was time for so much. Time for Tony to show in his eyes that he knew what he had said. Time for her to decide on heart rather than head and to despise herself for being able to destroy but not to make ugly. Time for Tony's knowledge to turn into a gesture towards her of his uninjured hand which she knew she would have with her for ever. Time for her to hope so young a baby would be sleeping, to ask forgiveness. Time to target her gold toy for the second time and to pull the trigger.

CHAPTER 15

She didn't know what time it was, time had stood still in that long moment, and she had no idea at what point it had resumed. But night came early to Hartshorn Manor and it could be that several hours of darkness still lay ahead before the summer dawn. She had so much to do in them she had to postpone realization of what she had already done, to acknowledge it would be to render her incapable of further action.

It was a sort of cruelty to Julian, letting time tick by while she waited for Nurse Evans, but Nurse Evans was her necessary first step. Before Mr. Colburn. Mr. Colburn would advise her not to try and make use of Nurse Evans, he might even attempt to restrain her, so she could go to him only when she was able to tell him that Nurse Evans was already their ally. As she would be, if Helen got it right. And Nurse Evans was the junior, mobile, member of staff on duty, answering to Sister on back-up duty in her office below.

But not answering to Sister tonight, when Helen had spoken to her.

She couldn't be certain, of course, she was taking another crazy risk, but she needed Nurse Evans. They both needed her, she and Mr. Colburn. One official figure, one person known to be sane, on their side.

The nurse on duty was supposed to walk the length of the corridors every half-hour. She must just have missed Nurse Evans, she seemed to have been standing there for so long, behind her half-open door. And what if the gnome came round first?

But the gnome never stepped beyond the west corridor, and Tony Edwards had been in charge of Dr. Webster's latest patient. *What fun, Penelope Dale!* Would she be able to go back into that room, even with Nurse Evans?

It was like waiting for a bus on a blind corner, it could be very near and you wouldn't know. Nurse Evans would appear suddenly in the corridor as she stepped through the door at the foot of the stairs from the staff quarters. Which she was doing, was actually doing, standing stock still as she saw Helen, then coming quickly up to her.

"What is it, pet, what is it?"

Helen put her hand on Nurse Evans's arm and gently pulled at it. Nurse Evans, concern in her face, allowed herself to be urged into Fiona's room. When she was by the bed Helen patted it, with increasing urgency until Nurse Evans sat down. Then Helen went back to the door, closed it, and stood with her back to it, her gold toy in her hand.

"Oh, dear, pet, is there something—"

"Sit down. Please." Nurse Evans had got to her feet, but collapsed backwards as Helen spoke, her rosy face suddenly and dramatically white.

"Don't say anything for a moment, just listen to me. I'm not Fiona Spencer and I'm not an idiot. I'm working for—British Intelligence —and I need your help. The new owners of the Manor have started to turn it into the sort of psychiatric hospital they have in the Soviet Union for people who won't conform. So far as we're concerned here, it's for people they want information from. Dr. Webster's their doctor. And Dr. Irving. And . . . Their woman patient has a lot of important information. The same with the man. He's American and Mr. Colburn's the American agent on the same track as me." Nurse Evans made a gulping sound, as if this latest revelation had brought the water level above her head. "The third person, the man brought in today—Nurse Rogers will have told you he tried to get away— he's important too. And he's my husband." She paused because she had to, and thought she saw understanding filtering the shock in Nurse Evans's abnormally large blue eyes. "Nurse Evans, I want to organize a snatch tonight for these three people. Before they're forced to give their information away. Before they're damaged or destroyed." She had to stop again and Nurse Evans held out a hand. Helen took a step towards her. "You've been so kind to Fiona, and I think you haven't been happy about the changes here. You might be part of them, I'm taking a dreadful risk revealing myself to you, more risk than you'll be taking if you trust and help me. And I don't want you to do very much. Just tell me if there's a telephone which isn't connected with any other telephone—I'll be able to tell if it's bugged—and then stand guard while I use it. If there isn't one, I'll want you to smuggle me out to a call-box. And then I'll want you to keep quiet when things happen later. That's all. Will you help me? Do you believe me?"

Nurse Evans said, sitting rigid on the edge of the bed, her hands clasped, "The baby."

"Yes. I've wanted a baby all my life and I'm nearly forty. I haven't been able to think about it yet."

"We talked in front of you about an abortion."

"That was grisly, but what else could I expect? I was just terrified someone might actually do something."

"Oh *God!* How could you bear it, going on doing Fiona. . . ."

"I had to. But I could bear it better with you on my side. You are on my side?"

"Oh, pet! I mean . . ."

"Call me pet, it's the safest name. And thank you. Now, it gets light so early, we must move. We've got to get them out tonight, before Dr. Webster comes and drugs them again and perhaps recognizes my husband." *That's Vladimir.* Julian had recognized Dr. Webster. If she hadn't been so distracted, she would already have thanked God that the doctor who brought in the latest patient had been Dr. Irving. "Of course! You can tell me the time!"

"It's ten minutes past midnight."

"That's wonderful, it could have been two o'clock."

"Poor pet. There's an outside line in the Resident Director's office. No one goes near there at night."

"Better and better. We've got one big advantage, by the way—they think they're absolutely safe here, they've no idea we're on to them."

"Let's go, then!"

"There's something else I have to tell you." Nurse Evans was leaping from the bed, but Helen motioned her back. "I was so crazed earlier on—after seeing my husband on the stairs, you can imagine" —Nurse Evans nodded her horrified understanding—"I went into the room where he is. He's the professional agent, I'm just an actress although I've worked for him before—and I went to pieces. I shouldn't have gone near him. When I was in there a young man I know of, no doubt posing as another of Dr. Webster's assistants . . .

this young man came in and was going to give my husband an injection, part of the breaking-down process, he told me, and—"

"He—told you? You spoke to him?"

"Yes. After I'd shot him in the hand to stop him giving the injection. Then when we'd talked a bit and he'd said . . . I shot him dead." It shocked her that the words had no more significance than if she had been saying them on stage.

Nurse Evans had scarcely recoiled and was leaning forward, lips parted, eyes bright, high bosom heaving.

"Call me Daphne. The gun, though. Where did you get the gun?"

"This is the gun." For the last few minutes she had been holding it as a worry bead. "I'm sorry, you'll understand why I had to keep it in my hand, I'm fighting real enemies, and not just for myself."

Nurse Evans nodded eagerly. "For your husband and the baby and England."

"Oh, my dear girl. Don't be too understanding or I shall break down. Listen. Before we go to that telephone—the man I shot is still on the floor in the room where my husband is. The hypodermic's somewhere in the wall and there's blood on the sheet. I need your help there, too. Now, there's nothing worse I can tell you."

"Let's go, then!" The enthusiasm was, if anything, greater.

"Does the gnome prowl regularly at night?"

"Not as regularly as I do. If we see him, shall we shoot him?"

"Not unless we have to." In horrified silence they stared at one another, as Helen realized it would be easier to shoot the second time than it had been the first.

"Those rooms have keys," said Nurse Evans at last. "We can take the key inside and lock the door while we're busy and just hope no one'll notice it isn't in the lock. Well, there's only the gnome." She stopped abruptly, a hand on the doorknob. "Are any of the staff with —them?"

"We'll talk about that later. In the meantime you're to be suspicious of absolutely everybody, it's the safest way. And promise me faithfully you won't say a word about this to anyone."

Nurse Evans's response came in an indignant hiss. "Of course I won't! Come on! I'm awfully glad you're not poor Fiona. I mean . . . Come on!"

Whatever Helen had anticipated, it hadn't been this schoolgirl keenness for action. But it was tempered.

"All right, pet," soothed Nurse Evans in the corridor. "If you want to have a little dance up here, that's fine."

Admiringly taking her cue, Helen began to dance and softly sing, and when they reached the door of the room where Julian was she took the key from the lock as she danced a circle, and then the two of them slipped inside and shut and locked the door before venturing the switch.

It had to be a relief to see by the meagre spotlight that Tony Edwards was still slumped down at the side of the bed, even though she started to shake and couldn't look at him directly. Nurse Evans put her in the chair and whispered to her to stay there, then speedily and efficiently transferred the body to the cupboard after confirming it was dead. Helen presumed from her back view that she was covering it with what was to hand. With equal speed and efficiency Nurse Evans then retrieved the syringe, put it back in the case with the other things which had spilled out, and put the case with the body, closing the cupboard doors. Then after a glance at Helen she reverently pulled back the bedclothes—in her one brief glance Helen saw that Julian was lying stretched out on his back, his hands still motionless at his sides—and turned the top sheet.

"No blood on the pillow," whispered Nurse Evans briskly, "and his breathing's all right although he's a bit far away. Now, if anyone looks in they won't notice anything wrong. All right, pet?"

"For the time being."

"No one's been trying the door. If we see anyone now, you've been a bit wilful, and I've followed you in here."

"Dear Daphne, my sixth sense has never served me so well."

It felt like one movement, coming out of the room, replacing the key, getting back on to home ground.

"Is Sister in her room?"

"Yes. She won't come out. Is Sister—"

"I'm going to telephone before I see Mr. Colburn."

"Oughtn't you to consult him first?"

"Yes. But I'm not going to start being professional now. I want that snatch tonight, and Mr. Colburn might tell me to wait until he goes tomorrow, and can ask for it in safety."

"Not when he hears about the body in the wardrobe, he won't."

"I wish I'd had you sooner. But all that explaining could delay things crucially. Let's go downstairs."

"You *are* active tonight, Fiona!" Nurse Evans gave a little giggle, and in case it was more than nerves Helen told her sharply that they weren't playing games. Nurse Evans didn't come back at her, but she was silent until they were on the stairs and she had let Fiona drift ahead. Then, babying her softly, she followed Helen inside the Resident Director's office.

The light over the front door was strong enough to be shining faintly through the uncurtained window, showing up the room like a still from a black and white film and making Helen drop to her knees, below the level of the window ledge, drawing Nurse Evans with her.

"There's the phone!" whispered Nurse Evans excitedly. "You can reach up for it and pull it down on the floor."

"That's what I'll do, thanks. Will you go back to the hall and keep a lookout?"

"Message received and understood."

Nurse Evans crawled out of the room quickly and quietly, leaving Helen to bring the Resident Director's telephone to the floor in one careful movement. She had been at fault in not remembering to ask Nurse Evans for a torch, but the light from outside was enough, as her eyes adjusted, for her to ascertain that the instrument was blameless.

The number she had memorized evoked an instant response.

"Rice Crispies here. Reporting from cornflake packet. Asking for an immediate snatch. Cookery book. One American." If she had done what she ought to have done, and seen Mr. Colburn first, she would have known the code name for his prisoner. "Also grape nuts. Brought in this afternoon." She heard the exclamation the other end. "All unconscious owing to drug treatment. Are you ready to receive information on entry and location of subjects?" She hadn't consciously assembled her mental page but it was there, all she needed to say set out on it. At the end she asked her second question.

"Will do?"

"Within the next two hours." There had been the briefest of murmured consultations.

"I suggest no shooting unless guns here in evidence. To my knowledge only three residents hostile. Look out for very small man probably behind door on first floor front of west corridor, second from stairhead. Good luck."

The man's voice told her to take care.

"Oh, I will. It's yours, now."

Thank heaven.

Inarticulately praying, she leaned up and replaced the telephone on the Resident Director's desk, then crawled to the door, standing upright as she opened it.

"That's where you've got to, pet!" Nurse Evans came forward from the shadows. "Let's go upstairs to bed, shall we?"

Fiona allowed a hand on her arm, and she and the nurse mounted the stairs together. At the top Fiona broke away and ran, twisting as she went, into her bedroom.

"I'll just tuck you up, pet." Nurse Evans closed the bedroom door behind them. "Are you going to Mr. Colburn now?"

"I must. It would be awful if the action started and he didn't know. Will you hover? I'll probably call you in."

Mr. Colburn, awakened as gently as she could manage from a noisy sleep, was very angry at the first thing she told him.

"What the hell authority did you have? You'll never work again."

"I don't want to work again. They accepted the request, anyway. I know I should have told you but there's so little darkness in July and it would have wasted so much precious time."

"You knew I was going to set it up for tomorrow."

"Yes. And if I hadn't discovered that the new patient was my husband I wouldn't have gone to the room where he was and had to—"

"Your husband? Julian Johnson?"

"That's right."

"He's—here?"

"I don't know how, or why. I saw him struggling on the stairs earlier—you must have heard him—and when we'd gone to bed I freaked out and went to him. Another of Dr. Webster's young men came in and was going to give him an injection. I—I found myself telling him not to and drawing my gun on him—"

"This gets rich. Your gun?" The stripes on Mr. Colburn's pyjamas showed in monochrome as he reared higher in his bed.

"Fiona's toy, you'll have seen it. I killed him with it. Not just because he was going to hurt Julian. Because so far as he was concerned I'd blown my cover." *She* had blown it, by going to the room where Julian was. And then she had killed because of her own stupid behaviour, Tony Edwards had died because she hadn't done her job properly. This was an extra horror, but it, too, would have to wait. "There was nothing else I could do by then. And then there was nothing else I could do but order the snatch for tonight, before they find the body."

"Jesus. The body. It's lying about the room?"

"No. It's in the cupboard with the hypodermic and so on, and Nurse Evans hid the blood on the bedclothes. I've recruited her pro tem. and she's having a whale of a time. She's very resourceful and entirely trustworthy. I knew that was the wrong thing to do as well, but I knew it would be all right. Mr. Colburn, you and I haven't any more to do now, except lie low and let things happen outside our rooms. We'll go home—you tomorrow and I on Friday—as we planned to do. Mr. Colburn? Look, I know I went mad but it was my husband and on top of everything else—"

"Okay. Okay. It's that nurse that's bugging me. If she's one of them the team that comes in'll be fouled up as well as you and me. It'll be the greatest disaster since—"

"She's not one of them. If she is, I'll shoot myself with this gun, I promise you." She had said that before she remembered the baby. There was so much to remember. And to forget, if she ever could.

"That'll help. Jesus . . . Okay, okay. Get back to bed now and stay there. And don't start anything else on your own."

"I won't. Good night."

Nurse Evans followed her into her room, closing the door again.

"He was angriest of all about you," said Helen as she climbed into bed. "So I didn't think there was much point in asking you to join us and putting us all at risk again. Don't be upset about that. He couldn't really be angry with me for calling the team in, in view of what I'd done, and I think he understood why I did it. I'm glad to be in bed, I think I need to rest. . . ."

Now, at last, whoever saw them would see nothing amiss. She was

shocked at her sense of relief when she should be in constant tor-
ment, shocked to know she was going to be able to sleep. Really,
though, she ought to try and postpone her self-hate until another
seven months had gone by.

"Oh, pet."

"Go upstairs now, and stay there if you can. If you can't, avoid the
west corridor. Come and see if Fiona's all right when it's over."

She must have been asleep before Nurse Evans closed the door,
she remembered nothing between hearing her steps across the room
and hearing the encumbered movement of feet along the corridor.
She lay tense but not paralysed, clasping her hands over the baby and
trying to interpret the sounds. Tramping. Stumbling. Thuds. Curses.
A warning shout. A muffled report. Another. Then feet on the stairs,
on the marble, strained and cautious like the feet of the men who had
brought Julian in. Please God they were taking Julian out. Another
shout, another bullet. Someone else shot, someone else perhaps dead.
She wanted to go to her door and look out, and that was what Fiona
might have done. But Fiona could equally well have stayed cowering
in her bed. Best to wait for Nurse Evans. . . . Freda and Geoffrey
and the rest, she had forgotten them. No innocent victims,
please. . . .

The door was opening and quickly closing, Nurse Evans was by
the bed.

"You all right, pet?"

"Yes, yes." She struggled upright. "Is it finished?"

"It must be. I went upstairs like you said but I came down before
it started and I went in the big ward and sat there. I thought they
might be frightened, honestly I did. Then I heard sounds, sort of
stealthy, you know. And then someone called out and there was a
shot and a second shot and I made myself stay there. None of them
had wakened up, which was a miracle. Then the sounds started to go
down the stairs and across the hall and then there were voices in the
hall and feet flying upstairs and then another shot. I went out to the
corridor then, I couldn't help it and there were sort of camouflaged
army men and—and—there was Mr. Mute, lying on his face and—
and Sister lying beside him, on her side against the wall, so big and
he was so small. . . . There was a gun on the floor. I only looked

out for a moment, I don't know how I saw all that but I did and I'll never forget it, not any of it. Sister's eyes were open. O-o-oh."

"Come here." Helen leaned forward and took Nurse Evans's hands and drew her up the bed and cradled her head until she stopped crying. "I told you it was for real. Sister—was one of them. And the gnome, of course. They were shot because one of them, the gnome from what you've told me, had fired a shot, and Sister must have been carrying a gun. You didn't see—any stretchers?"

"There may have been something in the hall. That was further away than I took in. There can't have been anything on the stairs, now I think of it, because Sister must have just run up."

"Are the bodies still there?" Helen stroked Nurse Evans's hair away from her forehead, up the edge of the cap she was still amazingly wearing.

"No! There's nothing there now, I think they took them away, too. The only thing that looked different was that a couple of the west corridor doors were open, and I felt that gave me a reason for poking about. Oh, pet, what I should have told you right away—your husband's gone. And—and the body, and Dr. Webster's other two patients. And the room the gnome used is empty."

"Oh, Daphne. Oh, thank you."

"I went upstairs then and wakened Matron. She really did seem surprised. I can't believe she's anything to do with it. So far as Sister's concerned, I said I'd gone to her first because she was on duty, but that she wasn't in her office, or anywhere else."

"That was absolutely right." It was as if she had handed on her expertise to this blonde vital girl. "You've been marvellous."

"I'm supposed to be on my way round, seeing if everyone's all right."

"You go and do that, sweetie."

"Message received. Now, pet, you go back to sleep."

Nurse Evans bustled to the door. She had only just opened it when Matron was standing there. Helen was interested to see that Nurse Evans was not disconcerted. But they had been whispering.

"Mercy on us!" said Matron, sagging heavily against the doorpost. "You were right, Nurse. They've disappeared. Simply disappeared. Sister too. And that little chap of the owners, although I'm not concerned with *him*."

Nurse Evans had a bit of difficulty transferring Matron to Fiona's chair, where she sat panting.

"Sister! Where's Sister?" Nurse Baines in a dressing-gown was also entering the room.

"Disappeared," said Matron. "Clean disappeared. Along with Dr. Webster's patients. I'll contact him in a moment. When I've got my wind."

Nurse Baines shrugged. She would, of course, already have taken care of Dr. Webster. Helen could see that the whole of Nurse Baines's body was very slightly trembling. "If there's nothing I can do I'll go back to bed."

"There's nothing any of us can do," said Matron, beginning to recover. "There's nobody to do anything for. All we've got is an open window on the west side and some footmarks on the carpet. Plus," said Matron, passing her hand across her forehead, "some other marks on the wall in the corridor which look like blood." Nurse Baines's eyes flickered, noticed Fiona. Helen got out of bed and put her hand on Nurse Evans's arm, whimpering.

"It's a wonder there wasn't a stampede this side," said Nurse Evans. "Three cheers for Ovaltine. It's all right, pet."

"Early one morning," sang Fiona. Helen didn't know if she had tried to make a joke.

"And it is, at that." Matron got to her feet and stood firm. "You go back to bed, Baines, you weren't on duty and you won't have anything to tell the police. You'd better stay around, Evans, keep an eye out for panic and be ready to answer any questions. Mr. Jenkins is ringing the police and—ah, here he is."

The Resident Director, in a short dressing-gown of quilted yellow satin, had now taken Nurse Baines's place at the door, just as Nurse Evans was successfully persuading Fiona to get back into bed.

"I've spoken to the police." Mr. Jenkins's voice was loud and toneless. Helen suspected he was in shock. "At first they wouldn't believe what I was saying and were almost offensive on the subject of practical jokes. However, they will be here directly. I left a message for Dr. Webster, Matron"—his glance was magnanimously forgiving Matron for not having undertaken the call—"with a female voice. Not Mrs. Webster, I think. . . . It's as if they've been spirited away.

Simply spirited away." He turned awkwardly, like a sleepwalker, to face Nurse Evans. "You were on duty, Nurse?"

"Yes, sir. But I'd just finished a tour and gone upstairs and when I came down for my next round—well, whatever happened had happened. It was only the open doors in the west corridor which made me suspect anything was wrong."

"You went down to Sister's office?"

"Of course, sir. Right away when I realized the three patients were —missing." Matron held her pudgy palms to the ceiling. "And she wasn't there."

"Any signs of—er—struggle?" The Resident Director put his hand up to the lapel of his dressing-gown, as if to loosen an imaginary collar.

"None at all. Except that her desk chair was leaning against her armchair as if she'd pushed it back in a hurry, and her door was wide open. She seemed to be in the middle of writing something, but of course I didn't look closely."

"No? Well, that was quite right, Nurse Evans, quite right. I must go down and lock the door so that the police . . . Dear me, it's something we should have done right away, I suppose. Are you all right, Matron?"

"I'm punch drunk," said Matron. "Like you, Mr. Jenkins. Have you seen Mr. Erickson?"

"Dear me, no. I wonder—"

"The door of the room he's been using, the new room," said Nurse Evans. "That was open."

"Oh dear, dear me!" The Resident Director went out into the corridor. "Perhaps we'd better have a roll-call. Matron . . ." Matron puffed out after him. "If you'd just like to see to it. . . ." Their voices faded and Nurse Evans quietly closed the door.

"Just what I need!"

"Daphne," whispered Helen from her pillow. "Did you see what Sister was writing?"

"Of course. But it was all figures. Arranged in little groups. D'you think it was a code?"

"I suppose so, I don't know, I don't know anything about things like that."

"What will the police make of it?"

"They'll have had their orders. They'll be very formal and they won't ask many questions. They'll ask the most from you, obviously. But you were marvellous."

"Thanks. It's true, anyway, except that I was listening to it all from the big ward. Is there anyone I should be careful of now?"

Helen hesitated, but decided not to give Nurse Evans any warning of Nurse Baines. Her ignorance was her best protection.

"Not especially, just keep your own counsel with all of them. And your boyfriend."

"You don't have to tell me that, although it'll be an awful temptation. Is there anything else I can do for you, pet, before Matron sets me checking on everyone?"

"Yes." Helen sat up in bed. For the last half-hour or so she had actually forgotten. "Please make sure no one who thinks he or she knows best gives me anything to induce a miscarriage."

It was a good feeling, to see that Nurse Evans was more shocked by this possibility than by any of the events of the night. When she had gone out and shut the door Helen drifted off to sleep, against the voice of the Resident Director along the corridor, saying how extraordinary, how preposterous, over and over again.

CHAPTER 16

She knew the quality of her awakening was different even before full consciousness returned. No need, any more, to tense into the day ahead. Time and space to look at the sunny square of window and think of the fields beyond it, stretch her legs out and then relax them. Ordinary, everyday life visible again on the horizon.

Which could make what she had done in her nightmare unbearable.

Too soon to let that fear lodge. And she would have to rejoice, for months yet, to feel as well as she felt this morning.

Mission accomplished.

Mission grossly, outrageously exceeded.

But Julian safe. And the house and garden and Toby.

Funny if after all this, alone and bewildered, Toby had let himself be run over. . . .

The mixture of laughter and tears was another warning. To permit herself no luxuries, nice or nasty, while she was still Fiona Spencer at Hartshorn Manor.

Only Nurse Baines, on duty tonight, to live through now.

Only Nurse Baines?

Even now, could they ever be certain they were safe?

"Here you are, pet."

"Daphne! Surely you shouldn't still be around?" She had waited until Nurse Evans had put the tray down and closed the door.

"I said I'd just do the earlier breakfasts before collapsing into bed and dying the death. Oh, pet, I'm sorry! The police were here, anyway, so there wasn't all that much night left."

Nurse Evans was as bright and energetic as ever, although her eyes were bloodshot and there were dark circles under them.

"Was I right about the police?"

"Yes. Hardly anything. It was almost funny, Mr. Jenkins kept trying to make them ask more questions, be more concerned than they were. I wouldn't be surprised if he reported them to the Chief Constable for negligence. I think Matron twigged there was something behind it all that didn't have anything to do with any of us. Except . . . ?" Helen shook her head, smiling, into the questioning glance. "Well, Baines didn't seem to be concerned, but that's Baines. And Elaine Rogers has a new boyfriend, she's not as interested in other things as she usually is. Chadwick's all concerned about the east corridor, of course, she's so desperately dedicated."

"I'm lucky to see you again in private. It's academic now, I suppose, but can you tell me about the set-up on the top floor? I mean, where did the gnome sleep, and did the owners have another room as well? Fiona could just have danced her way up, but I always felt that would be pushing it."

"There's just the one room—right at the end of the corridor up there, past our TV room and the linen room and the bathrooms and loos. It's a big room, we used to have a table-tennis table in it. The new owners took it over right away. The gnome was always in there until he started to sleep on this floor. When I saw him go downstairs once I found myself nipping up to the door and trying it. It was locked."

"So you've never seen inside since the Manor changed hands?"

"Never. I don't think any of the nursing staff have."

"You didn't see anyone going in apart from the gnome?"

"No. D'you think Sister did?"

"I think she must have done. Or he went to her. Did you ever see that?"

"Once or twice. To her office, that is, not her bedroom. And we wanted to ask her about him. But you couldn't ask Sister anything like that. Matron you could. But she just shrugged."

"Didn't anybody ever speculate? Wonder why the gnome's room was locked? And why he was so uncommunicative? I presume he didn't fraternize?"

"Heavens, never. We *did* speculate about the new owners, they were so sort of—faceless. Elaine was convinced they were an Arab syndicate. Mr. Mute made us feel a bit creepy at first, but he became a sort of fact of life, once we realized he didn't seem to be paying any attention to us. Then a few weeks ago we all received a duplicate sheet suggesting we pull our socks up and keep strictly to staff rules. That *was* creepy, we never knew just where it came from. We thought it must have been brought in from outside, although for all we knew Mr. Mute could have had a duplicating machine in that room of his. Poor Mr. Jenkins was very indignant—if I'd been him I'd have kept quiet and pretended it was my idea."

"Did you ask Matron and Sister?"

"Yes. They both seemed a bit annoyed and both said it was nothing to do with them."

Nurse Baines? Another one up on Sister, perhaps. "Don't the cleaners go into that room?"

"No. Sister said Mr. Erickson had a thing about anyone going into his room and was keeping it clean himself. Oh, pet, can you make it?"

At least the sickness seemed now to be confining itself conventionally to the mornings. Nurse Evans asked her anxiously how she felt.

"Very well, which horrifies me. I hope the baby won't have tendencies to violence because of—last night." This was one of the dangerous thoughts which was refusing to be dismissed.

"Of course not, that's ridiculous. You're not violent. You didn't want to"—Nurse Evans lowered her voice still further—"kill him."

"No." Hold on to that. And forget that if she had kept her head that cheerful young man would still be alive. And Julian still subject to his syringe. "You'd better go, Daphne, get some rest. I'll be grateful to you as long as I live."

"I enjoyed myself. I mean . . ." The blue eyes were abnormally large again, in apology.

"I know what you mean."

"May I see you again?"

"I'm afraid not. And if you did, I'd hope you wouldn't recognize me. There's just a chance though . . ." She was going to stick her neck out yet again. "Someone could get in touch with you. No guarantee, of course, it's not for me to say, but I should think it's possible if you're interested. Are you?"

"You mean . . . To help again. . . ."

"Yes."

The sleepy face was transfigured. "Oh yes! Please!"

"I'll say what's due. Off you go, now."

"I'll try to see you tomorrow before you go, but I'll say goodbye now, in case."

Helen was enfolded in a bear hug, and then Nurse Evans had gone, returning anticlimactically and possibly tearfully within seconds for the breakfast tray.

Despite its comparative simplicity the day would be a long one, with vigilance its watchword. The owners, now, would be very wary, but they would know that their photo ploy had failed. She couldn't be sure there was only Nurse Baines left. And Nurse Baines cornered, enraged . . . Singing and dancing would need an enormous effort. An effort she had to make before even leaving her room, because the door was opening.

Matron stood there, getting her breath.

"Good morning, darling. What's the little number entitled today?"

Helen moved from the middle eight bars of *Blue Moon* back to the main melody. "Ah yes, I had a young man once played that like a dream. If you'd seen me forty years ago . . . Now, darling, I've come to put your things together because your uncle's just been on to say he's back a bit earlier from holiday, owing to your aunt having contracted one of those Spanish tummies, and he's coming for you this very morning. That's very good of your uncle, I'm sorry you can't appreciate it, he's paid until tomorrow. I told him you'd been a good girl while you've been here. Though for the life of me I don't suppose we'd know if you hadn't." Matron was moving about the room, putting the few contents of the drawers and cupboards into Fiona's case. "I thought I'd wait until I saw him before telling him the sort of girl you'd been before you came. Woman, I should say, but there must have been someone else who thought he was looking at a girl. . . . Oh, dear me." Matron straightened up, puffing, and ruffled her rim of curls. "It won't be all that easy, but I think I'm the one to do it." Helen wondered if it would be done in her presence, and hoped not. But all that really mattered was that George was coming so soon to take her away.

"There!" Matron had the sponge bag in her hand, was feeling the toothbrush. "Damp it is. Good girl, you've used it. But you *are* a good girl, in a wicked world. You're not going to have a very nice time of it in the next few days, darling, but you'll be all right. Mother of God, I wish they'd leave you!" Helen hoped Matron was unaware of the trembling of her arm as she patted it. "I'll take your case down with me, I'm too near retirement to bother with my dignity. You come when you're ready."

Helen was ready then to leave her room for the last time, but Fiona was always dressed before the ladies in the larger rooms, and she thought she would look in on them, for once, with proper compassion. Mrs. Lockett was having trouble with her stockings again, sitting on the end of her bed and putting one on, shaking her head and taking it off and trying it on the other leg. One of the knitting ladies was mutteringly unravelling her work of the day before. Nurse Rogers should be on duty and was rather needed; she would probably be next door, with Freda's lot.

Helen heard the small sharp cry of pain before she reached the next half-open door, before she saw the back of Nurse Baines by craning into the gap.

"You tell me," Nurse Baines was softly saying. "You tell me what you know and stop pretending to be daft, and I'll stop hurting you. One of you must know something, one of you must have been sent in." A knitting lady stumbled past the narrow gap, whimpering and holding her arm. There was another cry, cut off. "It's got to be someone here," went on Nurse Baines, "and this is how I'll find out. There's no one else to find out, now. Come along, dear." Again the cry aborted. "I'll have to get to Miss Spencer today, it's her last. And that man . . ."

Mr. Colburn had walked past Helen, and past the gap in the doorway, to appear the other side of it and prevent her voicing her shock at him being suddenly and silently beside her. He caught her glance, gave a nod, then stealthy, cat-like, widened the gap. It was so quick, Helen couldn't say if Nurse Baines had started to turn round. Mr. Colburn's hand chopped at her white neck, visible where the long straight hair fell forward to either side as she bent over Freda.

She dropped like a rag doll and Mr. Colburn, ignoring her, went up to Freda and took the arm Nurse Baines had been attending to, stroking it with gentle murmurs. Then he went over to the first victim and repeated the process before taking each by the shoulder and leading them from the room.

Helen saw these things intermittently as she danced and sang about the corridor, and saw too that Nurse Baines didn't move. She had fallen in a heap and her head was at an unnatural angle.

Fiona ran ahead of the slowly moving trio, down the stairs and to the window by the front door where she tended to stand. Looking back now and then from her contemplation of the drive, Helen saw the ladies descend the first few stairs quite quickly, no doubt from the now invisible impetus of Mr. Colburn, then regain a pained bewilderment half way down so that their final descent was slow and distressingly vocal. Nurse Chadwick, emerging from the back of the hall with the trolley of fruit juice, was aware at once that something was amiss.

"What is it, darlings? Have you been fighting? Did you fall? *That's* going to be a bruise. You'd better come and sit down quietly and have a nice drink. . . ." Nurse Chadwick left the trolley while she took them, an arm round each, into the lounge, and was several minutes before coming back to retrieve it. Only then Mr. Colburn came in his usual jaunty way downstairs, straightening his tie.

At the foot of the stairs he paused while he and Helen looked at one another, and then it was she who nodded before dancing past him and out into the garden.

The kitten was there, and she said goodbye to it. It was impossible to imagine seeing Toby again. Or the house and garden. As if, because she had changed so totally, they had changed too. But of course George wouldn't be taking her home, even by a roundabout route. Julian wouldn't be at home, and he would be taking her to Julian. . . .

Was it a curse or a blessing that nothing, not even that prospect, was able to make her feel?

The only feeling she had was of slight amusement at the thought of the Resident Director in the face of murder following multiple abduction. The continuing complacency of the police would make a complaint inevitable. . . .

Nurse Chadwick was in the doorway. Either because of the fruit juice or because George had come. George was appearing in the doorway behind her. So it really was over. Not with a bang, with a whimper.

When she had danced half way across the lawn she could see George's expression. Grave concern. So the explanations had been given, Matron had already proffered the advice she wouldn't have wanted to give, as to George's best way of consigning Fiona's unfortunate acquisition to the past. Would Julian be well enough for her to tell him that afternoon? The question felt academic.

"Oh, my poor darling!" Yes, Matron had got it over. "I'm so sorry. So very sorry."

In the hall, it was clear that the Resident Director was as anxious to be rid of them as George was to go. It was just the difficulty of making the final move, deciding the latest platitude would be the last. The impasse was resolved by Nurse Rogers, screaming her way down the stairs.

"Baines! In room four! Her neck's broken. Oh, help. . . ."

"Perhaps I should go up with you?" suggested George. "Or perhaps there are still some police on the premises?"

Yes, the Resident Director wouldn't have been able to resist telling George something about the night.

"There are not!" shouted the Resident Director, dumb disbelief giving way to fury, pushing Nurse Rogers off his chest into Nurse Chadwick's ready arms. "There should be, but there are not! You had better be exaggerating, Nurse!"

"I'm not." Nurse Rogers hiccuped. "Baines asked me to let her take my duty this morning and I slept in a bit and then I went down to see her and . . . o-o-oh, she's on the floor in room four and she's dead."

"I'll go up with you." George was fractionally ahead of Mr. Jenkins on the stairs. Fiona began to whimper, staring large-eyed from her vanishing uncle to the near-hysterical Nurse Rogers.

"Ask Matron to ring the police!" The voice of the Resident Director drifted down, and Nurse Chadwick shepherded Fiona as well as Nurse Rogers towards Matron's office.

She didn't have to wait long, only the seconds of Matron's incredulity turning to action and the length of the telephone call. George came down alone, with a request that Matron would join Mr. Jenkins upstairs.

"It's all right, we'll see ourselves out." Nurse Chadwick said automatically that that was good of him, and flung her arms round Fiona. Nurse Rogers darted a kiss at her cheek.

George kept his arm across her shoulder on the way to the front door, and she went sedately enough. Struggling against laughter, Helen found herself helping him with the two locks. But there was no one in sight.

She danced round the car, her diaphragm heaving with the suppression of the laughter and George caught her and steered her to the passenger side and helped her in. She laughed, more and more helplessly and unhappily, until after a couple of turnings leading them to wider roads, George stopped the car long enough to slap her face.

Shocked, she thanked him for coming twenty-four hours early.

"Well, of course. Are you all right?"

"I think so. George, I killed a man last night."

"So I heard. In our game it's an occupational hazard."

"I'm not in your game."

"Last night you were. It's *your* news I'm choking on."

"I'm glad you can choke on something. Oh, George, I'm not angry with *you*. Will Julian be well enough to hear my news? Is he all right? Where is he? Where are we going?" She ought to want to know these things. And perhaps she did, the questions had rushed out without her deciding to ask them.

"He's in one of our houses, we're on our way. He's all right."

"The other two?" She had just remembered them.

"All right physically. For the rest . . . we can't say, yet."

"Julian hadn't been there long enough."

"No. I mean that, Helen. He hadn't. He's all right."

"Why was he there, George?"

"Because like you he broke the rules."

"What do you mean?"

"Julian will tell you."

"The man I killed was going to give him another injection."

"And you prevented it. Good."

"None of this is good. Don't talk to me like a child."

George didn't talk to her at all until they had done some rather complicated driving on the edge of London and ended in a lock-up garage, where there was another car.

"All change!" George said, then.

"Where next?" She could have been watching a crime series on television for want of something better to do.

"Another large house."

She thought of something, a penny very slowly dropping. "You don't think I should go home first, get some things, see everything's all right. The cat." Suddenly, agonizingly, she was feeling. "Oh, George, the cat!"

"Julian said one thing to me before I came for you, I popped in to see him after he'd come round. He said to tell you, if you asked, that the cat was with Margaret."

"That's his sister. Oh, George." She had asked, just. Earlier on she had been afraid Toby had been run over, but since then she had forgotten.

"And the things you'll need have already been collected. Your house is all right, too. Someone's there."

"I'm sorry, George, I'm impossible. Forgive me."

"Forgive us. We took three bodies out, by the way."

"Yes. The one just now was another of them. The last, she said so herself. She was saying it, torturing the poor little crones, having realized I suppose that she'd been double-crossed from inside, when the CIA man saw to her. I think she was in charge. Well, under the gnome at least. That's what the nurses called the little man . . . No, that's what I called him, Daphne called him Mr. Mute. . . . It seems the Americans were tipped off before we were. Do you know Mr. Colburn?" Somebody would have to stop her talking.

"I saw someone on the landing I recognized, so I suppose I do. Doze if you can."

Incredibly she could, and woke to find herself once more in the country, on a drive approaching a house at as great a length as the drive to Hartshorn Manor.

George parked outside the front door, then turned to her. She saw that he was suddenly nervous.

"Look, it's the last thing you'll be interested in today, but you're a bit of a talking point here just now. Something between a celebrity and a curiosity."

"You don't want me to start laughing again do you, George?"

"Heaven forbid. I just want you to realize you've been connected with something pretty remarkable. Not only have we nipped the first Anglo-Soviet psychiatric hospital in the bud, we've prevented any more. We'll see the Press get it. It'll give us a nation of paranoiac

Resident Directors, of course, but that's a small price to pay. . . . Let's go in."

"Please let me tell Julian about myself."

"No one else will tell him."

The façade was larger and more formal than the façade of the Manor. George rang the bell and the heavy white door was opened by a young man in a well-cut grey suit. There seemed to be quite a lot of young men in the same mould standing about the imposing hall inspecting notice-boards or talking in small groups. And a number of young women.

"I think a check-up and a rest," said George, partly to Helen and partly to the young man.

She was glad George had said the preposterous thing he had just said in the car. Otherwise her awareness of being surreptitiously watched would have felt sinister as well as uncomfortable. Now, the danger was that she might start to laugh again.

But two of the young men had whisked her away, into a lift and out of it, along a corridor and into a room which looked and smelt like a surgery. She climbed on to a couch, an older face leaned over her and smiled, and then she was stretching luxuriously in a bed and the same face was telling her she was fine and that she'd had a good long sleep.

She shot upright. "The baby?"

"You're still going to have a baby."

It was a nice room with an elegant fireplace and two sashed windows showing blue sky with clouds.

"What time is it?"

"Tea-time. You didn't have any lunch so you'd better have tea and then you can go and see your husband."

Tea was boiled egg with thin bread and butter, apricot jam and a very fine China brew, and while she was eating she realized she was wearing her own nightdress. As she was finishing a young woman came in and suggested she put her dressing-gown on to go along the corridor to Julian's room.

When she had knocked at a door the young woman went away and Helen opened the door and closed it behind her and walked slowly up to the bed where Julian lay propped up with pillows, watching her. There was a chair by the bed and she sat down and they looked at each other gravely before the instantaneous precipitation into each other's arms, which wiped out everything except what she had done the night before.

"Julian, darling, I don't deserve you, I don't deserve to have got away. I only got away because I murdered Tony Edwards, and I only murdered him because I'd been a fool." She didn't deserve, either, that it should help so much to tell it to Julian. "I aimed at his heart and I pulled the trigger. I shouldn't have been able to."

Julian was shaved but there were still the short spikes of hair under her frantic fingers.

"It was one or other of you. George has been in again this afternoon and told me everything. Oh, darling, I'm the guilty one, I shouldn't have let you go. I think that's why I went to see Edwards."

"You went to see Tony Edwards?"

She wasn't shocked only at that, she was shocked too that the few seconds of confession had so blunted the edge of her self-outrage.

"Yes. I thought I might get a clue to Pete and what he knew about you. And whether Edwards was involved. And I think I wanted to share risks with you, put myself in jeopardy too."

"Julian . . ."

"I tried to be clever and imply that my connection with Pete was sexual, but it hadn't occurred to me that Master Tony might start propositioning me himself. When he did, I told him he'd got it wrong, that my business with Pete was financial. Evidently I wasn't convincing, there was a touch of the Georgi Markovs—but only to put me out—and then I was at the Manor. He was clever, that boy, right up to passing out I thought I'd managed it. Oh, darling, with Tony Edwards it was kill or be killed. I hope I can make you realize!"

"I do realize, but it doesn't seem to help."

"You did it for me."

"I shot him in the hand for you. I shot him dead for myself as well." And the baby. But there were moments when she didn't want an excuse.

"Accept that."

Julian had accepted it, which was vitally important. There could be no prevarications here.

"And if I'd been up to the job I wouldn't have lost my head and gone to your room in the first place."

"Then if you must chastise yourself, chastise yourself for incompetence. Which it hardly was. If we were both stronger I'd shake you till your teeth fell out."

As it was, he took her in his arms again.

"What now?" she asked eventually. "Will you be in trouble?"

"There'll be a routine reprimand. I'm no longer in the field and I was right out of line. But I'm leaving the Service."

"Julian!"

"I've had it to the top of my head. And I've discovered that I no longer put it entirely first. I didn't go to that house in Camden Town on behalf of the Service."

"Down to me again."

"Because of you, yes. But it feels like a natural ending. I don't regret it."

"You may change your mind. George didn't tell you everything. I'm going to have a baby."

She realized as she spoke that she wasn't sure he would still be pleased. Although he didn't or couldn't speak at once, his eyes and then his arms were her reassurance.

"You didn't know before—"

"No. Oh no. It was while I was there. I kept being sick and it was awfully hard not to imagine I was being poisoned." She wouldn't tell him, not yet at least, that other people had known first and had made practical suggestions. "I've just seen the doctor and despite everything it's still there."

"You're not afraid?"

"Only of losing it."

"I shall still leave the Department. I've got some ideas. Everything's changed, hasn't it? Except the you-and-me."

She leaned down and put her head on the pillows. "Even now—we can't be absolutely and completely sure, can we, that we're safe? Dr. Webster—your Vladimir—Pete Irving, they won't go back to Hartshorn Manor, Nurse Baines will have seen to that, so they'll be at large, and we'll never be certain Pete didn't follow me home that time. That someone didn't follow me after the dinner-party. Not *certain.*"

"Helen, I—"

"Can you be *certain* you didn't tell them who you are?"

"I'm sure I didn't. But anyway, Helen, I—"

"Does Vladimir know you by sight?"

"I don't think so, I think I have that advantage, he's still in the field. But there's a chance—"

"He didn't see you, as it happens, only Pete and—Tony—saw you. But perhaps the little man Erickson did, and told—"

"I've seen Erickson's photograph, I don't know him. I don't imagine he knows me. But darling, if you'd just let me finish a sentence. There's a chance I may find something out this very day to make the uncertainty less. Make us more sure we've succeeded. Or more sure we've failed."

"Tell me."

"I'll be able to tell you later. I want you to rest again now. And meanwhile I *can* tell you that the letter which came for Versatile Actress after you'd gone came via *The Contemporary Review.*"

"Oh, Julian. . . . Thank you for seeing to Toby."

She hadn't wanted to go back to bed, and was amazed on waking to find she had instantly slept. Her own wristwatch was on the bedside table, telling her she had lost a further hour. She wouldn't lose any more, she wouldn't be kept any longer in bed, she would get up and see what was hanging in the wardrobe, try to make herself glamorous. After she'd found a bathroom.

Two figures were coming into sight along the corridor, pausing at Julian's door. Two men, perhaps it would be better to go back into her room and use the telephone . . . One of the men was Julian, she hadn't recognized for a moment his changed outline, and she started to walk towards them. The other man was younger than her husband. Dark, slight . . . *No, please, no. Oh dear God, no.* Cry out, pinch herself, close her eyes and open them again, it was still Pete. Pete looking as alarmed now as Julian, but having just been exchanging smiles with him. . . . *Pete and Julian. Another large house.* Julian had seemed all right, but he had been drugged. And if he was all right, Eleanor Philby had lived with Kim for years and not known. . . .

"Don't touch me! Don't come near me! Either of you. . . ." She screamed again as she turned and started to run back to her room.

The running, too, was part of the nightmare, she couldn't run fast enough, they were catching her up. If they caught her she would have to wake up, and if she was awake already she would have to black out, she wouldn't be able to bear it.

She just made it to her bed, slipping down on to the floor beside it as darkness descended.

CHAPTER 17

Julian was saying "Oh, Helen" over and over again, and she was wondering why. Then remembering she could no longer trust him. She pulled her hand out of his and tried to hide under the bedclothes.

He didn't touch her again. He said, "All right, I know how you must feel. Just listen to me. The man you know as Pete Irving, he's defected, he's come over to us. Did you hear me?"

She had heard him and she wanted to believe him, but it was such an easy thing for him to say, she had no way of checking it. She lay there unresponding and his voice went on.

"I told you, darling, I told you we believed the owners of Hartshorn Manor had no idea we knew what they were up to. That was because Pete had approached us, wanting to come over, and had told us as an earnest of his good faith what was going on there. He could have been telling us a fiction, or he could have been leading us into a trap. We couldn't take his word for it, we had to find out if it was the truth, and until you volunteered to go in for us we hadn't known how we could do it. One thing we were entirely sure of: if it was the truth he was on the level, it was too big a piece of information to have been authorized by his masters merely to make us trust him. Everything you said on the telephone last night tallied with what he had told us—"

"You mean you knew it all already—the layout of the house, Sister, Nurse Baines!" She flung the bedclothes away and lay glaring at him.

"We knew what Pete had told us. And when you told us the same things we knew we could go in. If your reports hadn't tallied we simply wouldn't have done anything, Fiona Spencer would have seen her week out and been taken home. What you were doing, darling, was more important than you realized, not less."

"You didn't expect me to be in the corridor when I was, did you?

Why should I believe you?" But she did believe him, and was angry now rather than afraid. Angry that he hadn't told her about Pete and spared her those moments of terror.

Her anger was fuelled by his smile. "Because you know that I would never lie to you. However, if you'd like me to bring J. to see you it could be arranged. You can hardly imagine that J.—"

"Why didn't you tell me Pete was all right?"

His smile disappeared in his astonishment. "I didn't know our defector was Pete! Even when you saw us in the corridor, I didn't know the man with me was someone you'd met! He contacted us under another name. I didn't tell you how we came to know about the Manor because the negotiations were so secret and delicate, and even if I had told you, you'd still have had the same shock when you saw Pete. Oh darling, I'm so sorry." She let him take her hand. "The baby's still all right. I promise there won't be any more ordeals for him."

"I'd forgotten about the baby. He's strong, isn't he?"

"As strong as you. How do you feel?"

"Tired. I thought I wanted to get dressed up for dinner, but I don't. *Pete.* My sixth sense isn't all that hot, I thought he was the villain of villains. And that Tony . . . I could have killed Pete."

"You didn't. Look, there's nothing I can say to make that easier for you, so I won't try. Just after you'd gone to the convent to study the real Fiona, by the way, Pete contacted us to say that the photo of you and Vladimir was a phoney. That was something in his favour, but not enough to make us risk going into the Manor without corroboration."

"How on earth did he get *here?*"

"When he got in touch about the photo he asked us to let him know when the balloon went up, if it did, which seemed to us fair enough—if we decided to go in it would mean we'd decided he was on the level. We took a voice pattern, and another when he arrived at the address we gave him after you rang from the Manor—lucky for him he wasn't there then!"

"I never saw any of the doctors there at night. Except that one time. . . ."

"Vladimir was alerted from the Manor—I suppose that nurse—and rang Pete to tell him to start fending for himself, just as Pete was about to leave the digs where they'd set him up, so he didn't have any trouble getting to the address we'd given him. The voice patterns tallied, and we brought him on here early this morning."

"Where did the Americans come in?"

"When he contacted us about the photo and the balloon Pete told us he was treating with the Americans as well, because of there being an important American at the Manor, and that he'd told them he was asking us for asylum. He contacted them first, in fact. Well, you'll know that."

"Mr. Colburn was definitely one up about it."

"We both had the same idea. To be honest, I don't think *we* could have managed anything from among our personnel."

"Mr. Colburn started out as an actor." She was amused to see the satisfaction in Julian's face. "Pete . . . I can't imagine it. . . . Julian, he can tell us things, he can tell us . . ." She was sitting up in bed, full of hope and energy. "And even if he *did* follow me home . . ."

"He didn't, actually, but as you say, he can tell us things. Would you like to see him? Oh darling, if you'd rather not. . . ."

She was wary again and it was showing in her face, but that was probably just a reflex from the recent associations with the name Pete.

"It's all right, I'd like to see him, if he's not in quarantine. I mean, if he doesn't have to be debriefed first."

"He does, before he's allowed any ordinary contacts. You're hardly that. Now?"

"Yes." Pete had become a myth, which should be shattered before it grew any more monstrous.

"No need to watch what you say, he knows who we are." Julian used the telephone, and then they waited hand in hand. By the time the knock came on the door her doubts were all at rest.

A young woman, maybe the one who had come to her room before, showed the young man in, then left closing the door. Pete came forward slowly, taking the upright chair and sliding it beside Julian so that Julian was between them. As their eyes met and held she remembered the moment in the kitchen of the flat in Camden Town. Pete was still assessing her. But now, perhaps, just to see how she had stood up to it.

He said eventually, almost with respect, "Mrs. Johnson, I think the best way is for you to ask me questions."

"Why did you come over?" she inquired at once. "And come to that, why were you with Dr. Webster and Co. in the first place?"

"Not from conviction. I was doing my GP training with a doctor —not Vladimir, he is a doctor but he doesn't practise. Officially, that is." He grimaced, then turned to Julian. "I was with a doctor I'll be talking to you about—"

"You're a doctor!" She heard her indignant exclamation.

"Yes." He grinned at her. "Penelope didn't ask, I would have told her that."

"You injected them! That's as bad as—"

"You killed Tony Edwards." He must have seen her eyes, because it was he who flinched. "I'm sorry. And it isn't a parallel, of course. But we've both done things we'd rather we hadn't. Shall I go on?"

"Please. I'm sorry."

"There was a patient. I thought—he wanted me to . . . I responded. It appeared I'd made a mistake." Julian squeezed her hand. "He 'told' my boss. Who said he would have to report me to the GMC. Unless . . . That's when I met Vladimir. There was a heady amount of money, too. And not an awful lot to do. At the beginning, nothing, except live in Camden Town with Tony. That—was no penance." Pete closed his eyes and she had to take hers off his face. "Tony's allegiance was ideological. He was my immediate boss."

"Tony—your boss?" She could never again list sixth sense as one of her qualifications. But she would never again want a job where such an endowment was a particular advantage.

"Yes. Between him and Vladimir, I was pretty neatly tied up."

"I hope it was hell for you. Oh God, I'm sorry. It's the amateur in me, still near the surface. Still making judgments. Forgetting I've lost the right."

"You haven't lost the right to deplore," said Julian gently. "But we'll get on better if we stick to facts."

"I know. Why did Tony write to Versatile Actress?"

"Partly because he really was concerned about his mother, he wanted her to carry an impeccable image of her only son, as much because he loved her as because it would be better for his—career—if she did. His mother was his one human place."

"You?"

Pete laughed, disagreeably. "He knew how to please me, to keep me to heel. Vladimir had been very clever. By sending me to Camden Town you could say he turned a predilection into an addiction."

His face for a moment was unbearable and she hurried on.

"You said partly . . ."

"Another reason was that he was always on the lookout for someone who might be useful to the cause. For one-off jobs like the phoney photo." She and Julian pressed hands again. When he had first recruited her, he had used a similar argument. "And I think there was another reason. A sort of devilment in him, a native necessity to invent and explore bizarre situations. If he had any weakness as a senior operative, it was that. And in a way it killed him."

"I thought—I was so sure—you were his senior."

Pete laughed again, more attractively. "We both spotted your amazing likeness to Dr. Bakewell. I had the opportunity to exploit it first, while Tony was tied up with his mother. So I was the one who had to disappear. Because I was the one connected with the uncle character, and anyway Tony was the one with the whiter than white image and the better natural gift for putting it across."

"All the official visitors to the flat," said Julian, "were satisfied. They looked round, of course, but there was nothing to alert them, least of all the deserted co-owner."

"And all the time," said Pete, "he was sole permanent occupant of one of their more important houses, with concealed access to the house next door."

"We caught up with that today." For the first time Julian had turned away from her.

"And plenty of evidence, I hope. Tony had no reason to believe, when he went to the Manor, that he wouldn't be coming back."

"But the other people there," she protested. "Dr. Webster would have warned *them*. . . ."

"There wouldn't necessarily have been any others. Self-confidence had reached smug proportions."

Helen's own newborn complacency was suddenly shot through with thoughts of her and Julian's safety. "About us. Julian tells me you didn't follow me away from the flat that time?"

"No. It wasn't considered necessary. If you hadn't rung Uncle

Mark, another letter would have come for Versatile Actress with an acceptable assignment."

She managed to suppress her shudder. "After the dinner-party?"

"They attempted to follow you then. And began to get a bit tense when they lost you, although they put it down to bungling on their part rather than skill on yours. After all, they had no reason to think you had their kind of connections."

"Then there was the letter, I know about that. The files . . ."

"*The Contemporary Review* files were broken into," said Julian. "There was nothing to find, of course."

"Nobbling a records clerk was discussed," said Pete, "and might have been implemented eventually. But they were waiting to see what the letter brought." He smiled at her, and although she couldn't respond she had to acknowledge that the effect was pleasing. "And now, of course, nothing."

"Dr. Webster never saw Julian?"

"Not on this assignment."

"Not on any other," said Julian.

"He wasn't secretly photographed when he was in Camden Town?" The awful possibility had only just hit her, and she clutched Julian's hand.

"No, no," soothed Pete. "There were no facilities."

"Julian didn't—say anything?"

"Not to me. And if he said anything to Tony . . ." Briefly he averted his eyes. "And Erickson's dead, and the nursing staff."

"We're in the clear, then?"

"You must be. All Vladimir'll be concerned with is getting out of the country. To Brazil rather than Moscow, he didn't get it right. You can forget him."

"Can you?"

He grimaced again. "I'll try. There was such disarray, he has no way of sorting anybody out."

"What will you do now?" One of the things she was looking forward to was thinking about other people again.

"I'll be all right. I'm hoping I shall be allowed to compensate."

Julian turned to look at him again. "It's possible." His gaze was back on Helen. "Will that do for now?"

"Yes. Thank you. Pete. I'm sorry about Tony."

"I'm sorry about a lot of things. I don't expect to see you again. I wish you well."

"And I you." Surely the Department had won a prize.

There was a knock on the door, response to Julian's finger on the telephone buttons. When they were alone again he asked her if she still intended to dine in bed.

"No. I'm going down."

"I'm glad, they'll be disappointed if you don't. There's a great deal of interest so far as you're concerned and I've no doubt they're hoping to recruit you."

"I won't be recruited."

"I know that. But take it calmly."

"And Julian, I can't be. If I could go into your room like that, stay there—I'd never be a hundred per cent reliable. There's someone, though . . . Daphne Evans, the nurse at the Manor who helped me. She was tremendous. Darling, I was rash enough to offer her a bit of hope. . . . At least you could start investigating her."

"I'll suggest it."

"Julian, tell me . . . Do you remember anything between being at the flat in Camden Town and being here?" She waited anxiously.

"Just bad dreams of being chased and caught." One of her memories, at least, was suddenly easier. "How did you know I was there?"

"I took a routine prowl because I saw the stretcher arriving with Pete going up the stairs behind it." She must wipe that picture out, now. "And then—I went crazy and went back again—"

"Don't let's talk about it, it's over. Margaret tells me Toby's a bit subdued and obviously missing us, but all right."

"Thank you. Oh, thank you, darling. I'm so grateful and I'm so glad about Toby. And about being safe, of course, although it's hard to take it in. I wish I didn't feel so *serious.* Relieved, happy, of course. But so *serious.* Solemn, even."

"I've got something which might help."

Julian reached into his jacket pocket and put an envelope into her hands. It appeared to have suffered some ordeal by fire, but the name of the addressee was still legible.

Versatile Actress in bold capitals and inverted commas.

She tried to give it back to him, her hands shaking.

"It's all right, go on. Have a look inside."

Inside were some charred photographs of a small posed group of formally dressed people. "I don't . . ."

"There's a piece of paper."

The folded sheet had escaped injury. It was a note from Albert Redfern to Dear Madam, saying he thought copies of the wedding photographs might be appreciated and wondering if she could see her way to being available one day over Christmas. *Vi said she'd try to persuade Mabel if I couldn't manage it.*

"It was handed over to the police, of course," said Julian, "by the magazine, when they saw those fatal words. And of course the police had to be prepared for the worst, and blew it open. They were very apologetic, offered to try and repair . . . Oh darling, that's better."

Tremulously, unfamiliarly, against her will, her lips insisted on stretching into a smile.

About the author

Eileen Dewhurst was born in Liverpool and educated at Oxford. As a free-lance journalist, she has published numerous articles, and her plays have been performed throughout England. PLAYING SAFE is her seventh novel for the Crime Club.